Beating the Odds

Beating the Odds

Sherrod J. Tunstall

www.urbanbooks.net

Urban Books, LLC
300 Farmingdale Road, NY-Route 109
Farmingdale, NY 11735

ISBN 13: 978-1-62286-573-4
ISBN 10: 1-62286-573-1

First Trade Paperback Printing September 2017
Printed in the United States of America

10 9 8 7 6 5 4 3 2 1

Distributed by Kensington Publishing Corp.
Submit orders to:
Customer Service
400 Hahn Road
Westminster, MD 21157-4627
Phone: 1-800-733-3000
Fax: 1-800-659-2436

Beating the Odds

By

Sherrod J. Tunstall

About the book

Brad Carter is a twenty-two-year-old man down on his luck. He loses his job, catches his woman in bed with another man, and he's days away from being booted out of his home. Wanting to get away from his problems, Brad and his boys go to a nightclub, where they meet a wealthy stranger who offers them each $50,000 to go to Rio de Janeiro and traffic cocaine back to the U.S. They jump at the opportunity and have the time of their lives in Rio. When it's time to return to the U.S. with the drugs, all hell breaks loose. Brad and his friends get caught, and being in jail is not what they had hoped for. They plan an escape that, ultimately, leaves Brad and his friends scrambling to stay alive. He's determined to make his way back home, but with many obstacles, including a beautiful woman who has captured his heart, Brad's survival journey may turn out to be impossible.

Dedication

This book is dedicated to all people who kept going with my career as an author. I came from a bad publishing experience with my first publisher and almost gave up on my dream of being an author for good. I just want to thank those people who pushed and kept me going in this industry, because without you, this book wouldn't be completed today. Mama, Brenda Hampton, Keisha Ervin, Darryl Chatman, Rose Jackson-Beavers, Fabiola Joseph, Matthew Ramsey, Jeffery Roshell, and William Fredrick Cooper, if it weren't for your wisdom and kind words, I don't know where I would have been. I thank you all from the bottom of my heart.

Acknowledgments

First off, I have to thank my Lord and Savior, Jesus Christ. Lord, I thank you that you gave me the gift of words and expression. This journey as an author has had its good times and bad, Lord, but you kept my head high and pushed me to be the best author I could be. Even when I almost gave up my dream of being an author, you always kept it in my mind to write and to stop hanging and being around negativity. When I cut certain things and people out of my life, my blessing from you came, and I thank you, Lord, and I love you.

Dear Lola,
Mama!!! Thank you for always having my back no matter what. Even though we have our disagreements and we argue, we always have each other's backs no matter what. You have been with me with this writing journey from day one, and I thank you for always pushing me to be my best. It was hard, but in the end it was all worth it.
Love you,
Your Baby

Darryl Chatman,
To the best attorney on earth, thank you so much for putting up with me all these years. Thank you for always having my back legally. Even though sometimes I don't understand some of this legal business and contracts, you always have my back no matter, and I'm glad Charles Price told me all about you. Thanks again, bro.

Acknowledgments

Brenda Hampton,

My literary angel/agent, God put you in my life for a reason. Thank you for always giving me literary advice and breaking down the industry for me. We been talking since 2009, and we stayed talking until we met face to face in 2012. It's like the old saying: People are in your life for a season, a reason, or a lifetime. I believe you are someone that will be here for a lifetime. Thank you for getting me this deal with Urban. Thank you and I love you. May God bless you.

I have to say thank you to my dad, Curtis, my siblings, Corey, Curtis Jr. and Jeana, Chris Renee, Mary L. Wilson, Wanda Graves, Fabiola Joseph, Ronald Gordon, Jonathan Royal, Matthew Ramsey, Qiana Drennen & DRMRB team, Millie Carter, Jeffery Roshell, Bronchey Battle, Johnna B, Kai Leakes, Nikki Michelle, and the entire Tunstall, Isabelle, Wilson, Johnson, Manuel, and Lowe families.

And to Carl Weber, my idol, and the entire Urban staff, thank you for welcoming me into your world and taking a chance on me. I won't let you down.

For all my readers out there who supported me from day one with my debut novel, *Spicy*, I thank you all for rocking with me, and I won't stop writing.

If you want to contact me with any questions or feedback, e-mail me at sherrodt05@yahoo.com, Twitter: @Sherroddaauthor, FB: Sherrod The Author, IG: Sherroddaauthor. Website coming soon.

Chapter 1

What a Day

Brad had just dropped a whole basket of french fries on the floor, making a loud noise. The new restaurant manager, La Bailey, aka The Bitch, was always on his back. Her face was twisted as she barked at him for making another mistake.

"Why are you always dropping shit? You know product cost money, lazy fat boy!"

Brad had taken a lot of bullshit from this woman, but cursing and insulting him in front of his coworkers and the customers was crossing the line. His nice switch went off, and his hood side was on the verge of coming out.

"Look, don't talk to me like I'm stupid," he said, raising his tone. "I'm warning you."

La Bailey didn't like to be challenged, especially when other people were around. Some stood with their mouths wide open, while others whispered and waited to see who would throw the first blow.

La Bailey stepped a few inches forward, speaking to Brad through gritted teeth. "You just dropped product on the floor, stupid! I'm warning you not to do it again, or there will be consequences."

"Don't yell at me if I'm not yelling at you! One more word and you're going to regret ever opening your fat mouth." Brad's light skin turned beet red, and his whole body started to tremble. He had to stand his ground.

Everyone was shocked to see him display so much anger. They never saw this side of Brad before, and it was almost scary. The Brad they knew was very nice, quiet, gentle, and laid back. La Bailey hadn't seen him like this either. Even she was shocked. Nonetheless, the evil glare in her eyes remained as she marched back into her office, slamming the door behind her.

Now that she was out of his sight, Brad felt embarrassed but relieved. He poured himself a cup of cold water and then found a rag to wipe the sheen of sweat from his forehead. He quickly got back to work, starting with picking up the fries off the floor.

It wasn't long before La Bailey opened her door and called out to him.

Shit! What does this ho want now? he thought. His anger had subsided, but after what had just happened, he wasn't sure if he would be able to control himself in La Bailey's presence again. He took a deep breath, and after going into her office, he took a seat, listening to her numerous complaints about him not following the rules.

"Your facial hair is too much," she said, peering over her glasses that sat on the tip of her pug nose. "You've been late three times since I've been here, and there are times when I've seen you standing around doing nothing."

Brad rocked low waves with a perfectly trimmed beard, so he wasn't sure what she was griping about. He admitted to being late three times, but only by minutes. As for him standing around, that claim was false. He'd worked harder than anyone else in the restaurant, and he hadn't been named Employee of the Month for no reason.

While stroking his beard, he narrowed his eyes, looking at La Bailey sitting with her legs crossed behind the desk. He didn't want to classify her as an angry black woman, but she sure as hell was representing.

"I don't know what your problem is with me, La Bailey, but I can tell you that this shit ain't funny. I work my ass off around here and—"

She quickly interrupted. "I do have a legitimate problem, and here's the deal. Our boss, Jon, put me in charge of this restaurant. I'm trying to get everything in order, and I don't appreciate people who slack all the time. This is a business, and—"

This time, Brad cut her off. "I know who the boss is, and I'm not knocking you for doing your job, but your position doesn't give you the right to talk nasty to people like you do. I'm grown, and so are you. You should know better, and if you want respect, you have to give it."

"Respect is something that you don't know anything about. You need to respect this place of business and do as you're told." She laughed, but he didn't see a damn thing funny.

"Listen, trick. I got one mama, and you ain't her. So are we done here, or would you like to speak to me about something else?"

She rolled her eyes, and with a tight face, she allowed her evilness to show. She was already an unattractive woman to Brad. He always thought she strutted around as if she were the prettiest brown-skinned woman in the world. With her shaved head and very thin frame, he didn't think so. She made claims about people telling her she resembled Beyoncé, but all he could do was laugh about that. If anything, that told him how messed up in the head she was.

Brad was also disgusted with La Bailey because she had the reputation of a whore. Her position came from her opening her legs, and everyone knew she'd slept with Jon to get the job. He even gave her a new car and an apartment in Town and Country, Missouri, an uppity part of town where affluent people resided. She literally thought that she was Ms. Rich Bitch, and to top it all off, she was married to a clueless, simpleminded man who thought she was a jewel. She'd told her husband that all the stuff she'd gotten was through the company. Brad figured her son came from the company, too, especially since he looked like Jon more than he did her husband. But like everyone else, Brad kept his mouth shut. It was none of his business, unless La Bailey continued to put him on blast.

She did, telling Brad exactly what else was on her mind. "I want you to clock out. You're fired, and no one—you hear me?—no one speaks to me like you just did."

Brad shot up from his chair like a rocket, releasing words that he had been dying to say to her. "Bitch, you can have this stupid-ass job! I wouldn't want to work another day with your trifling, messy ass. Good riddance, and don't forget to put my final check in the mail!"

She fired back, hissing at him so loudly that people outside the door could hear. "Messy? You're the one who is messy, fool. And as for your check, wait on it. I'll get to it when I can."

Brad tightened his fists. He was so ready to jump over the desk and crack her face, but the last thing he wanted was to be hauled out of the restaurant in handcuffs. He didn't have money for a lawyer, nor did he have bail money to get out of jail. With that in mind, he was able to maintain his composure. He loosened his fingers, and the only word that spilled from his mouth was, "Whatever."

La Bailey marched to the door then opened it. Everyone who had been listening in scattered as if they had been busy doing work. Brad was saddened by all that had happened, and as La Bailey began to rant to another manager about Brad, he ignored her. He clocked out and put up the deuces sign to everyone who looked on.

"And all y'all can kiss my light-skin ass!" Brad shouted.

Minutes later, Brad walked out of the building where he had been working for almost five years, still making minimum wage. He'd had bigger dreams than working at a restaurant, but he wasn't quite sure how to go about pursuing those dreams. For one, he could rap his ass off. He'd thought about pursuing that career, but everyone knew how difficult it was to break into the music industry. He was also skilled at drawing. Art was his second love, but most people weren't paying big dollars for artwork. He felt stuck, and it was so easy for him to settle. Now, though, he had to come up with a better plan—a plan that would help him satisfy his bills that were already tremendously behind.

Before Brad knew it, he'd driven at least seven miles away from the restaurant. The air conditioner in his car wasn't working; it was hot as hell. His shirt stuck to his sweaty skin, and the wrinkles on his forehead showed his frustration. He couldn't get La Bailey's words, "You're fired!" off his mind.

All he could think about was what he was going to do next, but after he pulled over at a gas station, he spotted a close friend who worked at the restaurant. Brad exited the car with a smile on his face.

"What's up, Stan?"

"What up, B?" They gave each other dap. "Why you off work so early?"

Brad looked away, trying to hide his disappointment. He then swallowed the huge lump in his throat before responding. "That bitch La Bailey fired my ass."

Stan cocked his head back and frowned. "What? Why?"

"Because I did something everyone in that place is afraid to do."

"And what was that?" Stan asked with a goofy smile.

"I stood up to her ass. Told her exactly what I felt, and she didn't like it."

Stan could only imagine how it had all gone down. He knew how Brad was when he got angry. It was funny to Stan, only because he was one of Brad's goofy friends. He knew how La Bailey was, and he would have given anything to see Brad crack her face. More than anything, though, Stan was a loyal friend. If any of his friends, including Brad, needed money, Stan would give them his last. He was only twenty-one years old, with a fat face that was real bumpy and a low-cut fade that did him no justice. He wasn't anywhere near as good-looking as Brad, but for some strange reason, some chicks appreciated his chubby frame and the thick Steve Urkel glasses on his face. Brad was sure it was Stan's personality that hooked him; he was undeniably a character.

"I wish I could have been a fly on the wall," Stan said, laughing. "And you know not to stand up to La Bailey. Everyone in that place either scared of her or kisses her ass, hard. I've never done it, and I'm surprised that she finally pushed you to your limit today."

"She did, and I just wasn't in the mood. The only reason I put up with her shit is because the economy is bad and people like me gotta keep they jobs. That's what I was thinking, but enough is enough."

"I feel you, man, trust me I do. But since you unemployed, what you gon' do?"

Brad took a deep breath. He wasn't sure yet, but he needed to think of something fast. "I got a little money saved up, and if all else fails, maybe I'll go back to school and take up a trade or something. Then I can find another job that's not related to the restaurant business."

"Man, good luck with that. You need money now. What you gon' do now?"

"Now, as in right now, I'm gon' go to my baby house and see what's up with her. Probably go catch a movie later and get some dinner. She ain't gon' be happy about me being fired, but she knows that I'll be back on my feet in no time."

"You know how women are, so I'll be praying for you, my brotha. Give me a holla later and let me know if I can help in any way."

They pounded fists then parted ways.

At the corner of Delmar and North Kingshighway Boulevard, Brad made a right and then parked his gold 1999 Toyota Camry in front of his girlfriend's apartment building. The second he walked inside, he saw that the elevator was out of order again. Already exhausted, he began to walk five floors upstairs to Nichelle's apartment. He knew that he needed to lose some weight, but even with a bulging stomach, Brad Julian Carter was a handsome man built like a linebacker. His smile and dimples were to die for, but his slanted, dark-brown eyes drew women to him.

Even though he was a big dude with confidence, at times he still wanted to feel better about himself physically. At one time, he had a goal to lose sixty pounds, but it was his girlfriend, Nichelle, who said he was fine the way he was. Plus, he remembered when Nichelle said she liked thick dudes. That was when he loved her hard. That really raised his confidence level and put his diet plans on hold.

Brad and Nichelle had their ups and downs, but she had been Brad's one true love for a little over two years. She accepted him "as-is," and Brad viewed her as the woman of his dreams. She was twenty-one, smart as a whip, and was a nursing student at STLCC-Forest Park.

She worked as a patient care tech at Barnes Jewish Hospital, and what Brad appreciated about her the most was how she often encouraged him to do better. He hoped that one day, when he got his life on the right path, Nichelle would be his wife, or at least his baby's mama.

By the time Brad reached Nichelle's door, he was panting and sweating like a dog in heat. His legs burned, and the Timberlands on his feet made climbing the stairs more difficult. He sucked in several heaps of air before sticking the key in the door. That's when he heard Usher & Rick Ross's "Let Me See" blasting. He made his way down the narrow hallway, not knowing that the high volume was the least of his worries.

The second he hit the doorway, he halted his steps. His eyes grew wide, and his heart fell to his stomach. Nichelle was on the bed with her legs wide open. Her loud moans echoed in the room, and her nails clawed the back of a muscular man who, obviously, had perfected his pussy-sucking skills. He moaned too, and as he expressed how delicious Nichelle's pussy tasted to him, Brad was speechless. He slowly inched his way into the room, soon realizing that the man between his woman's legs was his childhood nemesis, Garrett.

Garrett had always had it going on. His build was perfect. His brown skin was smooth and soft; hair was trimmed as if he visited the barber shop every day. His baggy jeans hung low on his waist, and with his shirt off, his muscles were in full effect.

Nichelle was getting served well. She was so aroused by Garrett's performance that she didn't see Brad standing there with shock and disgust written on his face. "Do that shit, baby," she said with her eyes shut tight. "I love how you make me feel. I . . . I needed this sooooo badly."

I can't believe this li'l ho, Brad thought as his stomach turned in knots. *Why did she have to do this shit to me, especially after two fucking years together? Two years and now this. What the fuck!*

Nichelle finally opened her eyes. They grew wide as saucers. "Brad! Wha . . . What are you doing here?"

Garrett snapped his head to the side, and after seeing Brad, he grinned. He used his tongue to take one last swipe at Nichelle's pussy before backing away from it. Without saying one word, he got off the bed and started zipping his pants. "Sorry about that," he said with a smirk on his face. "I couldn't help myself. I'm sure you already know how good she is."

As Brad continued to stand in awe, Nichelle hopped off the bed too. She hurried into her panties while keeping her eyes locked on Brad. "I . . . I'm sorry about this, but you should have called. Besides, I've been meaning to tell you a few things anyway."

Brad was so mortified that he didn't bother to respond. He didn't want to hurt Nichelle or Garrett, and he knew that if he stayed, he would definitely catch a case.

As he was going to the stairs, Nichelle followed him in her Mickey Mouse bathrobe. "Stop, Brad! We need to talk! You can't just leave without allowing me to say something!"

She snatched his arm, and that's what caused him to swing around and face her. "What's there to explain? You've been cheating on me with a nigga I've hated since high school! I wouldn't dare touch his leftovers, so you can march yo' ass back up to that apartment and let him finish what he started."

Nichelle ignored his harsh words, and since she'd been busted, it was time for her to face reality. She held on to Brad's arm so he wouldn't move. "Baby, I'm sorry you had to find out like this, but the truth is, sexually, you just didn't do it for me. I was never satisfied. I mean, you're a nice guy and all, but you're not for me. You could make some woman very happy one day."

She took a deep breath. "I . . . I need a real man in my life. I need a man who can bend me over like a slut, slap my ass and make it clap-slash-applaud him. You wanna settle down, but that's crazy. I'm only twenty-one and in college. I wanna have fun with as many dudes as I can. I don't want to hurt your feelings, but it's best that we be friends, if you want to still be that at all."

"Friends!" Brad shouted as his face shook and turned red again. "I gave you two fucking years of my life and this is how you treat me? You have the nerve to talk about what you need, but the truth is, I gave you exactly what you told me you needed and more. Gave you head, drank your cum, even pissed on yo' freaky ass. I was warned about you, and like my cousin said, all women are thots. Screw that love and happiness shit. Screw all you bitches, and all y'all gon' be good for is fucking!"

"I'm not a bitch, and to hell—"

Before Nichelle could finish her sentence, Brad raised his hand, slapping it hard across her face. She stumbled then fell back on the steps. While holding her face, she watched Brad rush down the stairs in anger.

"Trifling ass," he barked. "Never, ever again!"

With tears trapped in her eyes, Nichelle bit into her bottom lip, feeling dissed by Brad. "Fuck you, you fat-ass fool! I'ma get you back for putting your hands on me! I can promise you that, so watch your back!"

Brad was so disappointed by everything that had happened that day, and on the drive home, he couldn't help but shed a few tears. In his mind, men weren't supposed to cry, but this was horrible. He didn't know what the next day would bring, but as for this day, it couldn't get any worse. At least that's what he hoped.

**

Brad unlocked the door to his two-bedroom, one-bathroom house that he rented for $500 a month in University City on Canton Avenue. He went inside and tossed his jacket on a chair that was already piled high with clothes he needed to wash. He sat on his sofa looking over his mail. The cable bill was overdue, he was two months behind on his car payments, his internet was subject to disconnection soon, and his cell phone bill needed to be paid by the close of business that day. That wasn't going to happen, so he tossed his bills in the air then looked at the envelopes as they fell like rain and hit the floor. Staring at the floor, he hung his head low.

Brad couldn't help but think about how he'd been doing shit on his own since he was a child. His mother, Belinda Carter, had died in childbirth at the age of 15. He was raised by his grandmother, whom he called Mama Carter. Brad's father wanted a football career, and a child would have messed that up. When Brad was ten, Mama Carter was diagnosed with breast cancer, and on his twelfth birthday, she died. She was a loving woman who had worked as a bank teller and taught Brad he could be anything he put his mind to. With her gone, her brother took her house and any money she had. Brad was left with nothing and nowhere to go.

Remembering these things only made the awful day Brad had been having seem even worse. He went to the kitchen to get himself a cold drink. He found his last beer at the back of the refrigerator, opened it, and took a long drink. It felt good going down, and for a minute he felt better, but then the memories hit him again.

Brad remembered how his great aunt had stepped up to help him. Her old friend was the mother of Brad's father, Dewayne. Dewayne had become the football star he wanted to be, and his sneaky mother told him that taking in Brad would look good to his fans, so Brad went to live with him. But he barely spent any time with Brad, while he treated his other children from a previous marriage like gold. When Brad was fourteen, his father injured his right knee and lost his contract with the St. Louis Rams. With no money, left. Mainly because of his father's high spending and his semi cocaine habit, they had to move out of his luxurious six-bedroom, eight-bathroom mansion in Ladue, Missouri and downgrade to a small apartment in Bridgeton. From then on, Dewayne blamed Brad for everything that went wrong and made his life a living hell.

Brad was angry remembering how his father made him do everything around the house but wouldn't even give him food, even telling him he was the cause of both his mother's and grandmother's deaths. It was a terrible time and got worse when Brad was sixteen and his father got a job to play with the Toronto Argonauts. He took his other children with him and left Brad with a thousand dollars out of his three hundred thousand dollar contract to get by on his own. Dewayne left a note saying, *Don't spend it all in one place.*

Brad was so mad he burned that money and stayed with cousins and friends, working two or three jobs at a time, until he was able to get steady work and make a life for himself. He remembered that he promised Mama Carter before she died that he was going to make her proud of him, and he was determined to do just that.

Brad started to feel better, thinking about all he had been able to survive. He went back into the living room. Sitting on the sofa, he took another long drink and laid his head back, letting the alcohol take effect. He was about to turn on the TV until the doorbell rang. He lifted his head, wondering who had come to see him.

The second he opened the door, he knew it had been a bad idea. It was his landlord, Chris Stolle, a short, fat white man with glasses, who could give the actor Drew Carey a run for his money.

"What's up, Mr. Stolle?"

His hand was out and he tapped his palm. "I'm still waiting for my rent money. Do you have it?"

Brad wasn't even thirty days late yet, but Chris was the kind of landlord who wanted his money exactly when it was due. Brad's intentions were to pay the money next week, but so much for that.

"I kinda don't have it right now, but I will have it soon." *Now go away,* he thought. *Not today, please.*

Chris took a deep breath. "Look, Brad, you've been in this house for two years, and you're late again. I know the month isn't over yet, but I don't want you to go months without paying me like you did in the past. If you can't pay me soon, I will have to issue you a thirty-day notice and ask you to leave so I can rent this house to someone who can pay me on time."

Take this raggedy piece of shit then. You don't fix shit in this rat hole anyway. Family-Guy-looking bastard, thought Brad with a smirk on his face. "All I need is a little more time and I promise to get your money to you, okay?"

"You have until the sixteenth of this month. No rent and you go!" Without saying another word, Chris walked off the porch without turning around to see the wicked look in Brad's eyes and his middle finger that stood straight up, telling Chris where to stick it.

Sometimes, I really do hate white people, Brad thought while watching Chris get into his Mercedes. *Greed, greed, greed.* He also recognized that a lot of this was on him, and if he didn't come up with plan B fast, he was going to be fucked!

Chapter 2

The Deal

That Friday evening, Brad was sitting in the living room on his laptop, looking at his Facebook page and conversing with friends. He ignored all of Nichelle's messages, but when he examined her page, he saw recent photos she had posted of her and Garrett together. He still couldn't believe what she'd done, and as he thought more about his fucked up situation, he kept in mind what Mama Carter used to say: "God always makes a way out of no way." He held onto those words, and as he took a sip of his Snapple fruit punch, Drake's "The Motto (Remix)" ringtone went off on his cell phone. Brad looked to see who the caller was. His boy Tyler's number was displayed on the screen.

"What's up?" Brad said after pushing the speakerphone button.

"Shit. What you doin'?" Tyler asked.

"His ass probably bored," said another male voice in the background.

Brad smiled, knowing exactly who it was. "Is that Travis's crazy ass?"

"Yeah, that's him."

"What's up, fool? I called you the other day, but you ain't hit me back."

"Been busy," Travis said. "The struggle is real, but you do know what tonight is, don't you?"

Brad squinted while trying to think. "Naw, you tell me what's poppin' tonight."

"What? You forgot?" Travis asked.

"Forgot what?"

"Man, I can't believe you forgot about your cousin Swag's birthday party at that hot new nightclub, The Cartel, downtown."

Brad now remembered. He rubbed his forehead then released a deep breath. "Damn. I forgot about that. I didn't know he was back from vacation. Regardless, I need to get out of here tonight. What time y'all wanna hook up?"

"'Bout ten thirty," Tyler said. "And we're taking Travis's car."

"What?" yelled Travis.

The fellas laughed.

"Cool. I'ma holla at Stan to see if he wanna roll with us. The more, the merrier," said Brad, still laughing.

"That's what's up. Just tell that fool to be there by the time we get there," said Tyler before ending the call.

Later that night, things were on and popping at The Cartel. It was thick with partygoers there to celebrate Swag's twenty-second birthday, and there were several other parties in the process as well. The DJ blasted 2 Chainz's new joint that had the whole club jumping. Brad, Stan, and the twins, Tyler and Travis, were in the VIP section of the club, looking for the birthday boy, who was late. It was going on midnight, and Swag still wasn't there.

"Damn, where that fool at?" Stan asked.

"Don't know," Tyler said, shrugging his shoulders. "But he can be late if he wants to. Just like Brad was late for work all the time. You should've known that yo' ass would eventually get fired."

Brad didn't respond. He was trying to put that behind him. He was a little disturbed by Tyler's comment, but he was there to have a good time.

"For real, man? You out of work?" Travis asked, looking at Brad as if he didn't already know he'd been fired.

Brad answered, pretending as if it were no big deal. "Yeah, I was tired of that place and half the people in it. I got something else lined up. Just waiting to hear something back soon."

Travis shrugged his shoulders this time. "Well, don't sweat it. If you need a place to stay, I got you. My sofa bed is always available for as long as you need it. That is, until my lady comes over. Then yo' ass has to go somewhere 'til we done. That's the main rule if you stay wit' me, bruh."

Both Brad and Travis laughed, but Brad had mad respect for that. Who would want someone on their sofa while he's trying to get it on with his woman?

Brad would probably have to take him up on his offer if it came to moving out of his crib. He thanked Travis then they gave each other dap. Since junior high school, Brad and the twins had been friends. They had each other's backs, and with the twins being on the wrestling team, no one ever messed with them. They were muscular and cocky, with brown skin and hazelnut eyes. The only difference between them was that Travis had a low cut and was clean shaved because of his mailroom job at Fowlers Publishing. Tyler had cornrows and a thick beard. He was a barber at one of St. Louis's hottest barbershop/ beauty salons. He had high hopes of opening his own shop one day.

As the night went on, they continued to toss back drinks, dance, and converse with plenty of females who had made themselves available. Brad had halfway forgotten about his problems from earlier, especially after a female who was ten times better-looking than

Nichelle had given him her undivided attention. He was sitting at a table with her when Swag came in, garnering full attention from nearly everyone in the place.

Solomon Carter was his government name, but he was known on the streets of St. Louis as Swag. He was half black, half Puerto Rican, and considered one of the hot boys in the Lou. His light skin glowed with a tan, and his deep-set eyes lured women straight to the bedroom. He had mega money, a fly whip, and lived in a 3000-square-foot loft in the downtown area. Swag had two sons, Solomon Jr, aka Li'l Swag, and Namond. Both kids were by a fine-ass chick in the Lou, Zaria Mitchell. She was by his side tonight, and a trophy she was. Her skin was cocoa brown, and her long, jet black hair flowed midway down her back. Her eyes were slanted, and her hourglass figure showed well in the pink strapless dress she rocked, looking like it was painted on her. You could have a picnic on her ass, and many people had mistaken her for rapper Li'l Wayne's ex-wife, Toya Wright.

Another reason that Swag got his name was because he could dress his ass off. He had on a red-and-black long sleeve shirt, True Religion jeans that showed off his stallion-like frame, the new Jordans, and a platinum chain around his neck with a cross piece resting on his chest. To rep St. Louis, a red Cardinal's cap was on his head.

Everyone greeted Swag as he and Zaria made their way to the table where the crew was at. They all pounded and hugged him.

"What's up, fellas? Sorry I'm late, but nonetheless, I am here," Swag said with a big-ass smile on his face.

"Better late than never," Brad replied. "Good seeing you, man."

Brad looked at Zaria, who looked sexy as hell. "What's up, Z?"

"Hey, B." Zaria smiled. "Good seeing you too."

"Now that I'm here," Swag shouted, "let's get some more drinks and really get this party started! Drinks for everyone!"

The music cranked up, and everyone clapped, cheered, and wished him a happy birthday.

A while later, Brad had drunk so much that he made himself sick. The room kept spinning, and he was starting to feel dizzy. He couldn't even dance with the beautiful woman he'd been talking to for most of the night. Before she left him at peace, she eased her phone number into his pocket.

"Don't forget to call me," she said, whispering in his ear. "I have something real special for you, okay?"

Brad definitely wanted to know what that was, but tonight he wasn't feeling it. He just wanted to go home and lay his head on a pillow.

By 4:30 a.m., The Cartel was damn near empty. Everybody had a good time, and Brad was feeling a little more upbeat. All he probably needed was something to eat. He sat at a table with Swag, Stan, Travis, and Tyler, eating hot wings and talking shit like they always did when they hung out.

Swag, who had given Zaria money for cab fare an hour ago, had been rambling on and on about his vacation to Rio de Janeiro and Miami. He claimed that whenever he went to either place, he was partying every night and sleeping with some of the most exotic women he had ever seen.

"Maaaaan, those Brazilian females are some of the baddest women out there, bruh. All different varieties to pick from—light brown, Indian, and Latina. This Indian chick I fucked was a virgin. She was so tight; the shit felt too good! It's been a minute since ya boy had a virgin. And trust me when I say they are the best ones, for real."

Stan agreed. "True that, true that. You ain't speaking nothing but the truth."

For whatever reason, Brad assumed Swag had been nothing but faithful to Zaria. After all, she was the total package and then some in his eyes. "Man, what about Zaria? She's the mother of your boys, and she really loves you. If I had a chick like that, shiiiit, I would never even look at another woman."

"She's good, real good, but at the end of the day, all these tricks care about is the money and the dick. The only reason I'm wit' that gold digger is 'cause of my kids. I don't have to pay no child support right now. And at the end of the day, I wouldn't put a wedding ring on a thot's finger. Not now, not ever. Sorry, cuz, but I can't live that fairy tale life you and Nichelle got. Fairy tales always come to an end. You'd better believe that."

"I do believe, and I know all too well. Mine ended today when I busted Nichelle in bed with her legs wide open while getting her pussy sucked by another man."

"Daaaaaaamn," said the fellas in unison.

"Straight up," Swag said with his head cocked back. "I'm sorry to hear that. "What happened after that? I know you beat that ass, didn't you?"

Brad took a breath. "I wanted to, but I didn't. My whole day was fucked up. Got fired from my job, and when I thought I could get some loving and sympathy from my girl, that trick was hemmed up with Garrett."

Swag pondered for a second then snapped his fingers. "You mean Garrett, the one we used to jump for always talking shit?" He took a sip of his Heineken, waiting for Brad to reply.

"Yep, that sucka. That's exactly who it was." Brad visualized what he had witnessed earlier. The vision of Nichelle squirming on the bed and hearing her moans in his head angered him.

Tyler could see how upset his friend was. He knew Garrett as well, so he had to weigh in, "Man, I guess ol' dude ain't learned shit after all those ass whippings and from almost being tossed out of the window. He better be glad I stopped myself from tripping that day, but I still did a year in military school 'cause of that shit."

The fellas laughed as they reminisced about the incident that had everyone in the school talking.

"So, cuz, do you want me to take care of this dude and ol' girl for you?" Swag asked. "You know I got some contacts that will take them off the scene in a second."

Brad threw his hand back then picked up another wing. "Nah, I ain't fightin' over that slut. And as for Garrett, he can eat a dick for all I care. I'm done."

"I wouldn't waste my time either," Stan said. "But what about yo' job? How you gon' pay your bills?"

Swag pulled out a big roll of hundred-dollar bills. "Don't worry 'bout that, cuz. I got you. How much you—"

"No," Brad said, shaking his head. "I can handle this, and as a matter of fact, I will handle this."

"But, B, we fam, and fam help each other out when need be."

Brad tossed back a shot of vodka. "Sorry, but I learned a long time ago not to take handouts from nobody. I have plans to get through this on my own."

Just as Swag was about to speak up, they were interrupted by a man with a deep Portuguese accent. "Evening, or should I say good morning, gentlemen."

They all turned around and saw a Brazilian man who was six foot two, in his mid-forties, fair-skinned, with black hair cut in a Caesar. His thick eyebrows and round-shaped dark eyes made him look mysterious. He was very handsome with strong features, and sometimes people mistook him for being Arabian. What they could tell right away was the man had money. His navy blue Giorgio

Armani suit, white Gucci dress shirt, silk navy blue Gucci tie, black Prada leather loafers, platinum Burberry watch, and diamond wedding band confirmed his status. The suit showed off his muscular frame, telling them that the stranger worked out on a regular basis.

The stranger was not alone, and standing to his right was a woman with flawless chocolate-colored skin, almond-shaped eyes, a cute button nose, juicy heart-shaped lips, and long, jet black curly hair that flowed to the tip of her ass. She looked ready for the runway, with firm breasts and long legs. An Aidan Mattox gold one-shoulder dress enhanced her figure, and Jimmy Choo sandals were on her feet. The fellas were in awe as they looked at her. She made Swag's girl look like a welfare queen.

There was a man standing behind everyone. Dark shades shielded his eyes, and his large frame made him look like he could break someone in half in an instant. His thick mustache was a bit awkward, and the black suit he wore was tailored.

Swag stood up to address the man next to him. "Armand, what's shaking?"

They shook hands as everyone else looked on, a bit confused about who the man was. Swag looked at his crew. "Fellas, this is my boss, Armand Castro." Swag looked over at the sexy model chick next to Armand. "And this is, uh, uh . . ."

"Milena," she said in a seductive voice.

Swag was in a trance with how beautiful Milena was, but from the corner of his eye, Armand's bodyguard removed his shades to shoot Swag an evil gaze.

"Let me try this again," Swag said jokingly. "Armand, these my boys, Tyler, Travis, Stan, and my cousin, Brad. Fellas, this is my boss and his lady, Milena. Their body-guard is Sandino."

They all greeted each other. Minutes later, a waitress brought a chair for Armand, and Milena sat on his lap. He then ordered several bottles of Moët for everyone at the table. That got everyone's attention, especially when Armand gave the waitress a hundred-dollar tip.

"Thanks. I'll be back wit' y'all drinks soon," the waitress said, giddy as ever. She walked away with a big smile on her face like she had just hit the number.

Swag rubbed his hands together. "So, Armand, to what do I owe this pleasure?"

Armand laughed. "I wanted to wish my best employee a happy birthday."

Brad thought, *What has Swag gotten himself into now? This dude is always in some shit.* Brad knew his cousin was a hustler. He did everything from selling dime bags, selling bootleg movies, being a stickup man, to gambling.

"Thanks, Armand. I appreciate that."

The waitress came back with three bottles of Moët and champagne glasses. Just before she left, she poured Moët into their glasses. "Have a good evening, gentlemen." She walked away.

Once the giddy waitress left, Armand lifted his glass in the air. "To Swag. Happy birthday, and many more to come, just so we can continue to do business together. To Swag!"

"To Swag," everyone shouted before sipping from their glasses.

Armand wasn't done giving his praises just yet. "First off, Swag, I have to say good job that you did in Miami. I hope the money was good."

"My bread always be good, and thank you very much." Swag smiled then sipped from his glass again.

The fellas remained quiet as they listened in, but plenty of thoughts ran through their heads, especially Brad's.

What the hell is Swag into now? Brad thought. *This doesn't sound good, but I sure would like to get my hands on some of Armand's money.*

Damn that suit, Tyler thought. *I wonder how much it cost. I wish I could afford to wear something like that.*

My ass ain't never been to Miami, Stan thought as he guzzled down the Moët. *I want to go there, just to feast my eyes upon all of the beautiful women. Swag is one lucky dude.*

I would fuck the shit out of Milena, thought Tyler. *Damn, she fine. I wonder if she would be interested in a brother like me. If she look over here one more time, I'ma need to see what's up.*

The attention transferred back to Armand when he spoke up again. "I have another assignment for you. And if you'd like, your friends can help you with this task, especially since it may be too big for one person."

Brad almost choked on his drink, but they were all ears.

"Tell us more about it," Swag said. "More so, how much and when?"

Armand laughed then squeezed Swag's shoulder. "I'll get to that soon, but how about this? I fly all of you out to Rio de Janeiro in the next few days, first class. You stay a few nights, party, shop, have sex . . . do whatever your hearts desire. But after your stay, there are some packages I need you to take from Brazil to Los Angeles. There is a man whom I know will pay you all big, big dollars. Something like . . ." He paused to light his Cuban cigar, and as everyone leaned in to hear how much, Armand whistled smoke into the air.

"How much?" Stan said with excitement in his voice.

Armand smiled then laughed again. "Fifty grand each."

All of their mouths dropped wide open. Swag was the first one to speak up. "Shit, I'm in! Count me in right now!" He reached for Armand's hand, shaking the shit out of it.

"We are too," Stan, Travis, and Tyler yelled. "Let's go now."

Brad was the only one mulling things over. He hadn't said one word yet. Swag pushed his shoulder, attempting to knock him out of the trance he was in.

"Cuz, you in or not? Tell us now. What's it gon' be?"

Brad remained in deep thought. *Damn, ain't this drug trafficking? I don't know if I should do this or not. What if we get caught and go to jail? But then again, fifty Gs would save my life right about now. I need to pay these bills. I could pay my rent up for a year or just move into a new place altogether. Get a new ride, take some classes at Flo Valley, and while I'm looking for another job, try to collect unemployment. Fuck it! What in the hell do I have to lose?*

Brad smiled as he reached out to shake Armand's hand too. "I'm in."

"Great," Armand said with his pearly white teeth on display.

Milena got up from his lap. He stood up then snapped his fingers at her. "Oh, umm, get that for me, dear."

She opened her Gucci bag then pulled out a rolled-up plastic Ziploc bag, placing it on the table.

"Happy birthday, Swag! Enjoy, fellas. See you all soon."

Armand gave everyone a pat on the back before he and Milena walked off, holding hands.

Swag unrolled the Ziploc bag, noticing right away that it was cocaine. "Ahhh, damn!" He laughed and rubbed his hands together. "This is the real good shit!"

The crew looked at Swag like he was crazy.

"Yo, cuz, when did you start snorting that shit?" Brad asked.

"Don't worry 'bout it. The question is, do y'all want some? There's plenty to go around."

Travis backed away from the table. "Nah, man, I can't even mess wit' it. They check my piss at work, and I ain't about to lose my job."

"I'ma just stick to my weed," Tyler said.

"Me and you both," Stan added.

Brad was highly disappointed in his cousin. All he did was stand and reply, "I'm ready to go."

"Cool," Swag said, grabbing the bag and putting it in his pocket. "More for me. Now, come on, cuz. I'll take you home."

They parted ways, feeling uneasy about Swag but excited about the offer Armand had made.

Things were quiet between Brad and Swag in his black Ford F-150 pickup truck, but the radio blasted an old Jadakiss song that had Swag bobbing his head. Brad had questions about the journey they would soon take, so he lowered the volume and looked at Swag.

"How long have you been trafficking?"

Swag nodded his head to the song while looking at Brad. "What?"

"Fool, you heard me. When did you start drug trafficking?"

Swag turned off his radio, put a Black & Mild cigar in his mouth, then lit it. Blowing out the smoke, he said, "About a few months now."

"Man, you gon' get yo' ass caught up one of these days, and I hope it won't be soon. You got your girl and your sons to think about. You don't want to put yourself in a situation where you have to make calls to them from jail, do you?"

"Hell no, but I gotta do what I gotta do to support myself and my fam. Jobs ain't exactly hiring high school dropouts, and if you got a record like me, forget it. And I ain't flippin' no burgers or cleaning these crackers' dirty-ass toilets for pennies." Swag took another puff of his cigar. "Plus, I make more money trafficking than I did being a stick-up kid or selling dimes when I was working for that Puerto Rican dude."

"Yeah, I remember that. You were working for one of the most powerful criminal families in the Lou. Getting paid too. How the hell did you get wit' Armand?"

"One of my boys hooked me up wit' him. I saw how my boy was living in a nice condo and had three brand new cars. All I had was an old school Cadillac that was barely making it, and a shitty apartment. Armand asked if I wanted to go to Brazil to take some drugs to Paris. I did it and got my fifty Gs. From then on, I was hooked."

Brad sat speechless while in deep thought. *Why did I agree to make this trip? What if we all get caught? Damn. Is it too late to change my mind?*

Swag smiled. "Before long, you gon' be hooked too. Fifty grand looks good in your hands, and I bet you'll want to keep the money flowing."

"All I wanna do is get some shit paid off and maybe get a new place and a new car. That's it. After that, I'm done. A second trip I will not commit to."

"Yeah, whatever," Swag said, pulling his car in front of Brad's house. "Take it easy. See you soon, and get a lot of rest, a'ight, cuz."

"Most definitely."

Brad reached for the door handle, but Swag stopped him. "B, I almost forgot. Here."

Brad took an envelope from Swag. When he opened it, there were several hundred-dollar bills inside.

"Swag, man, I can't take this. I already told you—"

"Shut up and put yo' pride aside. We blood, and we gotta stick together. Now take it and don't worry about paying it back."

They pounded.

"Thanks," Brad said. "I will pay you back, sooner rather than later."

That's what Brad hoped. If everything went according to the plan in Rio, he would be back on track. If not, it would be a major setback for sure.

Chapter 3

The Ice Queen

While looking over submissions from advertisers and photos of models to put in her magazine, CEO and Publisher Taylor Monroe appeared frustrated. Her team had given her garbage to put in *Brazilian Kouture,* her upscale fashion and entertainment magazine. It had been the best fashion and entertainment magazine in South America for the past nine years and was still going strong. She threw all of the photos and ads on the round glass table before getting up to address her team. Editor-in-Chief Ramon, Entertainment Editor Sabrina, and Sports Editor Braxton paid close attention.

"This is all terrible. December's issue is dedicated to the men of South America. Plus, *Brazilian Kouture* is an upscale fashion magazine, not a blog. You all have to go back to the drawing board and give me something that says *Brazilian Kouture,* 'cause this shit isn't it." Taylor walked over to her desk then plopped down in her chair. She narrowed her eyes and shot her team a dirty look that implied how pissed she was.

"Bye!" She waved them off. "Go find me something I can use! Thank you!"

Everyone left her office with frowns on their faces.

Taylor had been in the fashion world for twenty-seven years. She had been in love with fashion ever since she was five years old, due to having the best of everything from the time she was born.

Taylor's real name was Selena Luis, born to Iris Cortes, whose family in Brazil was known for a gun smuggling operation. Her father, Cruz Luis, was head of the Colombian Mob known for smuggling cocaine all over the globe. When Iris and Cruz hooked up, and with both of their families' crime backgrounds, it was a match made in heaven. When Selena was born, they spoiled her to death, and money was coming left and right. They were living a lavish life in Bogotá, Colombia.

Selena was about nine years old when her parents sent her to London, putting her in one of the best boarding schools for girls. When her family gave her a weekly allowance, she would have the malls in the UK on lockdown. But the one thing she loved buying were fashion magazines from *Vogue* to *Elle*. Selena was determined to live the glamorous lifestyle no matter what.

She was eleven years old when an agent from Wilhelmina Models approached her in her school uniform while she was shopping the mall with one of her friends who was tall, blond, and beautiful. The modeling agent was from New York and wanted to sign her right away. With the blessings of her parents, she changed her name to Taylor Monroe, taking the last names of her two favorite actresses, Marilyn Monroe and Elizabeth Taylor. She did her first runway show for Versace in Milan. After her big fashion debut, and for the past seventeen years of her supermodel career, she walked the runways of Paris, New York, and Japan. She even worked with every top designer from Chanel to Dior and graced the covers of every magazine from *Vanity Fair* to *Bazaar*.

She'd dated and slept with all types of men and women from black to Italian, Iranian, rappers, political figures, doctors, and corporate executives. By the time Taylor was twenty-eight, she was the richest supermodel in the world. That was also when she hooked up with Brazil's notorious drug kingpin, who was worth billions. After two months of dating him, she married him. She wasn't ready to have any children yet, and her husband wasn't ready for her to ruin her perfect body. So instead of having a child, Taylor formed her own magazine back in Brazil. It was her way of giving back to her country.

It had been one of the hottest magazines in South America ever since, but there were two things she hated about her business. For one, her husband was an investor in the company; therefore, he walked in and out of the company when he felt like it. Secondly, he did all of the hiring, from editors to the gardeners, many of whom he was sleeping with. She wanted to fire ninety percent of the staff but couldn't because of her husband. If she could, she would blow up the whole building.

Taylor got up from her chair and looked at herself in a full-length mirror. She resembled the Colombian actress Sofia Vergara. Her fair skin was flawless, her honey-brown hair fell down her back, and her brown eyes were big and round. She went over to the rack of clothes sent to her by designers. Deciding which one to wear for the MMA fight that night, she turned around, startled that Ramon was behind her.

"Oh my goodness, Ramon. Don't ever do that again." She held her chest while taking deep breaths.

"Sorry, and I didn't mean to scare you. But can I talk to you for a few minutes?"

"Is it very important, Ramon? Because I have to get ready for a very important engagement this evening." She went over to her desk and sat. Ramon walked over to the chair across from her desk, but before he took a seat, she yelled at him. "Stand!"

He trembled from the sound of her loud voice and remained standing.

Silence fell over the room as Taylor ignored him and looked at her computer.

"Taylor, me and the team feel that having a men's issue for next month is kind of stressful. Plus, we feel that having Desmond Diaz on the cover of an elegant, high fashion magazine would send a bad message to our readers."

"Oh, really," Taylor said, still looking at her computer. Deep inside, she was pissed.

"Yes, and as Editor-in-Chief, I feel that we should sell to the women of today in South America. I think we should have a strong woman on the cover, like Gisele Bundchen or Beyonce. It could make us cross over to the United States."

Asshole, thought Taylor with her eyes glued on the computer. That was one of the many things she hated about Ramon. He thought the magazine was his and everything should be his way. If it were up to Taylor, he would've been gone a long time ago.

She winced and looked at him with her boss-bitch attitude. "Ramon, look at this office. This is my damn office. Not yours, and not anyone else's."

Taylor's office was all white with a touch of classic and contemporary furniture.

On the walls were photographs of her in her modeling days, along with black and white photos of her idols, the late legendary actresses Elizabeth Taylor and Vivien Leigh. She even had big paintings of Marylyn Monroe and Elizabeth Taylor in their younger years together, which had cost her a pretty penny.

"If this makes any sense to you, I'm the CEO, publisher, and head bitch in charge of this magazine. I decide what goes and doesn't go in this damn magazine. Your job is to make sure you keep those untalented bastards in line. If you can't do that, maybe you should go back to modeling again and fuck up miserably." Taylor smiled. She knew Ramon hated when she bought up his failing career as a model. He was one of the top male models in South America and Europe. When he thought he could make extra money doing porn, that career move messed his modeling career up royally, which led him to drugs and escorting, until Taylor's husband cleaned him up and made him Editor-in-Chief.

Taylor waved him off. "Go, please. I'm tired of looking at you. Don't come back until you have some better ideas for the magazine."

Ramon cut his eyes at Taylor before marching out of her office with a twisted face.

After he left, Taylor went over to a clothing rack, searching for something to wear. She wasn't giving up until she found the right dress and heels. Nothing seemed to jump out at her, but just as she set her eyes on an elegant dress with a bell sleeve, her speakerphone buzzed. Taylor walked over to her desk and pushed the intercom button.

"Yes, Maria."

"Taylor, Milena's here to see you."

"Thank you. Send her in, Maria." Taylor went over to her chair and sat with a wide smile on her face. "I wonder what my protégé has for me today."

Within moments, Milena came in looking beautiful without a drop of makeup on. She rocked a Catherine Malandrino jumpsuit and flip flops. Her long hair was in a ponytail. She smiled at Taylor as she strutted over to a chair in front of her desk.

They had been best friends for three years, ever since they met at the MMA match in Sao Paulo that Taylor's husband had forced her to go to. She preferred to be at a fashion show in Milan or at a shopping mall with some of her closest friends. But during the fight, Taylor went to the ladies' room, where she met Milena, an aspiring model who was waiting for her big brother, Desmond

Diaz, to fight. She had offered Taylor a seat next to her, and since Taylor took a liking to Milena, she accepted.

At the fight, Taylor immediately fell head over heels for Desmond. After he won the match, she had to meet him, because she couldn't get him off her mind. One thing led to another, and when all was said and done, Milena and Taylor became the best of friends. One of the things that Taylor liked about Milena was that she was like a younger version of her. When Taylor built up enough confidence to talk to Milena's brother, Milena offered to be Taylor's husband's new toy. Taylor loved her even more, and they kept the game of playing with Armand while Taylor was developing a loving relationship with Desmond. Taylor wanted to make it official one day and use the information Milena was giving her to get rid of Armand.

"Darling, you are looking so stunning in that outfit," Taylor said.

"All thanks to your husband. He spent millions on me back in St. Louis." Milena laughed.

They high fived each other.

"So, what is the scoop on Armand in St. Louis?"

"Well, one of his traffickers, Swag, and his friends are coming to Rio in a couple of days to traffic cocaine from here to California."

"Really? Where is he putting them?"

"In one of his apartments in downtown Rio."

"Excellent." Taylor smiled evilly.

"What are you going to do with that little bit of information I gave you?"

Taylor shrugged and waved off the question. "Don't be so nosy, darling. It's for me to know and you to find out."

Right then, her phone buzzed again.

"Yes, Maria?"

"Taylor, the limo driver is here."

"Thank you, Maria. Tell him that I'll be ready in few minutes."

Taylor got up from her desk and stood behind a dressing screen to get ready for Desmond's fight.

"So, where are you going?" Milena asked. "You and Armand have a date?" She knew that would tick Taylor off.

"Ha, ha, very funny," Taylor said. "I'm getting ready for the fight tonight at the HSBC Arena." She pulled down her pants and panties.

"And Desmond?"

The sound of his name turned Taylor on. "I'm getting ready for him too."

"So, what excuse did you give Armand this time?"

Taylor stepped from behind the dressing screen looking runway ready. "Please. He'll be too busy fucking his three while his ten is having a better time."

Milena laughed. "Come on. Let's go downstairs so I can get my hair, nails, and makeup done. And as for you, you'd better be on your best behavior tonight. Promise that you will."

"I don't make promises that I can't keep."

They both laughed then left Taylor's office together.

That evening at the HSBC Arena, MMA superstar Desmond Diaz was in the cage, beating the shit out of his opponent, The Beast, with kickboxing, boxing, Brazilian jiu-jitsu and plain old whip-ass techniques.

Not wanting to be in the noisy crowd or having sweat and blood on her sexy dress, Taylor decided to watch the fight in Desmond's private dressing room. Desmond had everything in there she would need from roses to champagne, whipped cream, strawberries, chocolates, and honey. It was just a matter of minutes before he would return to the dressing room, and after he won the fight, the crowd went wild. So did Taylor. She watched on the flat screen as Desmond talked to reporters, who were asking him how he felt about another win. The reporters also questioned him about rumors pertaining to him going to Hollywood to star in films. Desmond answered everything but said "no comment" to the Hollywood question.

Taylor could tell from the look on his face that he was in a hurry to get to the dressing room. She quickly slipped out of her dress, leaving only her heels on. She looked at her body in the full-length mirror and licked her lips.

Damn, if I was a man, I'd fuck me too.

She put on Desmond's robe then waited. Minutes later, there was a knock on the door. Taylor stood in the middle of the room looking ready to eat.

"Come in," she whispered.

Desmond came into the room, locking the door behind him. His body dripped with sweat, and several bruises could be seen on his face and hands. He still looked sexy to Taylor. He was six foot nine, with cinnamon-colored skin, a muscle-packed body, light gray eyes, and a bald head, and Taylor was eager to wrap her legs around the twenty-four-year-old MMA superstar.

Desmond had won black and white belts, a gold medal, and many World MMA awards. He was trained by his father and grandfather, who were former MMA champions. He owned his own martial arts studio, House of Diaz, which helped inner city youth in Rio. He also owned a five-star restaurant, an MMA gear shop, and a health spa/gym. He was voted sexiest man alive by *People* three years in a row. Plus, he'd been on the covers of *Sports Illustrated*, *ESPN*, and *GQ*. Even Hollywood movie directors had been calling him and his agent's phone like crazy. They wanted him to star in action films. Directors believed that with Desmond's body and strikingly good looks, he could be the next Vin Diesel. Most of the roles he was offered were turned down. One was about a slave turned bounty hunter, which was later given to a famous comedian turned Oscar winner. Another was a starring role alongside action hero legends.

With all of his fame and success, the ladies were all over his jock, but it was Taylor who had stolen his heart. He would do anything to make her officially his.

Desmond's eyes scanned Taylor up and down as he slid his robe off his shoulders. His manhood increased by several inches and was soon rock hard.

"Congratulations, champ," Taylor said, slowly walking over to him. She wrapped her arms around him, kissing his lips gently.

His hands roamed her ass before he squeezed it. "Damn, Pinky, that's what I'm talking about."

She loved when he called her Pinky, and she was on a serious high when he picked her up and rushed her over to a dresser. With one swipe of his hand, he knocked everything off the dresser and sat Taylor on top of it. They continued to kiss while Desmond caressed and massaged her 38C breasts.

"Mmmmm," she moaned as she felt moistness building between her legs.

Desmond slipped his index and middle fingers inside of her pink walls. After coating his fingers with her heavy glaze, he put them in his mouth to taste her.

"Damn, Pinky, you taste real good."

"Good? How about I show you better."

She pushed his head down low, causing him to get on his knees, spread her legs apart, and dive in.

"Ahh, shit," she groaned.

Taylor played with her nipples before her hands went down to Desmond's head, forcing him deeper inside of her pussy to make her cum. "Ahhhh, fuck me, baby! I want more! Give me some more!"

She said the magic words for Desmond, who quickly got up from his knees. He licked his wet lips then pulled down his shorts with the help of Taylor. His penis was a thick ten inches long that always filled her to full capacity.

"You ready, Pinky?"

She nodded and smiled like a kid in a candy store. "Yes, D. I'm always ready for you."

He navigated his dick inside of her, and within seconds, the room filled with heat. Their lips and bodies smacked together. Desmond slapped Taylor's ass and tore into her like a beast.

"Ahhhh, mmmm, yessss!" she shouted as she enjoyed the feel of him sliding in and out of her pussy. "I've been wanting this dick all day!"

"Now you got it, so use it allllll to your advantage." Desmond groaned while holding on to Taylor's hips. He felt his dick pulsating, and all he could say was, "Ohhh, shit!"

They kissed to calm him, but as Desmond sucked and licked Taylor's nipples, he caused her to cum. She wrapped her arms around his neck, squeezing it tight. "Shit, D, I wanna taste my cum! Let me taste it, okay?"

Desmond had no problem with that. He eased his dripping wet dick out of Taylor's coochie then backed away from the dresser. Taylor dropped to her knees, sucking her juices off of Desmond's dick while jerking him off.

He could barely stand. His legs trembled as he gathered a bunch of her hair in his hand. "Ahhhh, daaaamn, Pinky! You give good head, baby. Damn good head!"

His eyes rolled to the back of his head as she continued to suck him. She then put two fingers in her pussy, attempting to make herself cum again.

"I'm about to bust," Desmond crooned.

"Please do. Cum in my mouth and give me every drop!"

Desmond jerked his dick and flooded Taylor's mouth with white cream that dripped from her mouth.

They were happy about their long overdue sex session, and they couldn't wait to tackle each other again. As Desmond sat in a chair to regroup, Taylor sat on his lap. One of her breasts was in his mouth. He was gearing up for round two.

"I hate to interrupt you, but you must get dressed now. You have a press conference, and I don't want you to be too late," she told him.

"Okay, coach." Desmond kissed Taylor on the lips and then stood up. "I gotta do this conference meeting, but I promise I'll be back."

"Hurry. I'll be here when you get back."

He put on his shorts, flip flops, and his robe. He kissed Taylor on the forehead before saying those magic words she loved to hear. "I love you, Pinky."

"I love you too."

Taylor was on cloud nine after he walked out. She couldn't stop thinking about Desmond. All she wanted was to get rid of Armand so she could spend the rest of her life with the man she loved. She pondered a plan, one that would give her exactly what she wanted. When something good came to mind, she lit a cigar and smiled.

Chapter 4

Welcome to Brazil

For the past few days, Brad had been thinking about the situation he had gotten himself into. Now, he was at the airport sitting, waiting, and thinking of all the shit that could go wrong on the trip to Rio.

What if we get caught? Other countries' prisons are a lot worse. Will I ever see American soil again? But what if everything goes according to the plan and we all get our fifty Gs? Yes!

Brad looked at his friends. Travis had his headphones on, nodding his head to Alicia Keys, Tyler was reading *Ghetto Love* by local St. Louis author Mary L. Wilson, Stan was looking at porn on his cell phone, while Swag was on the pay phone getting clear instructions from Armand. Brad's feelings were up and down, and as the clock ticked away, he started sweating bullets.

Damn, why did I agree to do this shit? Maybe while no one's looking I can make a run for it. But then what would I do for money? There is no way in hell I'm going to work in a low-paying restaurant again. And fifty Gs is a lot of bread to get me by for a minute.

His thoughts continued, and he didn't even notice that his cousin was shaking his shoulder. Back to reality, Brad shifted in his seat to look at Swag.

"Yeah, what, man?"

"Here's your passport, man. Now, cheer up and let's go get on this plane," said Swag, handing him his passport along with the other guys'.

Brad knew his final decision was to proceed with the trip. He put the passport in his back pocket. He shook his head as he got up. His stomach felt queasy. He looked out the window at the American Airlines plane and whispered, "Goodbye, St. Louis."

The thirteen-hour flight to Rio was long and tiresome. It was shaky, too, and the ongoing turbulence made Brad feel as if his life was about to end. Instead of being fearful, Brad kept himself occupied with music and watching movies on the small screen in front of him. Conversation with the fellas helped the time pass, and before they knew it, the plane had arrived at the Galeão International Airport in Rio de Janeiro, Brazil.

With the exception of Swag, none of them had ever been to a place like this. They were in awe as they looked around at people from different nationalities. After they got their luggage, Swag informed them that a limousine would be waiting for them outside. And sure enough, it was.

The driver, who was dressed in black, spotted them right away. He opened the doors to the limousine with a wide smile on his face. "Welcome to Rio, gentlemen. I can assist with your luggage, and then we must go."

The driver helped everyone put their luggage in the trunk. Some of their bags went on the back seat. There was not much conversation going on, and like Brad, the others were still weighing the negative and positive aspects of being in Rio. They kept checking their surroundings, and the only one who seemed one hundred percent comfortable with all of this was Swag.

"Lighten up, fellas," he said as they climbed inside the spacious limo. "All this quietness is working me. We're in Rio, y'all. Look around and enjoy yourselves, because we are in Rio!"

They all smiled—even Brad, who had started to accept that there was no turning back now.

As the limo coasted away from the airport, Brad let down the window to sniff the air that was a mixture of sweetness and gasoline. He couldn't believe how breathtaking the city was, and the people were some of the most exotic-looking people he'd ever seen. Using his smartphone, he took photos of the high mountains, the sky blue waters of the Atlantic Ocean, and of some of the landscape areas that were unique in their own way. He posted the pictures to Facebook, and as they neared the city, he posted more pictures of buildings and sandy white beaches, where he hoped to chill.

Tyler and Stan had their windows lowered too. They were yelling at fine women walking down the street, telling them how sexy they were. "Aye, let's hook up tonight, a'ight?" Tyler said to one woman who ignored him. "Damn, baby, it's like that? Okay. That's cool."

Everyone laughed as the women kept brushing them off, but they did not give up. They tossed back champagne in the limo, and Swag lifted his glass so they could toast.

"Here's to having a lot of fun, meeting a slew of beautiful women, and soon having a lot of dough in our pockets," Swag said.

They clinked their glasses together, definitely drinking to that.

When they arrived to the exclusive apartment building where they'd be staying, Swag instructed the gang to follow his lead and not to make asses of themselves. They removed their luggage from the limo, and while carrying the luggage in their hands and on their shoulders, they walked inside the expensive place that was fit for the cover of a magazine. Ceiling fans hung from the high ceilings, palms trees were visible in large ceramic vases, clean white sectionals were here and there, and stone wall accents surrounded glass elevators.

The people surrounding them had nothing but money. It breezed through the air, along with plenty of heads that were held high. Some of the people looked at the young men with snootiness and fakeness in their eyes. They smiled but surely didn't want to. None of the fellas tripped. They started to feel hyped about being in Rio, and as they made their way to the elevator, their eyes continued to wander, especially Brad, whose eyes were glued to a wall-to-wall fish tank that sat in the middle of the floor.

"This is . . . I mean, wow. I ain't never seen nothing like this before," Brad said.

"Me either," Travis countered while looking around as well. "I could stay here for the rest of my life."

Tyler agreed as they got on the elevator, taking it to the thirteenth floor. The elevator opened, and Swag led the way to the room they were staying in. They couldn't wait to go inside. The second he opened the door, they all rushed in, with the exception of Brad. He'd seen a beautiful woman coming out of her room. She had his full attention.

Her skin was a creamy mocha chocolate, and she had mesmerizing, almond-shaped brown eyes. Her cheekbones were high, and her shoulder-length hair was in a ponytail. She wore a white dress shirt, black pants, and black work shoes. The fact that she didn't have on any makeup made her even more attractive.

She walked by Brad, slightly glancing at him. He turned around and was completely under her spell. She pushed the down button on the elevator, but as she waited for it to open, she pivoted to look at Brad again.

Damn, I can't believe God made a woman that damn fine, he thought. *And she's looking at me like I can get it.*

Their eyes stayed locked together until Tyler rushed out of the room and grabbed Brad's arm. "Come on, B! Man, what's up? You need to come in here now and see this place!"

Not wanting to break the woman's spell, Brad slowly turned his head to look at Tyler. "Wha . . . What did you say? I didn't hear you."

"I said come inside. You been out in the hallway for a minute."

"I know," Brad said before turning his head to see if the woman was still there. She was gone. "Damn."

"Damn what?" Tyler asked.

"Nothing. Nothing at all."

Brad went inside the apartment, still thinking about the woman he had just seen. His thoughts, however, quickly shifted to the apartment he stood in. He was completely blown away by how the place looked. He felt like a celebrity in a celebrity's crib. Huge windows surrounded the place, and views of Rio could be seen for miles and miles. The contemporary furniture was made of brown wicker, and the hardwood floors looked as if glass was on top of them. The open space had a chef's kitchen, and a living room and sitting room with a mini bar. The fellas were already getting their drink on, and Swag invited Brad to join them.

"B, put yo' shit in the bedroom and come get a drink. Bedrooms are down the curved hallway over there to the left."

Brad slowly walked down the hallway, admiring the exquisite paintings on the walls. He entered the first bedroom he saw. It was decked out with black and white décor and more contemporary furniture. A double-sided fireplace sat in front of a king-sized bed that had numerous pillows stacked on top of it. Yet again, the windows surrounding the room provided a beautiful view of the city, as well as of the Atlantic Ocean.

"Damn, if this is how a drug trafficker lives, I'ma have to come here more often."

He put down his bags then checked out the unbelievable bathroom with a circular shower. It was big enough to fit ten people inside, and the tub with columns beside it was even bigger. All Brad could do was shake his head before joining his friends again. They were still tossing back drinks while Jay-Z's latest hit blasted through the speakers.

"Brad, come over here, man," Swag yelled. "So, what do you think? Are you with me on this or not?"

After seeing all of this, Brad was unquestionably with Swag. He nodded and smiled. "Yes, I'm with you. All the way, cuz. All the way."

Swag picked up five bottles of Moët from the bar, and then he reached for five wineglasses. He filled them to the top, and everyone grabbed one for themselves.

"Come on. Let's go out on the patio," he suggested.

They trailed behind him, and as they stepped on the patio that stretched around the entire apartment, they examined the view. The ocean was mind-blowing, and they could see the Christ the Redeemer statue overlooking the city. The soothing breeze was just right, and none of them could think of another place they would rather be right now.

"Hold your glasses up!" Swag shouted.

They all did.

"To Rio!" Swag shouted again.

They yelled in unison. "To Rio!"

***

After a few hours had gone by, the fellas were comfortable in the apartment. Stan was in his room, asleep. Tyler was drinking liquor non-stop, while Brad, Swag, and Travis were trying to decide where to go that night.

"Let's just go to the beach," Travis said while lying on the sofa with his shirt off. All he had on was a pair of jean shorts and a cap on his head. "I hear them Brazilian chicks be havin' all they ass and titties out while on the beach. I definitely want to see what's up with that."

"I don't mind the beach," Brad said, looking over at Swag. "But I wanna go to a club. Cuz, do you know a club or something we can kick it at?"

"As a matter of fact, I—" A knock on the door cut Swag off. "What the hell?" Swag was shirtless too, showing off his perfectly sculpted Adonis chest. He was a regular at the gym, keeping it together. Plus, he was inked to the nines with tattoos. He had a tribal tattoo on his upper chest. On his right arm, he had one of Li'l Swag when he was first born. On his left arm was a tattoo of Namond at his current age. One on his back depicted praying hands. The words on top read: *Fear No Man But God.*

He got up and opened the door. Armand was on the other side.

"I kind of figured that was you," Swag said, smiling. "Come right in."

They pounded before Armand entered the apartment. He was wearing a tropical shirt, tan khaki shorts, and flip flops. He was also followed by Sandino, who always had a straight mean mug on his face.

"What's popping, San?"

Swag held his hand out, but like always, Sandino left him hanging. Swag laughed it off then turned to Armand, who was more pleasurable. He shook hands with the others, asking if everything was good.

"Not good, but great," Tyler said, full of alcohol.

Travis agreed. He, too, was tipsy.

"Man, this is a nice crib you got," Brad said to Armand.

Armand loved when people paid him compliments about the structure and the décor of his apartment. Armand smiled at Brad. "Thanks. I'm glad you like it. With the kind of money you're going to make, you may have you one like it real soon, big guy." Armand turned to Swag. "By the way, I need to talk to you about something important. Do you mind taking a quick ride with me?"

Swag shrugged his shoulders then laid his drink on the table. "Sure. But do you mind if Brad come too?"

"No problem. The more the merrier."

Brad was excited about spending more time with his future boss. He hurried to change into his khaki shorts and colorful flowered shirt that was missing a few buttons. His trimmed beard was perfectly fine, but since his hair hadn't been brushed, he put on a tan cap to cover it up. With clean white tennis shoes on, he left the apartment to meet Swag, who now had on a red tank top to show his muscular arms, and Armand at the elevator. They seemed to be involved in a deep conversation, but as Brad approached, they went silent.

"Ready?" Armand said as the elevator opened.

Brad nodded. "Ready as I'm ever going to be."

Several minutes later, they arrived at Diamond's Bakery Boutique. It was such a beautiful day outside, and with the sun shining bright, a soothing breeze kept rolling in. Armand, Brad, and Swag sat on the front patio while Sandino stood guard with his arms across his chest.

"Before we get started, gentlemen, let's get something to snack on." Armand looked over at a waitress in a white and black uniform. Her back was turned; hair was in a sleek ponytail. "Yo, waitress!" He snapped his fingers and yelled "Come here!"

The waitress immediately turned around and rushed their way. Brad was in a complete spell again. It was the same woman from the apartment building. She looked even better up close. She flashed a smile at everyone at the table, but her eyes locked on Brad for just a few seconds. He was overjoyed.

Damn. Even her teeth are beautiful.

"Hello. Welcome to Diamond's Bakery Boutique. What can I get for you gentlemen today?"

From her accent, Brad could tell she wasn't from Brazil.

Before anyone spoke up, Armand gave a quick introduction while squeezing the waitress's ass cheek. "Guys, this is the owner of Diamond's Bakery Boutique, my girl Diamond. Diamond, this is my friend Swag."

"Hello," Swag said. "I think I've met you before, but I can never be too sure."

Diamond nodded.

"And this is Brad." Armand pointed to him.

"Hi," Diamond said, waving and blushing.

Brad was so lost in her beauty that he struggled to get out a simple word like, "Hello."

Armand cleared his throat. "Diamond, get us some *pão de queijo* and lemonade."

"Sure. I'll be right back."

Before she walked away, Armand playfully smacked her ass. She didn't flinch, just kept it moving.

"You know you got good taste when it comes to women," Swag said to Armand.

"Yeah, but you have to watch that one. She cost me plenty to get." Armand pulled out a Cuban cigar. Brad wasn't sure what that meant, but he was sure that whatever Armand was involved in, it was illegal. He kept his mouth shut and just listened in.

"Armand, what do you want to talk about?" Swag asked. He could tell that Brad was uncomfortable about what Armand had said.

Armand lit his cigar then took a long drag before blowing smoke in Brad's face.

Normally, Brad wouldn't take that kind of disrespect, but he had to remember that he wasn't in St. Louis anymore, and from what he heard about drug lords in foreign countries, they were not to be messed with.

Swag, on the other hand, was proud of his cousin for not even flinching. He took a deep breath, thinking, *Brad passed the test.*

Armand thought the same thing too. He smiled at Brad then looked at Swag. "Swag, you know the procedure, so just lay low for a few days. You and your boys have a good time, go shopping, relax on the beach, sex a slut or two, do whatever you want, and I'll be in touch in the next few days."

"Okay, but what else did you want to holla at me about?"

Armand reached in a bag he was carrying then pulled out a stack of cash. He eased it over to Swag, whose eyes had grown wide.

"What's this for?"

"For you and your friends to have a good time. I didn't have much to talk to you about. I just wanted to give you that. Enjoy, and ring me if you require anything else."

Swag looked over at Brad, who appeared just as shocked as he was.

Armand looked about and saw another limo pulling up, knowing it was his time to leave. "Look, guys, I have to get out of here. I have another appointment." Armand stood. "The other limo will take you two back to the apartment. Enjoy your *pão de queijo* and lemonade," Armand said. "Swag, please walk me to my limo."

Both Swag and Brad slowly got up from the table. Armand gave both the guys a pound. Just before Armand left, Brad felt a hand on his ass. He quickly swung around.

Armand stood, smiling, whispering in his ear. "Damn, big boy, you have a nice ass. If you ever have a desire to make me feel good, just let me know."

Brad's face was twisted as he sat back down in his chair. His frown was clearly visible. He wasn't sure what that was all about. Swag didn't seem to appreciate Armand's words either, but he didn't say anything as he walked Armand to his car.

In moments, when Swag came back, the cousins laughed at the whole "Armand smacking Brad's ass" situation.

"I can't believe he did that shit to you too!" Swag shook his head in disbelief.

"He slapped you on yo' ass too?"

"Yeah, but I just told him I don't go that route."

"If he do that shit again, I will speak up. I let him slide just because," said Brad, still looking disgusted and starting to shake. "Ugh!"

"I feel you. We definitely don't want to mess things up. I can't wait to spend all this cash. We need to get with the fellas and discuss everything we gon' do," said Swag, placing all the cash in his pockets.

Just then, Diamond came back with a tray with their cheese rolls and lemonade. "Here you go, gentleman. Anything else I can get you?"

Swag bit into a roll, looking up at Diamond. "Nah, that's cool, ma. We got it from here."

Diamond nodded. "Okay. Be back to check on you both."

"Whateva," Swag said, taking a sip of his lemonade and waving her off.

Diamond looked over at Brad with a slight smile before walking off.

Brad looked at her from the back. *For a small-frame woman, like my boy Sir Mix-a-Lot used to rap, baby got back.* Brad picked up a roll, taking a bit and licking his lips. He continued to look at Diamond, who was assisting a customer and taking another employee to clean up a mess on the inside of the bakery.

Swag knew from the look in his cousin's eyes that he wanted this girl, but Diamond was a no-no. Swag snapped his finger in Brad's face.

Brad once again was broken out of Diamond's spell. He looked at Swag, pissed. "What?"

"Yo, man, eat yo' cheddar biscuit or roll or whatever this bread is!" Swag shook his head, taking another bite.

During their time at Diamond's Bakery, Brad and Swag had three baskets of *pão de queijo* and five of the most delicious cupcakes they'd ever had. Brad knew his belly was full, but his mind was only halfway full of Diamond. He had to get to know this chick. She was a true vision and a rare beauty. To him, she was a puzzle that just had to be solved, and Brad was up for the chase for his diamond in the rough.

Swag cleared his throat as he got up, patting his six-pack abs. "A'ight, cuz. I'ma take a piss 'cause that lemonade is running through a brotha." Swag then let out a big belch that had everyone in the bakery looking their way.

"Excuse me, everyone!" shouted Swag, laughing. "Them baked goods just hit the spot!"

Brad laughed, shaking his head. "Dude, you sick."

Everyone in the bakery looked at Swag with disgust, almost losing their appetites. Some mumbled under their breath, saying, "These black Americans."

"A'ight, cuzzo, I'ma hit this restroom and then we out," said Swag, rubbing his stomach again.

"Cool," said Brad, taking one last bite.

Swag walked out, shouting, "Where the bathroom?" and laughing, knowing he was drawing attention and getting under the customers' skin.

Brad shook his head, still laughing. "That fool." He took a sip of his lemonade.

Within moments, Diamond switched her fine ass back over to Brad's table.

She tapped Brad on his shoulder. Brad turned and smiled from ear to ear. It was Brad's plan to just keep looking at his mystery lady.

"What's up, ma," he said, putting on his player smile.

"Sir, are you and your cousin done with your lemonade and meal?" Diamond asked, holding a bin to carry away their dishes.

"Yeah," said Brad, real suave.

Diamond twisted her lips, knowing what he was doing, but she couldn't show she was enjoying it. "Can I remove your dishes. Please?"

Brad sat back in his chair and tried to bring out his inner swagger. "Of course, ma. Go right ahead."

Diamond began to place each dish in the tub carefully. She made sure not to look Brad's way. But Brad wanted to break the ice and try to get to know Diamond.

"Diamond, this is truly a nice place you have. And the pa—de Qu—whatever they were, along with the cupcakes and lemonade, were off the chain."

Diamond took a quick look at Brad and continued to put dishes and trash in the tub. "Thanks."

Brad smiled at her. "I haven't had lemonade that good since my grandma passed." Just thinking about Mama Carter made him even more confident to talk to Diamond.

When Diamond was done putting dishes and trash in the tub, she took a wet dish cloth and slowly wiped the table.

Brad could tell that Diamond was playing hard to get, but he wasn't giving up just yet. "I love to see a young and independent woman do her thing. How long have you owned this place? You look much too young to have a spot like this. How old are you, sixteen or something?"

He forget the cardinal rule: Never ask a chick her age. *Damn, I hope she don't judge me for that one.*

Diamond looked up at him, still wiping the table. "No, I'm nineteen. I'm not independent, and I don't own this place." She cleared her throat. "Armand's name is on the lease."

Okay, I got her talking, even though I struck a nerve, thought Brad, starting to sweat.

"Do you have a napkins on you, bae?" he asked.

Diamond went into her apron and handed some napkins to Brad.

He slowly took them from her soft hands. "Thanks, ma." Brad wiped his brow.

"You're welcome, sir," Diamond said as she wiped down Swag's chair.

"You must really like to clean, uh . . ." said Brad, but hit himself on the knee, thinking he had screwed up. *Smooth, Brad. Real smooth.*

"Yeah, Armand likes this place clean from head to toe," said Diamond.

Brad laughed, reminiscing about the days working in the restaurant. "I remember having to do this shit back home."

"Home?" asked Diamond in amazement. "Where's home for you?"

"I'm from St. Louis, Missouri. Maybe you could come visit me sometime. I can show you a good time in the Lou," Brad said, rubbing his hands together.

Diamond shook her head. "Oh, I don't think Armand will allow that. I haven't left Rio in ten years. Now, if you'll excuse me . . ."

Before Diamond could walk away, Brad grabbed her arm.

"Do you need something else, sir?" Diamond asked, looking at Brad's hand on her.

Brad let go of her. "I'm sorry to grab you like that, but . . ."

Think of something to win her over, you idiot.

"Oh, uh, Diamond, since we're going to be neighbors for the next few days, I was wondering if you and I could go on a date. You can show me the sites of Rio. Maybe we can get a bite to eat or a drink. What do you say, Diamond?"

Diamond took a deep breath. "Look, I don't want you to get hurt. Don't even look at my apartment door. I've been Armand's property since I was a child, and—"

Diamond stopped talking when she looked up to see a man in a dark suit looking at her and Brad. The last thing Diamond wanted was for one of Armand's goons to kill him.

Diamond bent down and whispered in his ear. "Be careful. Like Nicole Kidman said in the film *Moulin Rouge:* You're bad for business. Good-bye, and stay away from me." Diamond looked up to see the man in the suit coming their way. "Good-bye." She ran back into the building.

Brad watched her run back inside like she stole something.

"Hey! Cuzzo!" shouted Swag.

Brad looked back to see Swag with a man in a dark suit. He got up, still thinking about Diamond and still holding the napkins she gave him.

In the limo, Brad and Swag were quiet. Brad's mind was on the conversation he had with Diamond. Even though it was short, in his mind, it was still sweet.

Swag looked over at his cousin. "What's up with you, cuz?"

Brad shook his head, smiling and looking at Swag. "Man, Diamond. Before I leave Rio, I would definitely like to get me a piece of Diamond. I could just . . ." He couldn't get his mind off of her.

"Man, don't mess wit' her," Swag advised.

"Why not? Baby was eyeballing me for real. Didn't you see her?"

"I saw her, but I'm telling you this as your cousin. Don't mess wit' that girl. You'll get us both in big trouble. She stays on the same floor we on, but when she comes by, don't say shit, a'ight? Not one word!"

Brad wasn't sure why, but he promised Swag that he wouldn't say one word to Diamond. Thing is, he wasn't sure if that was a promise he was going to keep.

Chapter 5

Nightlife

That evening, the fellas decided to party at one of Rio's hottest nightclubs, The Nuth. The club had an exotic jungle theme to it, but it was very upscale, with some of Brazil's most beautiful women and biggest ballers. The music was off the chain in the club. All eyes were on the fellas, and everyone knew right off that they were Americans.

The fellas were having a good time on the dance floor with some of the finest women. Travis and Tyler were dancing with Japanese twin sisters. Stan was at the bar, talking mad game to this sexy Latina who couldn't speak a word of English but smiled at him anyway. Brad was making good conversation with this Afro-Brazilian woman, pretending that he was talking to Diamond. Swag took this fine-ass Indian girl back to the limo and fucked her real good while thinking, *Damn, what a night.*

Coming home from a long day at the bakery, Diamond went into her apartment, took off her dirty uniform, and slipped into a nice hot bubble bath. As she let the soothing water relax her tense body, she thought about her little conversation with Brad. She didn't know why, but she felt good vibes coming from him, just as she had when she saw him when she was coming out of her apartment earlier. Even though, in her mind, he was desperately trying to get close to her, she couldn't. She didn't want him to get hurt on account of her. She had seen enough pain, hurt, and loss for one lifetime.

Brad, thought Diamond, feeling more relaxed. *Could he be the one?*

After her bath, she slipped into her white pajamas. She looked in the refrigerator to find some dinner, but all she saw in there was a salad with more vegetables and fruit.

She sighed. *I can't live like this.* She removed three oranges, along with a bottle of water, then went to the living room to watch reruns of her favorite show, *City of Men.*

As she was watching TV, the door squeaked open. She snapped her head to the side to see who it was. It was Armand, holding a bag in his hand with that same devilish grin on his face.

"Hello, my little Diamond."

She sighed and barely wanted to speak. "Hey."

"What's the matter with my precious jewel?"

Diamond was not in the mood for Armand. She turned off the TV then got off the sofa. "I'm tired. I had a long day at the bakery. All I want to do is go to bed."

When she tried to go down the hallway, Armand blocked her path. "Not until you open your gifts."

"Can I open them tomorrow? I'm really beat." She tried to go around Armand again, but this time he grabbed her arm tightly. She squinted her teary eyes. "Ahhh, you're hurting me."

"I said I have gifts for you. Now, come on." He dragged her back into the living room then shoved her down on the sofa.

Diamond blinked away her tears. She kept thinking, *Be strong.*

Armand placed the bag of gifts in front of her. She wasn't excited, because she already knew there was a catch. Her name was on the bakery, but she didn't own a damn thing. It all belonged to Armand. He figured Diamond and the building were his property. It was his money that paid all the employees and bills for the business. He never gave Diamond a cent of the money. The way he paid her was through shelter, clothing, and food. To him, she had cost him enough already.

"Now, open your presents," Armand commanded while rubbing the back of her head.

The first box she opened had a beautiful grapefruit-colored Diane Von Furstenberg Zarita lace dress. *Even though he's an asshole and a greedy bastard, he has good taste in clothing,* she thought. She opened up the next box and saw a pair of nude-colored Christian Louboutin leather python pumps. The last gift took Diamond's breath away. It was a sunflower diamond necklace from Harry Winston. It was 363 round diamonds, twenty-five carats in a platinum setting. Diamond suspected that Armand had spent a pretty penny on that necklace. She lifted it from the box and placed it against her neck.

"Be careful with that shit. You're wearing that tomorrow night, and I don't want you to damage it."

"Tomorrow? Why?" Diamond asked curiously, knowing that Armand never took her anywhere. She was either in her apartment all day or in the bakery with no pay.

"There's a man from New York who wants to do business with me. I need a beautiful woman by my side that will make him want to be partners with me."

"Why don't you take your wife?" Diamond lowered her head. She didn't like being used.

"What did you just say to me?"

"I said, why don't you just take your wife? She was a supermodel. She's beautiful, well-known, glamorous, and she's a successful businesswoman. I'm none of those things."

Armand was insulted. "How dare you suggest that I take her! That bitch's mouth is too big. She will blow the business deal with her talk of her years in the fashion world and her magazine. So, no! All I need for you to do is to be quiet and look exceptional. Got it?"

She nodded while holding her empty stomach.

"What the hell is wrong with you?"

"I'm just hungry."

"You have veggies and fruit in the fridge."

"No. I need a steak, chicken, or some of my cupcakes."

"Hell, no! You'll get fat, and you're worth too much to get fat on me. Next you'll wanna have a baby. That will make you even more fat and ugly. If I find out you ever ate a steak or sweets, that'll be the last thing you'll ever eat."

The last time Diamond had a good meal was at nine years old. From then on, it was strictly veggies, fruit, and mineral water. Even though she worked at the bakery, she was never allowed to eat her own creations or take any home. The last time Diamond did, Armand locked her in her apartment closet for three months, giving her minimal food and water. He would sometimes check the entire apartment to make sure that she didn't eat anything she wasn't supposed to have.

"So, how are you goin' to thank me?" Armand displayed an evil grin.

Diamond fidgeted with her fingers. She looked down, already knowing exactly what he wanted. "Thank you for the gifts," she whispered.

"No." Armand unzipped his pants and pulled out his hard, five-inch dick. "Thank me now."

The sight of his penis made her sick, because she knew that he'd slept with plenty of women around the world without using protection. "Armand, not tonight. I don't feel well."

He grabbed her by her hair, forcing her to get down on her knees.

"Ahhhh!" Diamond screamed.

He slapped her so hard that her head jerked to the side. "Shut up and thank me!"

Diamond stared at his manhood for a moment before putting it in her mouth.

"No funny shit, slut!"

She sucked on his salty dick like her life depended on it—which it did. And while Armand's eyes rolled back, so did hers. *This asshole.*

"I'm about to cum! Faster, you dirty bitch!"

After two measly minutes, all she could do was shake her head. Armand forced his dick deeper, spraying his semen down her throat. She gagged while looking up at him with sadness in her eyes. He patted the back of her head as a reward for doing a great job.

"You are worth everything at your parents' expense. Your family stole from me, costing me money and causing bloodshed, so it was only natural I took their most precious treasure. Now we're even"

The thought of her parents pissed Diamond off. *I gotta get out of this hellhole soon!*

Chapter 6

Conquer and Destroy

It was a beautiful, sunny day on the beach in Ipanema, a neighborhood located in the southern part of Rio de Janeiro. Taylor was looking luscious in her yellow-and-white two-piece bathing suit, lying on her beach towel, wearing Fendi glasses and reading *I AM IMAN,* by her mentor, Somalian supermodel Iman. Taylor had thought about writing her own autobiography one day, but for now she had too much on her plate with her magazine, her miserable marriage, and figuring out how to be with Desmond.

She stopped reading to look at the waves in the ocean and even at the people who strolled by. There were plenty of women, in particular, lying on their beach towels, on their stomachs, with their backs and asses out, trying to get a tan. Taylor thought about how much she had missed a woman's touch, and then she glanced at several men who were either playing in the water or playing soccer. Their bodies and faces were just as desirable, and once Taylor got a glimpse of what half of them were packing in their Speedos, she realized why she was so in love with Desmond. His package was all that, too, and she regretted being married more with each day that passed.

Being without Desmond was painful, but thinking of him caused a tingly feeling to stir between her legs. She immediately crossed her legs and tried to focus on reading her book.

"Taylor!"

She heard the female's voice from a distance. Taylor looked up and saw Milena walking along the beach with five other women. They were all attractive and were fitting for her magazine.

Taylor stood to greet them, but first she air-kissed Milena's cheeks. "Mmmm, how are you, my dear?" Taylor said. "Well, I do hope."

"Superb, but let me introduce you to the girls." Milena looked at the Japanese twins. "This is Yoshi and Aoki."

The girls nodded.

Milena looked at the Latina chick. "This is Sasha."

"Hola señorita," Sasha said.

"Hola," Taylor countered.

"These two are Ocean and Star." Milena pointed to the Afro Brazilian and the Indian woman.

They both waved at Taylor.

"Good afternoon, ladies. Sit. Please sit so we can chat."

All of the ladies put their beach towels down and sat in a circle.

A devilish grin crept on Taylor's face. "Well, ladies, how did you do with those American boys?"

"We did good. They were a hit at The Nuth," Ocean said.

"What else? Did they say why they were in Rio?"

"The one I was with said they were on a free vacation, which was a favor from a friend," Star said.

Ocean interjected. "And that's also the one she screwed in the car, you slut!"

"Oh, shut up! I felt bigger and better dicks in me than that American bastard. It was like watching water boil."

All the girls laughed.

"Shhh," Taylor shouted. "Let's get back to business! What else did you girls learn about the Americans?"

"Nothing much, but we're taking them to Club Zero Zero tonight. We plan to get them highly intoxicated to get more info," Aoki said.

"Excellent," Taylor replied.

"Club Zero Zero?" Milena questioned.

"Sí," Sasha said.

"I'm going there tonight with my latest flame. We're having drinks with Armand and his mistress."

"More good news," Taylor hurried to say. Her cell phone alarm went off. "Sorry, ladies. I have to go now. I have a lunch date to get to."

Taylor got up and grabbed her book and towel. Under it was a purse full of money for the women to splurge. They were sure it would come in handy.

Two hours later at the Sheraton Rio Hotel and Resort, Taylor walked into the hotel suite with her hair flowing down her back, showing off in a sleeveless yellow scoop-back dress and Alexander McQueen thong sandals.

"You're late," a man said in a dry tone.

Taylor turned around to see Rio's police chief, Duke Pinto, sitting on the sofa. He was a handsome man with peanut butter skin, a medium build, a short afro, and a thick beard. The olive green button-down shirt he wore went perfectly with his khaki pants and brown leather shoes. Taylor couldn't resist a compliment before taking a seat next to him.

"Sorry I'm late, darling, but I had to get ready, and I couldn't figure out what dress to wear. I have to look good for you too."

Duke licked his lips. He couldn't deny that Taylor was one sexy woman. "Yeah, babe, but working out and Botox injections won't last forever."

Taylor twisted her lips. "Eat me!"

"We can save that for later." Duke tried to slide his hand under her dress, but she slapped his hand. "Okay. Let's get down to business."

"Let's." Taylor rolled her eyes.

"What new info do you have on that son-of-a-bitch husband of yours?" Duke tossed back a gulp of his whiskey.

"My girl, Milena, said he has that American boy named Swag with him. This time, the American brought four of his friends to transport cocaine back to the United States."

Duke nodded and sucked his teeth. "Good. Good. Where are they staying?"

"At my husband's apartment building, where he also keeps that Belizean whore of his."

Duke laughed. "How long are they here for?"

"I don't know. That's why you need to act fast. Tonight the men are going to Zero Zero with a few girls I hired to keep an eye on them. Armand will be there as well, having a business dinner with another dealer. That whore will be by his side, which suits me fine."

"Okay. I'll have an undercover cop keep an eye on those Americans."

"Good. And soon you'll have Armand."

"Yeah, and the governor will get off my back. I'll then be a hero to the people of Rio."

This bastard, Taylor thought. *Hero, my pretty ass.*

"Taylor, there's one thing I don't understand about this whole situation. Why did you want to help me and the governor bring down your husband?" Duke asked.

"Because . . ." Taylor paused to touch Duke's leg. Her thoughts switched to Desmond. "It's personal, very personal, and I'm sure you wouldn't understand." She shot Duke a seductive grin.

He giggled then inched in closer to Taylor. "So, after I lock your husband up forever, I was wondering what your future plans are."

To marry Desmond and get the hell out of Brazil, she thought as he continued to fill her head with his bright ideas.

"'Cause you're going to be single, and I was wondering if we could get together. You know how much I want to be with you, and . . ."

Taylor glared at him with disgust. She drifted off as he continued to go on and on about the future he wanted with her. *Please, you idiot. I only give my goodies up to the rich and famous or for the right price, and you meet none of those qualifications. Not one, so stop fooling yourself. This is all Desmond's.*

Taylor interrupted his rambling. "I'll let you know something soon." She licked the tip of his nose as she got up. She strutted to the door then blew him a kiss before walking out.

That fast, Desmond was back in her thoughts. *First a bath, brush my teeth to get his taste out of my mouth, and then my Desmond.*

Chapter 7

First Encounter

Club Zero Zero's vibe was hot that night. It was so thick with partygoers that you could barely move. They were playing the latest music by both North America and South America's hottest artists.

Armand walked in, looking sharp in an olive-colored Ralph Lauren suit and black Armani loafers. Diamond was by his side, shining in her new outfit and looking like a real trophy. Her MAC makeup was on point, and her hair was full of loose curls. She had all the men in the club turning their heads, wondering where Armand had found another beauty. The two of them found their table, where many of their guests already were.

A six foot four Italian man stood up with his hand extended. "Mr. Castro, nice to see you again."

They shook hands.

"Please, Bruno, call me Armand."

Armand had wanted to do business with Bruno Bello, a well-known mobster, for some time now. He was the leader of the Bello crime family that had been around for decades. They were known for drugs, illegal gambling, money laundering, loan sharking and other activities that were all covered up by the Bellos' multi-billion-dollar empire. From law firms to construction companies, real estate firms, and even record companies in St. Louis, Chicago, Los Angeles, Italy, and Tokyo . . . they owned it all. Now he wanted to expand his empire into Rio, and he was there to make a connection with the right partners.

Diamond couldn't believe how handsome Bruno was. In her eyes, he resembled HBO's *True Blood* actor, Joe Manganiello. He had the body to match, which showed well in a white Perry Ellis suit and his Kenneth Cole shoes.

Bruno's eyes shifted to Diamond. "Armand, who is this sexy bombshell?"

He eyed her up and down like she was melted ice cream on his lips that he wanted to lick. His stare made Armand furious, but he had to remember that he was conducting business and Diamond was his key to success.

"This is my lady, Diamond."

Bruno reached for Diamond's hand, kissing it. "Mmmm. You truly are a diamond, babe."

A female cleared her throat at Bruno's table then rolled her eyes. To Diamond, the woman was extremely attractive, and she could tell that she was a model. She rocked a sleeveless cowl-neck dress with Michael Kors red heels. She sparkled in a David Yurman diamond necklace with matching oval earrings. Her hair was black, with Chinese bangs resting on her forehead.

"Diamond, this is my date, Milena."

"Hello," she said.

The waiter came to take their drink orders.

"Let me get a *caipirinha*," Armand said.

"Make that two," Bruno replied, giving the peace sign.

"A red wine for me," Milena said softly.

Before Diamond could say what she wanted, Armand said, "Get her water."

Milena looked at Armand. *Asshole.* She looked over at Diamond, who had so much sadness in her eyes. *This girl has a story to tell.* She wasn't sure what it was, but she really didn't care, especially when the DJ played a hit song by Brazil's up-and-coming underground rapper,

Love Bullet. His song "Mimi" was off the chain. There was a touch of Tyga, Trey Songz, and Kanye West all wrapped into his music.

Milena got up and snapped her fingers. "This is my song." She pulled on Bruno's suit jacket. "Come on, Bruno. Dance with me."

"No, babe. I got business to take care of." He pulled out a Cuban cigar.

Milena looked over at Diamond. "Come on, girl. You want to have some fun, don't you?"

Before Diamond could say anything, Milena took her hand, pulling her out of the chair. They hit the dance floor, dancing wildly and sexy as ever. Armand narrowed his eyes as he looked over at Sandino, who was standing by the bar. Sandino knew what that signal meant.

Outside on the patio Brad, his crew, and the girls from The Nuth were enjoying the cool night air and drinking. Brad looked at the dance floor to see who or what the crowd was looking at. He couldn't really see, but the second he went inside, he saw his dream girl, Diamond. She was dancing up close and personal with Milena. That, of course, made him smile.

Once the music quieted down, the crowd shifted in another direction, causing Brad to lose sight of her. He kept peeking over the partygoers, and that's when he saw her enter the ladies' room with Milena.

While in the ladies room, Milena was touching up her makeup. She glanced at Diamond, who was washing her hands with a sad look on her face.

"Are you okay, doll?"

"Yes, but I . . . I just wish I could go home," Diamond answered.

"Don't worry. Armand and Bruno's meeting will—"

"No, not that home." Diamond cut her off and started to cry. "I just want to be free and be my own woman."

Milena had a whole new view of this woman, one very different than what Taylor had described. She cleared her throat.

"Come on. Let's fix your makeup."

Once Milena was finished getting Diamond's makeup together, she opened her purse and pulled out her card. "If you need anything, call me."

Diamond nodded. "Thank you."

Milena walked out.

Diamond threw the card in the trash. "This won't help me. Armand doesn't let me use the phone." She sighed. "I hate this. I wish my real prince charming would come to save me from this hellhole."

The second she left the bathroom, she was face to face with Brad, who had a sexy smile on his face. She looked at Brad with amazement. To her, he was so handsome, even for a big man. There was a strange chemistry between them each time their eyes connected. It was a feeling that Diamond had never felt, and in the moment, all they could do was smile at each other.

"What's up, ma?" Brad said.

"Nothing, sir." Diamond quickly put her head down, afraid that Armand would catch her eyeing another man.

To Brad, there was something mesmerizing about Diamond. She was like a puzzle he just had to solve, no matter what the consequences were. He took his hand and lifted her head up.

"None of that 'sir' stuff. Just call me Brad or B, a'ight?"

She blushed.

"So, what you doin' up in here?"

"I'm just being the whore of the night for Armand and his latest contact. I hate living like this." Realizing that she was telling too much of her personal life to Brad, she paused then turned her head.

Brad was determined to get more information from her, but he wasn't sure if it was the right time. Nonetheless, he got Diamond to face him. "Don't worry, ma. Things will get better."

Diamond blushed again.

"Yo, me and my boys are outside. Do you wanna join us?"

"No, I can't. I have to get back."

"Come on. Just for a minute." Brad took her hand, and she nervously followed behind him.

"Brad, stop. No, I can't." Diamond was so frightened as she looked out for Armand and Sandino. There was no sign of them.

Thank God. I don't want them to see me, and I don't want anything to happen to Brad.

"Chill, a'ight? I'll protect you, so come on."

Brad kissed her hand, trying to put her at ease. For whatever reason, she felt safe with him.

When they reached the outside, Brad saw most of his crew. Stan, however, was nowhere to be found. Tyler and Travis were on the dance floor, dancing with the twins. Swag was tonguing Star down.

Brad and Diamond sat down at the table, talking. When Swag spotted his cousin, he was pissed. He shook his head, thinking what a big mistake that was. His attention diverted back to kissing Star, especially since she started touching his hard muscle that was growing larger by the second. In an instant, she made Swag forget about the trouble Brad was going to get himself into.

A waitress came to the table, asking for their drink orders.

"Let me get a Bud Light," Brad said.

"Water," Diamond said dryly.

"No, get her a Coke."

"No, Armand said that'll get me fat."

"Forget what Armand said. You're skinny enough."
Brad frowned as he looked at the waitress. "Coke and a
Bud Light. Thanks."

The waitress left, and Brad still couldn't believe that he
was sitting face to face with his dream girl. "So, have you
lived in Rio all your life?"

Diamond felt comfortable with Brad, so his question
didn't bother her one bit. "No, I'm originally from Belize."

"Belize, wow." He was amazed. "How did you get to Rio
then?"

"Yeah, I had a beautiful life in Belize," Diamond said,
smiling as she remembered the happy times of her life.

Brad loved her smiles. It made her glow.

"But all that changed when I was nine years old."
Diamond choked, trying to hold her tears back.

Brad rubbed her shoulders. "Ma, it's okay. What
happened?"

Diamond paused, fretting about the terror of her past.
"Armand."

Brad's heart dropped. "That bastard, but yet that
pedophile." Thinking about it made Brad's blood boil.
"Damn, ma."

Diamond's head just hurt thinking of the pain Armand
had put her through the last ten years of her life. She
never cared about anyone but her parents, but being face
to face with Brad after their last talk at the bakery, she
felt comfortable. In a weird way, she cared about what
happened to him. Looking into his eyes, she could tell he
had a beautiful soul.

"Brad, for the last time, be careful around Armand. I
don't want him to hurt or even kill you on account of me."

Brad shook his head, laughing. "Ma, don't ever worry
about that. I ain't afraid of that *Goodfellas* mob prick
wannabe. I'm from the Lou, and I can get just as dirty as
these assholes in this country."

Diamond breathed hard like she was about to have a panic attack. "Brad, I'm serious." She paused for a moment, trying to collect her thoughts. She felt tears coming down but quickly wiped them off. "Brad, that demon has taken so much from me. He took my identity, my dignity, and my—"

Before Diamond could say another word, Armand came up to their table. "Well, well, well. There you are." Armand smiled at her, but Diamond knew he was only smiling because Brad was at the table. She could tell in his eyes that he was pissed off.

"What's up, B? You and your friends having a good time in Rio so far?"

"Yeah, man, it's cool." Brad looked behind Armand only to see his sidekick, Sandino.

"Great. Continue to have fun, and I'll see you soon. Meanwhile, my Diamond, we should go now." Armand held out his hand.

Brad looked at Diamond's eyes. He could tell that she was scared shitless. If Sandino weren't around, and if Armand weren't so powerful, Brad would've spoken up and taken Diamond with him, but he didn't want to deal with any confrontations. He also didn't want to do anything that would stop him from getting his hands on those fifty Gs.

Diamond took Armand's hand and stood up. He put his arm around her waist, and just for a split second, Diamond turned her head to take one last glimpse at Brad.

To him, something in her eyes was screaming, "Free me from this prison." But just like that, he was distracted by Sandino snapping his fingers in his face. Brad cocked his head back, looking at him.

Sandino shook his head then lifted up his shirt. Brad saw his gun that was a warning for him to back away. After that, Sandino walked away.

Damn it! If we was back in the Lou, things would be on and popping. Brad was heated.

From a short distance, Swag smiled and shook his head. *That'll teach him.*

Chapter 8

Where Do I Go from Here?

The next morning, sunlight hit Taylor's face as she slept peacefully after a night on the town and a steamy lovemaking session with Desmond. She woke up with white sheets covering her naked body. She looked over at the other side of the bed to see that her man wasn't there. Nonetheless, she smiled, got up out of bed, and went to the bathroom, examining herself in the mirror. Her thick, curly hair was all over the place, but she managed to put almost every hair in its rightful place. She looked at her face, which was bare without a touch of makeup. She didn't look bad, but Taylor also knew that she wasn't getting any younger or sexier. She needed to rid herself of Armand fast, and she was eager to have Desmond's child, just one, so she could instantly regain her figure. She was willing to put forth the exercise, especially for something that she wanted and dreamed of quite often.

She laughed as her head filled with these thoughts. And then she turned to the Jacuzzi tub, where she and Desmond had made love a million times. Just thinking about it made Taylor wet all over again

Before going downstairs, she put on one of Desmond's shirts and boxer shorts. Wearing his clothes made her feel more connected to him, but living with him would be even better.

His villa was definitely up to her high standards. It was three stories with seven bedrooms, five bathrooms, a workout room, a trophy room, and a game room. All of the furniture in the home was mixed with urban and classic in white, black, and brown hues. She wouldn't change one single thing, and it pleased her heart to love a man who had very good taste.

When Taylor couldn't find Desmond in the workout room or in the kitchen, she went into the backyard, where he had a zen garden. It was full of plants, flowers, trees, a big swimming pool, and a statue of Buddha. The outside scenery was to die for. You could see the city of Rio, as well as a clear view of the sandy beaches and mountains.

Taylor looked over and smiled when she saw Desmond meditating. He was wearing only his sweatpants and was barefooted while sitting cross-legged. She slowly walked over to him, not wanting to bother him. He looked like a handsome statue, one that she could keep in her possession and hold onto forever.

Taylor quickly turned her head after hearing a bird chirping. It held her attention for a brief second, until she felt a tug on her arm.

"Ahhh." Taylor was being pulled down and ended up lying on top of her man. They both laughed and shared a passionate kiss.

Desmond searched deep into Taylor's eyes. Even though she was fourteen years older than him, he always felt he was with a young lady. "You're always so beautiful. How can you look so sexy this early in the morning?"

Taylor laughed and kissed Desmond's cheek.

He softly touched her face then she kissed his hand. "So, Pinky, did you think about what I said last night?"

Taylor knew exactly what Desmond was talking about, but she didn't want to screw up the romantic mood, especially so early in the morning and after a night of makeup sex. She played the dumb blond model role.

"What was that?" she asked.

"You know what I'm talking about." A serious look was fixed on Desmond's face.

Damn, will he just leave the subject alone? He's so messing up my mood. Taylor faked a giggle. She tried to kiss Desmond again, but he stopped her.

"No," he said in a firm voice.

Taylor sighed. "Come on, Dez, don't mess up the mood so early in the morning." She planted kisses on his cheek before making her way down to his chest and nipples.

"Pinky, when are you going to tell your husband about us?" Desmond put his hands behind his back.

Taylor's good mood was over. She had to deal with reality. She looked at him. "What did you say again?" she asked.

"You heard me. When are you going to tell Armand about us?"

"Soon. Very, very soon." Taylor tried to play it down as if it were no big deal.

"Pinky, soon expired a long time ago. I'm tired of sharing you with that Al Pacino, *Godfather* wannabe faggot. I don't want another man inside of my woman. And—"

"Baby, trust and believe Armand hasn't touched my pink lips in three years. So it's all yours, Dez. But leaving him isn't that simple."

He cocked his head back after hearing the breaking news. "Why's that?"

"For one, he's a big drug lord here in Rio, and I don't want to see you or me killed. Also—"

"Baby, fuck all that. I ain't never scared. Remember, Pinky, not only am I a MMA fighter, but I'm a street fighter too. I got some partners in Colombia who're in the Colombian mob. They've been after Armand's ass for years. They can take him out of the picture just like that." Desmond snapped his fingers. "Believe that shit."

"No, I don't want to take any chances of getting you killed." Taylor thought about her family, knowing that they would kill anyone in a second for screwing over their daughter. Still, she didn't want to bother her parents, who were now retired from the life of crime on South Beach but still had the game on lock. If only Desmond knew who she really was.

"But there's my magazine, *Brazilian Kouture*. Even if he doesn't even find out about you, if we do the whole divorce thing, he'll try to take the magazine away from me. He's a big investor in that magazine, and he'll take what I worked for nine years to build."

"Baby, forget all that! I got money. I can take care of us. Got any more excuses? I can take care of Armand, and your finances will be okay once you're my wife. Now what?"

Taylor took a deep breath and thought about all of the consequences of leaving Armand for another man. Her head started to hurt, especially since Desmond wouldn't let it go.

"Look, Pinky, I love you and all. You're my world, my baby. I wanna one day marry you—hell, if it was possible, I would marry you right now. I want you to be the mother of my kids. If you think it's too dangerous for us to be together, just let me know now. Otherwise, I'm giving you thirty days."

Taylor was in a state of shock. *What? No man or woman has never, never, ever left me, no matter what the situation was. I get who and what I want with no questions asked. This new generation of young, rich, and famous men and women are something else. Dez better be glad I love his ass, because five years ago, I would have gotten off his body and went to next richest and sexiest thing out there.*

Taylor tried to stay strong on the outside, but on the inside, she was crushed about the ultimatum that Desmond had given her. Desmond knew he had Taylor right where he wanted her. He loved Taylor with all of his heart and soul, but after three years of their secret love affair, he was tired of sharing her. He wanted her all for himself. He was tired of his father and friends telling him that Taylor was a gold-digger or an old-school whore. They said that she was doing her best to stay in the media once Desmond made it to global mega superstardom.

Of course, Desmond had some of the sexiest women in the world on his jock, and they were hoping to be the next Mrs. Desmond Diaz. No matter how much he was tempted, or how his father and friends tried to set him up, his heart belonged to his Pinky. Still, if she didn't get that shit together with her husband, he was seriously going back to his playa days.

"Pinky, daddy loves you, but you gotta choose who you want to be with. You have thirty days to do what you have to do. If I don't hear from you by 11:45 p.m. that day, it's over for good. Do I make myself clear?"

On the inside, Taylor felt weak. She didn't want to lose her one true love, but she didn't want him to lose his life. She didn't want to lose her life either, or her business. She cleared her throat, holding back her tears. "Crystal clear."

They smiled, and right at that moment, he felt an erection in his pants. Taylor started to rub the lining of his penis.

"Pinky, you gon' make that go down one more time."

Taylor was out of it at the moment. "One more time?" She looked at him like he was crazy.

"Yeah, after you make daddy's dick go down, you can't have none of this until you get rid of Armand once and for all. Only then will my dick be all yours."

She would be no good without Desmond's loving. All she could think about was getting rid of Armand a.s.a.p. Taylor kneeled down, pulling off Desmond's sweats to see his long, thick cinnamon stick, looking delicious as always. She gave Desmond the best blowjob he'd ever had, while toying with his balls.

"Ahhh!" Desmond groaned. "Damn!" While rubbing Taylor's head and licking his lips, he was hoping she would leave Armand for good.

Chapter 9

Going Down

At the apartment that afternoon, the fellas were trying to relax after a wild night of partying. Brad was on cloud nine after spending a little time with Diamond, his forbidden fruit. He wanted to pay her a visit, but he found out that she hadn't come home that night.

Brad sat at the table on the balcony, not eating his lunch of *salada de fradinho com camara*, a fresh shrimp and black-eyed pea salad. He also had two slices of *lombo de porco assado*, which was roasted pork tenderloin, sautéed greens, and a *pão de queijo*. He just couldn't get his mind off of Diamond. She had him intrigued in many ways. He wondered why she hadn't come home, and he was worried that Armand had done something to her. He hoped she was okay, and his mind couldn't shake his thoughts as he gazed at the beautiful scenery.

"Boo!" Brad jumped before turning around to see Swag, who had scared him shitless.

He laughed. "Got yo' ass."

"Damn, man," Brad said, holding his chest.

Swag joined him on the balcony. "Sorry. I didn't mean to scare you, but what were you thinking about?"

"Not much. Just enjoying the view."

"Yeah, this place is something else, ain't it? Nothin' like home."

"Nope. Especially when it comes to a woman," Brad said, catching himself. "I mean, the women here got it going on."

"B, I know you were referring to Diamond. You still thinking of her?" Swag reached over and took a slice of Brad's pork tenderloin. "You gon' get yourself into deep trouble with that girl. That's Armand's property. Leave that girl alone, okay?" Swag chewed the meat before pulling out a Black and Mild.

"You really need to quit smoking." Brad attempted to change the subject.

Before Swag could say anything, they heard voices coming from the living room. They went inside, seeing that it was Armand and Sandino coming in to greet the men. Armand shot Brad a cold look, but Brad knew what that was all about. All he cared about was if Diamond was okay.

"Fellas, listen up. I'm feeling a lot of bad vibes in this part of town. Cops are everywhere, so I need you all to pack your belongings and come down to the limo. You have ten minutes to get downstairs."

"What?" Brad shouted.

"Right," Tyler said. "What's really going on?"

"Are we still getting paid?" Travis asked.

Armand and Sandino didn't answer. All they did was exit the apartment.

All of them had confused looks on their faces, and they didn't know what to expect. Swag took control of the situation.

"Come on, y'all, let's just go. Let's move! We gotta go! Get your shit packed now," Swag said.

No one liked Swag's tone, but they all went to their rooms to pack their belongings. There was a limousine waiting for them in front of the apartment building. The fellas got in, and the driver sped off. Brad turned to look out the back window. He spotted a car pull up in the place of the limo, and two hefty men with muscles got out. Right in the middle of them was Diamond, still in the same dress, but it was now wrinkled and torn. She had no shoes on her feet, and her hair was all over the place. Her head hung low, and her eyes were focused on the ground. Brad shook his head. He was grateful that she was still alive, but pissed at the same time. He balled up his fist, wondering what in the hell Armand had done to her.

As they entered Diamond's apartment, one of the men pushed Diamond on the sofa. She was frightened, just as she had been for the entire night. The men quickly exited, but seconds later, Armand came, making Diamond even more fearful. He sat beside her, but she slowly eased back. Armand yanked her toward him, and this time she didn't move.

"There's nothing to be afraid of my Diamond, especially if you learn to play by my rules. Sorry I had to punish you by locking you up in the cage. After ten years of being together, I thought you would learn to love me."

Diamond rolled her eyes and looked at him with an evil gaze. Her look prompted Armand to smack the shit out of her. Diamond screamed, holding her face.

Armand pointed his finger in her face. "Listen, you stupid little bitch. You better start respecting me. You think that fat, light-skinned nigger can give you what I've given you? Huh? He will never, ever know the value of you, so don't ever think or speak his name again. 'Cause next time, you'll be in a casket. Do you hear me?"

Diamond softly cried and didn't respond.

Armand yanked her hair, pulling her head back. "I said, do you hear me?"

Diamond thought she was looking at the devil himself. She nodded. "Yes . . . yes I hear you." She cried even harder.

Armand let her hair go, shoving her head forward. "Now, go get yourself washed up and get ready for me."

She looked at him for one moment and then went to the bathroom to turn on the shower. She lay down in the tub, letting the water fall on her. She cried uncontrollably, hoping the water would clean what she thought was her ruined body.

I hate him. Why did this happen to me, God? This was not the life I dreamed of as a child.

There were several hard knocks on the door. Diamond knew exactly who it was. She twisted her face, showing disgust. She hated everything that Armand had done and taken from her: her family, her innocence, her self-respect, and her freedom.

"Yes?" she said.

"Hurry up! It doesn't take all day to get cleaned up. You got two minutes."

Diamond embraced herself as her body trembled. "Okay." Continuing to cry and while holding her face in her hands, she said a little prayer. "Lord, I need help. Please send someone to save me from this hellhole. Please, I can't live like this anymore."

She swallowed the lump in her throat, held her head up, and felt more determined than ever to get out of Armand's grasp.

Chapter 10

I'm Here, but I'm Not Here

For the past two days, Taylor was going stir crazy without seeing, hearing, or feeling Desmond's touch. If she weren't a fashion icon, a businesswoman, and didn't care about her reputation, she would be at home in her bathrobe, crying, eating chocolates, and listening to sad love songs. She knew that she had to get Operation Get Rid of Armand Castro done fast. She thought long and hard about what Desmond had said: "Tell your husband about us or I'm out. One month or it's over." Taylor couldn't afford to lose the only man she had ever loved because of her powerful husband.

She sat in her office, looking flawless in a gray Armani dress suit with silver Jimmy Choo leather pumps and a David Yurman pearl, diamond and 18K gold pendant necklace, which Desmond had bought her. Her makeup was flawless, and her hair was pressed straight and styled in a bun. Her eyes were locked on her computer screen as she looked at photos of Desmond.

She didn't want to be in her office. Hell, she didn't want to be in her place of business period. She was around people she hated and hardly had any control of who stayed or left. At that moment, she regretted marrying Armand instead of manipulating or controlling him. He sure flipped the script on her, and she didn't even know it.

"Taylor!"

Taylor jumped as she saw Ramon looking at her like she was crazy. "Yeah, Ramon. What?"

"I need the reports on the Versace account."

She looked back at her computer screen. "I'll get them to you later."

Ramon paced back and forth. "No, Taylor, I need them now for next month's issue."

Taylor shot Ramon a wicked glare mixed with an "Oh no he didn't" look.

"And people in hell want ice water, but it doesn't mean they get it," she shot back. She rolled her eyes at him. "You'll get it tomorrow, okay?"

Ramon twisted his lips and sucked his teeth.

The intercom sounded, and Taylor pushed the button. "Yes, Maria."

"Taylor, Milena is here to see you."

"Send her in." Taylor looked back at Ramon. "Bye!"

Ramon rolled his eyes and walked out of Taylor's office, bumping into Milena, who was coming in.

"Excuse you!" shouted Milena. "There are some ignorant bastards in this dump."

"Tell me about it," Taylor commented dryly. "Hey, doll," she said, getting up from her chair.

The ladies hugged, air kissed, and went over to the sofa. Things stayed quiet until Milena cleared her throat. "So, uh, what's been new with you?"

Taylor stared at her best friend for a few seconds before tears cascaded down her face. Milena consoled her.

"Hey, doll, what's wrong?" asked Milena, concerned for her best friend.

Taylor calmed herself down and wiped her face. "Well, two days ago your brother gave me a choice to either be with him or Armand."

"Forgive me for saying this, but that's not a hard choice."

"I know, and I want to be with Desmond. He's my heart and soul. Everything I am. I love that man more than I love myself and my collection of designer shoes." Taylor laughed a little. "But it's not easy leaving Armand. You know how powerful he is. Hell, if he finds out I'm with Desmond, he'll have him killed. If anything ever happened to Desmond, I don't know what I would do."

"Shh, hun, it's okay. You know my brother and father know people that will take Armand off the scene like that," Milena said, snapping her fingers. "Chica, I never seen you this emotional. You must really love my brother to be feeling this way."

Taylor nodded.

"Don't worry. After your plans are in order, you and my brother will be together."

"And speaking of the plans, what was up with the dinner with Armand, his guest, and that li'l whore of Armand's?"

"Well, they were discussing building a casino here in Rio, but Bruno was talking some shit about making it an illegal gambling spot, plus a whore house. You know your husband went along with it."

Taylor sighed. "Men. Always thinking with their dicks." *This could be some useful info for Pinto,* she thought with a smile.

"Did the girls get any more information from our American guests?"

"Nothing that we can use for Pinto, but Sasha said she did see the big one with that girl . . . What's her name?" Milena thought for a moment. "Diamond! They talked for a few moments until Armand came."

"Oh, that li'l harlot. What did she have to talk about?"

"Taylor, hun, I wouldn't be so hard on the poor girl."

Taylor cut her eyes and threw her hand back. "Why shouldn't I be? She's been fucking my husband."

"Because, I talked to the girl and she seemed pretty nice. Just scared. She had these sad eyes that look like she wanted to be freed. I think we should help her, instead of trying to kill her. You should talk to her woman to woman."

"I'll think about it." Taylor stood up. "Now, if you'll excuse me, I have to meet Duke for lunch and plans."

"Okay, but fix that makeup first."

"Shut up!"

They laughed

At the Sheraton Rio Hotel and Resort, Taylor came in ready for business. She sat across from Duke, who was smoking a cigar and reading a Stephen King novel. Duke looked up from the book and put the cigar in an ashtray.

"On time today, I see," he said.

Taylor didn't have time for any of his offhand comments. She was there to handle business quickly and get back to Desmond. "Look, let's get business started, okay? I have another engagement to go to later."

Duke smiled. "Of course. What do you have for me?"

"Armand had that business dinner with mobster Bruno Bello here in Rio. I think they're doing an illegal gambling and prostitution ring here by using a casino."

"Interesting. I'll have my men keep an eye out for this Bruno Bello."

"Excellent."

"So, do you have any other information for me?"

Taylor had a dumbfounded look on her face. "At the moment, there are no other updates."

"Well," Duke said, taking a puff of his cigar. "I know that your husband has moved the boys out of that apartment and put them in one of his homes in the slums."

"Interesting," Taylor said, smiling.

"We have an undercover cop posing as a limo driver. He took the Americans there."

"Then why doesn't he just call the cops and bust them right there?" she asked.

"It's not that simple, because he has bodyguards all over that place. Hell, he has a six-year-old boy that will shoot you dead in the face in a second, so I don't want to take any chances and have the governor even more on my back."

Taylor twisted her lips. "Okay." She glanced at the clock and saw that it was quarter to one. "I have to get back to work to deal with that idiotic staff of mine. I'll call you to schedule our next meeting."

"You do that." Duke nodded and stared at her like he wanted to eat her alive.

Taylor made her way toward the door only to be grabbed by Duke on the way out. She looked at him like he had just lost his mind.

"What about our date?"

Taylor didn't appreciate him grabbing her, so she snatched away from him. She then pretended to be dumbfounded once again. "What are you talking about?"

"You know damn well what I'm talking about. When I get through with your husband, you're going to be lonely, and you'll need someone to keep you satisfied. So how about dinner, a movie, and sex?"

Taylor thought Duke was damn disgusting. The only man for her was Desmond, but she didn't have to tell Duke anything. All she did was laugh. "I'll let you know. Until then, be patient. We have some serious work to do, and I don't want anything to mess that up. Agreed?"

Duke agreed. He watched Taylor strut away as if she were on a runway. He intended to be patient, but after his job was done, Taylor was going to be his.

Chapter 11

Taking Care of Business

Hot, sweaty, and sticky, the fellas had spent the last four days in a small *favela* in the slums of Rio. The north or south side of St. Louis had nothing on the slums of Rio. Streets were dirty, kids were begging for pennies, drugs were everywhere, and people were looking through trash cans for food.

They were in one big room with a sofa bed, a table with two chairs, and an open bathroom. It was nasty as hell, with roaches and rats running around. Feces was on the floor, and the smell of shit breezing through the air made everyone want to throw up. The guys tried to stay awake just so they didn't have to sleep in a place like this. It had no air conditioning, running water, or electricity. They were sweating bullets, and all of them had their shirts off.

With Brad and Stan being big dudes, they wanted to go outside to get some air, but Swag told them both to stay inside. The place they were in was heavily guarded by Armand's henchmen, and with one wrong move, those men would blow your heads off without giving a damn.

For Brad to beat the heat and keep his mind off the crazy situation he'd gotten into, he tried to divert his attention to Diamond. He kept wondering if she was okay, dead or alive by now, and if Armand was emotionally, physically, and sexually abusing her.

Brad picked up his shirt to wipe his chest and stomach. He wished he were back in St. Louis, and he even wondered if Armand was still going to give him and the others the fifty Gs.

"Shit," he said underneath his breath. "I'm never doing this shit again. I don't know how Swag can do it."

There was a knock at the door that interrupted Brad's thoughts. Armand and Sandino came in.

"What's goin' on, fellas?" Armand had a stern look on his face, even though he was turned on by seeing the guys with their shirts off, sweating all over. He was so in the mood for some American chocolate, and the one who interested him the most was Brad. Brad had a tattoo of a bulldog on his right shoulder, and another tattoo of a necklace in the center of his chest. For some strange reason, big men always made Armand's dick hard, like it was starting to do now, but he had to remain focused on why he was there.

"You all look like shit," he said.

Some grunted, the others kept quiet, because they were fearful of what was going on—everyone with the exception of Swag.

"What's the word, Armand?" Swag asked, knowing what time it was.

"Put your shirts on and let's go!" Armand demanded.

"You don't have to tell me twice," Stan said, rushing to put on his shirt.

"Me neither," Travis added. He was ready to go.

They all put their shirts on and grabbed their bags. The limo was outside, so they hopped in, not knowing where they were headed next.

Within minutes, the fellas were back in downtown Rio. They went back to the same apartment building they had stayed in when they first arrived. Going inside the building, Armand led the guys to the elevator, this time taking them to the second floor. Brad was pissed because he wanted to go back to the apartment they were in before. He had an idea why Armand didn't want them on that floor. All he wanted to know was if Diamond was okay. He knew that sneaking up to see her would be risky. Armand probably had goons guarding that apartment around the clock, waiting to kill him.

They walked down a hallway, stopping and watching Armand as he opened the door. That apartment was smaller and plainer than the one they were in before. They no longer felt like kings. It had old-fashioned furniture, and all the walls were painted purple.

The fellas followed Armand inside. They were confused, and when Tyler opened his mouth to ask what was going on, Swag encouraged him to be quiet until Armand informed them of what to do next. Armand snapped his fingers, and Sandino handed Swag a big duffle bag.

"You have forty-eight hours to get this shit together. Let's go, Sandino." Like always, Armand and Sandino left in a hurry, closing the door behind them.

As soon as Armand and Sandino left the apartment Brad, Stan, Tyler, and Travis all took deep breaths of relief.

"Damn, man. I'm glad that shit is over," said Stan, wiping the sweat off his brow.

"Bruh, you ain't said nothing but a word," said Brad, flopping his ass on the sofa.

Stan joined him, sitting beside him.

Brad took another breath, looking at Swag. "This is some scary shit. I feel like I'm in *Scarface* right now."

Tyler laughed. "Dudes, I don't know about y'all." He took off his shirt. "I ain't washed my ass in four damn days. I'm 'bout to hit this damn shower."

"Not if I get to it first, ugly!" shouted Travis.

Before the brothers could race to the bathroom, Swag whistled.That got their attention.

"This ain't play time. This is some real shit!" Swag shouted as he looked over at Brad and Stan. "B! Stan! Get y'all big asses up!"

They did.

"Swag, what's up wit' you, man?" asked Stan, pissed.

"Stan, shut up! All y'all in the bedroom now," said Swag, walking into the bedroom.

The fellas followed Swag in the room. Swag flipped the duffle bag over and dumped out bricks of cocaine on the bed.

"Damn!" Brad shouted, never having seen that much cocaine in his life. "What the hell, Swag?"

"Man, shut up and help me cut this shit so I can get it packaged!" yelled Swag, pointing at the bricks.

Brad shook his head in disbelief. "I can't believe I'm doing this shit! I hope that fifty Gs is worth it."

"Me and you both," said Travis in shock from the sight of all that cocaine.

Swag got on his knees, pulled out a box cutter, and began working on the first brick. He was looking up at Brad and Travis with a pissed look on his face. "You both in it now, so deal wit' it. Stop talkin', get on y'all knees, and help me get this shit together." He looked over to Tyler and Stan, who stood their dumfounded. "All y'all."

The fellas kept their mouths shut and helped Swag with the bricks.

After fifteen straight hours of cutting and packaging the cocaine, it was finally over. The fellas came out of the room sweating and shaking like crazy. They all were under a little haze from being in a room with cocaine.

Brad, Tyler, Travis, and Stan had never experienced any shit like this before. They felt like they were in the 1991 movie, *New Jack City,* in the scene in the crack house, where the workers were butt naked, packing up the drugs.

Swag, on the other hand, was getting frustrated because he had to teach the fellas how to cut, measure, and pack cocaine. Normally, when he would get a big order like this, it would take him five and a half hours to complete.

Brad and Stan sat back down on the sofa. Tyler and Travis sat at the table. The room was so silent you could hear a pin drop. That was, until Stan started wheezing like crazy. He knew while he was packing that some of the cocaine went up his nose. Plus, being in a room that was small and full of funk was messing with his asthma royally. Stan went in his pants, taking two puffs of his inhaler.

Swag was the last to come out of the room looking like nothing had happened. This was the norm for him, except for having to be the teacher of his naïve friends, who didn't know shit about the cocaine game.

Swag folded his arms. "Y'all a'ight?"

They all nodded.

"I'm about to wash up a little bit first. Then, Brad, you can go next, and so on," Swag said. He went into the bathroom and closed the door.

After Swag finished, Brad went in next. In the hot shower, Brad washed and scrubbed his body hard, until his light skin turned beet red. He felt so dirty. His dirt wasn't from being in the *favela* or being in a room filled with cocaine that would be any drug user's dream. The real dirt was in his mind as he wondered what the fuck he was doing. This type of lifestyle was not him at all. He was just some simple dude from the Lou that had potential to one day be great, but now he was in training to be a drug trafficker.

He scrubbed his face, trying to wipe off the dirt and tears. "Damn, Mama Carter. I know you disappointed in me, but if you could ask the Man—"

Before Brad could finish his prayer, a loud bang came at the door.

"B, can you hurry it up? Other folks wanna shower too!" shouted Stan.

"Dude, shut up!" Brad laughed.

After Brad was finished, he came out wearing a red shirt, white shorts, and white Nike sneakers. The rest of the fellas went in the shower, washing the funk and cocaine off their bodies.

The fellas were a little more relaxed after having hot showers. Stan, Travis, and Tyler were at the table, playing a game of hearts. Brad and Swag were sitting on the sofa, watching a show on TV. It was completely in Portuguese, but they still tried to follow along with the storyline. No one was upbeat. This trip and drug ordeal was taking a toll on everyone.

Just when things were starting to feel relaxing, a knock came at the door.

Swag went up to the door, but before he opened it, he looked at his boys and said, "Let me handle this. Don't say shit."

He opened the door, and there stood Armand, with Sandino by his side. Armand had a twisted look on his face.

Before Swag could say anything, Armand spoke up. "Let's go. Leave your shit. It will all be taken down to the limo."

"Come on, y'all." Swag grabbed the duffle bag that held of all the packaged cocaine.

The others didn't like what was going on. There was too much back and forth, too many orders, and they didn't know what the hell was going to happen next.

Nonetheless, they did what they were told and kept real quiet, hoping and praying that all of this would be over soon. They trusted Swag, so they followed his lead.

While on their way to the basement, Brad's gut told him something was about to go horribly wrong. His stomach was queasy, and his legs were weak. With each step he took, it felt as if he were on his way to hell.

They all kept looking at each other, and when they got downstairs, Armand turned on the lights. The basement was muggy. Dust particles stirred around, and spider webs were everywhere. Stacked against the wall were more bricks of cocaine and piles of money. There was a clicking sound that caused everyone to snap their heads in the direction of the sound. Sandino stood with a machine gun in his hand.

"Yo, Armand, what's up with Sandino and the gun?" Swag asked with thick wrinkles across his forehead. "Is all of that necessary?"

"Swag, you know I trust you. I just need a little insurance, in case your boys get some smart ideas about taking my money and drugs."

Armand reached in his pocket, pulling out a nine.

Brad's, Travis's, Tyler's, and Stan's eyes were bugged. They wanted to make a quick run, and following Swag's lead didn't sound like a good idea anymore.

"What's with the guns?" Travis asked. "We not about to die, are we?"

"Right," Tyler said. "I just want to go home right now. Forget about the money. Forget about all of this shit."

Armand ignored what they'd said. He nudged his head toward Swag. "What are you waiting for? You know where the masking tape is, so start taping the shit on. All of you take off your clothes, except underwear."

"Take them off for what?" Brad shouted. "Hell no! I'm not going out like that."

"Neither am I," Stan said, standing with his hands folded. "Show me the way out."

As Armand lifted his gun to Stan's head, and Sandino's eyes started twitching, Swag asked the fellas to cooperate. "Please. This is all about hiding the goods. I know y'all don't like this shit, but we've come too far to back down now. Just cooperate and this will all be over with soon."

They all looked at each other, and figuring that there was really no place to run to, the started taking off their clothes. What they didn't expect was for Swag to start taping the drugs on their bodies. They thought the masking tape would be used to tie them up. Even though they were nervous about the drugs being attached to their bodies, this was something they had all signed up for.

With the guns still being aimed at them, everyone was now dead silent. No one wanted to piss off Sandino or Armand, not even Swag, who was happy to see his boys cooperating. He was done, and minutes later, Armand led them back upstairs.

They were about to get into the limo when they heard Armand shout, "Nooooo!"

They looked at Armand, and he pointed to a limo that had pulled beside them.

"What's up, Armand?" Swag asked.

He spoke through gritted teeth. "Shut up, boy. Get in the next limo, now!"

They all were confused and stood as if cement had been poured over them.

"Get in the limo now!" he yelled again.

The fellas rushed to get in the limo, not knowing where they were going with cocaine taped on each of them. Armand shut the door, and as he spoke to the new limo driver in Portuguese, he slapped an envelope in his hand.

The limo pulled off, and all Brad could think while gazing out of the window was, *Lord, protect me.*

Chapter 12

Time Bomb

"Yes, sir," the man said. "The boys are on their way to the airport. Have everyone ready."

"All right. Thank you," Duke said with a smile on his face, rubbing his hands together.

The man turned off his cell. He and Armand laughed.

"No one can bring down Armand Castro. Once they catch Swag and his crew, no one will ever bring that shit back to me," said Armand, still laughing.

The man nodded. "Yeah, you know how those stupid American black niggers are, especially with that no-snitching shit."

The man laughed as he lowered his head to sniff the cocaine in front of him. He had all of the free cocaine he wanted in Armand's basement, with unlimited access to not only the cocaine, but to Armand's money too.

"Officer, thank you for portraying the limo driver. Your boss has been trying to bring me down for years. I can't believe he was so close. Someone close to me must be working with him." Armand looked over at the officer snorting cocaine like crazy. "Officer, what updates do you have?"

The officer lifted his head then wiped white powder from the tip of his nose. "Once a week he goes to the Sheraton Rio Hotel and Resort on his lunch break."

"And? What does that shit have to do with him almost busting me?" Armand didn't like when people spoke in riddles. He also didn't appreciate this stupid mother-fucker snorting his shit nonstop and having the audacity to work for the government.

He reached in his pants pocket, pulling out photos. Sandino snatched the pictures then gave them to Armand. He flipped through the photos of Duke going to the hotel. Another looked as if Taylor was going in behind him moments later. The third one was of Taylor coming out, and the fourth photo was of Duke coming out minutes later. Armand tossed the pictures in the officer's face.

"What the fuck is this shit? This photo is my whore of a wife, possibly going to screw one of her many sex partners. How does this shit help?"

The officer shook his head. "No. I think your wife is giving info to Duke about you and your organization."

Armand couldn't believe it. He shook his head. "I don't think so. I make sure none of my business is in my house where she can hear it. Besides, all that bitch cares about is how she looks and how much money I give her ass. No way!"

The officer was high as hell when he got up. He staggered a bit but somehow managed not to fall. "You must be really blinded or really stupid. Anyone can see this woman is playing you for a sucker. The truth is, you ain't nothing like your brother! Your brother was way smarter than you."

Armand wasn't sure where this attack came from, and his blood started to boil. He grabbed the officer by the back of his neck, squeezing it. "What did your ass just say to me, you crackhead toy cop?"

"I said your weak ass ain't like your—"

Armand winked at Sandino. In an instant, he pulled the trigger on the gun in his hand, firing one bullet in the center of the officer's forehead. Blood splattered and dotted Armand's clothes. He was standing too close. The officer's lifeless body fell to the concrete, hitting it hard. Armand watched his brain ooze onto the floor, and all he did was smile.

"Don't fuck with the real kingpin of Brazil." He was so aroused by what had happened, and while looking at Sandino, he patted him on the back. "Get this shit cleaned up and bury this cokehead."

Sandino nodded. Before walking away, Armand gathered a gob of spit in his mouth, releasing it right in the officer's face. "Piece of shit," he said then headed upstairs, dialing his cell phone.

Moments later, a female picked up. "Hello, darling."

"Be at my place in a few. My dick is hard."

While at the airport, the fellas were on pins and needles, waiting for their flight to board. They tried to act normal and look like tourists, but that was difficult to do. Their eyes kept shifting around, they kept looking at each other, and every time they saw a police officer, they held their breath. Brad was about to have an anxiety attack, so he rushed into a bathroom stall, taking deep breaths to calm himself down.

"Okay. It's almost over with. Everything will be fine, and we'll be back in the Lou in no time."

He stayed in the stall for about ten minutes. After washing his hands, he met up with the fellas, and they went into a gift shop, pretending to look for things to take back home. Stan put on a traditional tribal mask and started dancing crazy. Swag slapped him on his shoulder.

"Man, take that shit off. We don't need you to bring any attention to us. Damn," Swag said.

"Just chill, all right? Besides, what's up with your ass putting your hands on me?" Stan took off the mask.

"This is business, so don't act like no ass. Let's go to the Burger King stand."

While at the Burger King stand, the fellas ordered burger meals and sat at the table in silence. Brad looked around and had a strange feeling that he and his boys were being watched. Plus, his mind was on Diamond. He wondered if he would ever see her again. He was so in a daze that he didn't realize Stan was throwing fries at him.

"Brad!" Stan threw three ice cubes at him, finally getting his full attention.

"What do you want?" Brad threw some ice at Stan but missed.

"You seem lost. You okay?" Stan asked.

"Just can't wait for this shit to be over so I can get my money."

"Me and you both," Tyler replied as his chest started to itch from the tape. He tried to scratch, but Swag slapped his hand.

"Fool, you crazy? Don't do that shit here," Swag said.

"Man, this tape is itchy. Got me sweating too."

"Man up! Damn!" Swag took a sip of his soda. "Now, here's the plan to make this a good getaway: When it's time for us to get on the plane, we won't line up together one by one. We'll just get in line. Brad, you go first, then Travis, Stan, then Tyler. Me last. Got it?"

Everyone nodded, except Brad, who was still in a slight daze. He couldn't believe this was actually happening. Swag hit Brad on his head to get his attention.

"What?" Brad rubbed the side of his head.

"If you over there thinking about that bitch, forget it. She ain't yours and never gon' be yours. Get yo' mind right so we can take care of this business. A'ight?"

Brad nodded. "Yeah, man, I hear you."

The announcer on the intercom informed passengers that the plane from Rio to Miami was ready to board. Swag ordered Brad to go first in line, and one by one the others waited to board. Brad was sweating bullets. He wanted to vomit but definitely didn't need the attention. What caught his eye were two muscular men in black suits. They had shades on and were walking toward the line, looking directly at him. He quickly shifted his head, trying to ignore them, but as they got closer, he saw one of the men reach for Tyler and Travis. The other reached for Stan and Swag.

"Come with us," one of the men said. "Don't make a scene and don't say a word."

As they started to walk away, Brad held his breath, hoping that they didn't suspect him as well. He felt horrible for his boys, but as the line kept on moving, he moved right along with it. That was, until another man tapped his shoulder. When Brad turned around and looked into the man's beady eyes, all he heard was, "Come with me. Now!"

Everybody was staring and whispering as the fellas were being whisked away by the angry-looking men. Poor Brad wanted to pee on himself. Travis and Tyler wanted to run. Stan was shaking his head, having plenty of regrets. And Swag was wondering how in the hell things went so wrong this time.

Chapter 13

Testify

One by one, the fellas were taken into the airport security office and ordered to strip out of their clothes. Their stomachs were tied in knots, and they were scared shitless, especially with guns being pointed at them.

"Maybe you stupid Americans didn't hear me. I said strip!"

In an instant, and fearing that they would be killed, the fellas immediately stripped down. There were bricks of cocaine taped to Tyler, Travis, and Stan's chest.

Brad and Swag took off everything except their shorts.

"You fools think I'm stupid! Take those shorts off too!"

Brad and Swag slowly pulled down their shorts. The cocaine bricks were taped to their legs.

"This must be some kind of mistake," Swag said as if he didn't know how the cocaine had gotten there.

The men laughed, and one of them ordered the fellas to face the wall.

Stan and Travis started crying. They begged the men to have mercy on them.

"Please don't do this," Stan said, refusing to turn around. "I . . . I didn't know what I was doing. We made a big mistake, and I don't deserve to die."

"Neither do I," Travis said with tears streaming down his face. "None of us deserve to die, and if you let us go, we won't say shit to nobody."

The men looked at each other, laughing again.

"The Americans are idiots. How foolish can they be?" one said.

One of the men's phone rang, so he stepped out of the room to answer. Within minutes after he left, three officers came in to remove the drugs from the fellas. Maybe they weren't going to be killed after all, Brad thought, and as the drugs were taken off him, he felt a little relieved.

"Are we free to go now?" Brad asked in a frightened tone. "You got the drugs, so we should be free to go."

"Close your mouth and put your clothes back on," one of the officers said. "In the meantime, I don't want to hear one word from any of you."

They remained tight-lipped as they put on their clothes, but once they were dressed, they were asked to turn around. Following the officer's rules, no one said a word. There was plenty of head-shaking going on as the cuffs were put on, and plenty of tears. After that, they were escorted out of the security office. Many people looked at them with disgust; some laughed and pointed fingers.

"What did they do?" one lady asked another.

"That's a shame. I bet they had drugs on them," a man said to another while shaking his head.

Brad felt so ashamed. Like the others, he lowered his head and didn't dare to make eye contact with anyone. He never thought in a million years he'd get arrested for anything like this. He wished that he could turn back the hands of time.

Once they were at the police station, the fellas were questioned by Duke in a small interrogation room that had concrete walls and one door. The look in Duke's eyes was very intimidating. He threatened them with "If you don't tell me where you got the drugs from" or "Who do you work for" or "You're going down big for this" speeches, but no matter how intimidating Duke was, the fellas didn't want to snitch. Yes, Armand had done them wrong, but they viewed him as one dangerous dude. They thought jail time was better than dying at a young age.

Duke looked at an officer standing by the door. "Since none of these motherfuckers want to talk, just book them. I'm not going to waste any more of my time. Maybe after a few days behind bars, somebody will be willing to speak up."

The fellas looked at each other, hoping that none of them snitched. When the officer informed Duke that the jail was too full, tiny smiles crept on their faces.

Duke slammed his hand on the table. "Then what in the hell am I going to do with these Americans? They can't run free in the station."

"Maybe we can put them in the elevator for a few days, until the prison has room."

"And how do you suppose we keep them in the elevator without them escaping, officer?"

"Just shut down the elevator system. Give them enough food to last two or three days. By then, the prison will have some room."

Duke sighed. He hated the idea but didn't have a choice. "Fine, put them in the elevator, but make sure it's completely shut down. Understand?"

"Yes," said the officer before he left the room.

Duke was pissed. He looked at the fellas, one by one. "Wipe those smirks off your faces. I don't think you all understand how serious this is, and if I have anything to do with it, all of you will be behind bars for years and years to come."

After that comment, their faces fell flat.

Duke knew that the governor was going to be all over his ass. Without the boys' confession and a statement from the undercover officer passing as the limo driver, whom he had been trying to reach for hours, he didn't have a case to bring down Armand.

"Damn!" He shouted then pushed the chair in front of him. "I guess it's time to call this whore with the bad news."

Nearly an hour later, the cuffs were removed and the fellas were shoved into a small elevator that could barely fit them. The officer tossed them a duffle bag with sandwiches and milk as he laughed. "Don't eat it all, especially you two fat boys. Hopefully, that'll last three days." He pushed a button, making the doors close.

Brad was the first to rush up to the door, banging on it and pushing all of the buttons to see if the elevator moved. No luck.

"I'll show yo' ass something fat!" Brad was heated. He wanted to punch something or somebody, and punching the elevator door allowed him to let off some steam.

"Man, cool out," Swag said, staying calm.

Brad swung around to face him, but Stan spoke up before he did.

"Cool out? Man, don't say shit to us, because this is all yo' fault we in this bullshit! I've been trying to keep my mouth shut, but now that we're alone, I could just fuck you up for getting us in this mess!" yelled Stan, pissed off to another level.

There was no question that Stan's blood was boiling.

Swag stepped forward, moving to face Stan. "Listen up, motherfucker! I didn't put a gun to your head and make you come to Brazil, so don't put this shit on me. All you saw, bruh, was dollar signs."

Stan cut his eyes before walking a few inches away from him. "Fuck you, man. I hate yo' ass. You ruined my life."

Swag pursed his lips. "Bruh, what life? All you did was work at McDonald's and Wendy's. Yo' ass still living wit' ya parents and taking care of that trick of a girlfriend who everyone knows would suck a dog's dick in a second. And man, can she suck. Ask my friend." Swag grabbed his dick, laughing.

"You son of a bitch!" Stan lifted his fist, charging at Swag. Travis and Tyler pulled him back, while Brad pulled Swag back.

"Naw, Travis and Tyler, let that fool go. Come and get some of this. I have a feeling you really don't want none," Swag said.

Brad was always the peacemaker when things like this happened. "Come on, y'all. We all friends, and we gotta stick together. Fighting won't help us one bit."

Swag snatched away from Brad. "Friends my ass. Fuck that and fuck him!"

"Yeah, nigga, fuck you too!" Stan shouted after he was released.

Brad knew Swag and Stan didn't mean anything. He had to figure out how to get the hell out of there, get back to St. Louis, and hopefully find out what happened to Diamond along the way.

Chapter 14

Sick

Climbing out of the limousine, Taylor knew that she was the shit, rocking finger waves with her Bobbi Brown makeup on point. Her hourglass figure showed well in a sleeveless white Akris Punto cotton peplum blouse, brown Ralph Lauren denim jeans, and white-and-gold Giuseppe Zanotti sneakers.

She was at Ipanema Beach for a photoshoot for Desmond's spread for the upcoming cover of *Brazilian Kouture.* It was a beautiful day outside—a clear blue sky and high waves in the ocean. Taylor wandered around, trying to look for Desmond and trying to keep things in order, since Ramon claimed he was sick from food poisoning.

As Taylor was thinking how hard it was to find good help these days, she felt a tap on her shoulder. She turned around to see Hervé Gallet her friend and a world-renowned French fashion photographer. Hervé, for the past thirty years, had taken photographs of some of the world's most beautiful supermodels, including Taylor, and landing them on the covers and pages of *Cosmopolitan* and *Marie* Claire. Now he was going to take some sexy pictures of Desmond Diaz.

"Bonjour, Hervé, darling." Taylor said with a smile.

Hervé kissed her hand. "Taylor, *mon beau papillon,*" he said, calling her a beautiful butterfly.

Hervé's French accent was thick. He was five foot five, in his mid-fifties, with gray hair, a thick mustache, and droopy brown eyes. His body, which was average, showed well in a black tank top and tan khaki shorts. "By the orders of Ramon, I'm supposed to do this shoot and make the cover even sexier. I have brought my new muse with me."

Taylor wasn't happy about him bringing someone else, but she put on her best red-carpet smile. "And who is that?" she asked falsely, knowing exactly who it was.

"Kitana!"

Kitana Cho, better known as supermodel/Oscar nominated actress, immediately took center stage of the entire set. Even without makeup, she was a total knockout. She was a 19-year old mix between Russian, Romanian, Japanese, and West Indian with long, raven-colored hair, icy blue eyes, and an olive complexion. She was a younger version of actress Angelina Jolie for sure.

Since the age of fifteen, Kitana had been taking the fashion and movie industry by storm, appearing on the covers of over a dozen magazines from *Elle* and *Glamour* to the *Sports Illustrated* swimsuit issue. She also had an amazing acting resume, appearing and starring in several American/European sitcoms and blockbuster films. She was the first ever supermodel to get an Academy award nomination for best actress in a thriller playing a teenage psycho killer.

Kitana walked over to Taylor and Hervé wearing a two-piece gold swimsuit by Victoria's Secret. It looked painted on her.

"Did you call me, sweetheart?" She air-kissed Hervé's cheeks.

"Yes, my little swan. This is Taylor Monroe, my former muse and CEO of *Brazilian* Kouture."

Former muse? Taylor thought. *Please, I'm a muse wherever I go.* Taylor continued to hold a fake smile. "Hi. Nice to meet you, Kitana." Taylor extended her hand.

Kitana rolled her eyes at Taylor. "Same here. I'm always willing to help the less fortunate in the fashion world."

Taylor's eyes grew wide. She was stunned. Not only did Kitana leave her hanging, but she called her the less fortunate one in fashion. *Oh, no this little bitch didn't. She must not know who she's talking to. She may be hot on the scene now, but I have bigger contacts that could take her off the scene so quickly it would make her head spin.*

A red sports car pulled up, and Desmond got out looking even finer than Taylor remembered him. He sported a black-and-white tropical shirt, denim shorts, and sandals, but he wasn't alone. His father, Baron Diaz, a legendary MMA champion turned coach, was with him. He was a handsome man with smooth, dark brown skin, bedroom eyes, and a neatly-trimmed afro. For a man in his late forties, he kept himself in nice shape, which showed in the tank top, shorts, and sandals he wore.

Taylor was in a trance. She didn't even realize that her assistant was tapping her shoulder. When she finally turned to look at her, there was a twisted look on her face. "What do you want?" Taylor asked.

"Taylor, since Kitana and Mr. Diaz are here, do you want me to lead them to wardrobe, hair, and makeup?"

"Sure. Now, go." Taylor waved her off then clapped her hands. "Come on everyone, let's move it! Time is money. Let's go!" She put on her Linda Farrow Luxe sunglasses, walking away as if she were worth billions.

***

The shoot was going extremely well. Desmond was posing like he had been modeling for years, looking like a piece of cinnamon cocaine with his sexy washboard abs and black shorts from his own line.

Taylor licked her lips while thinking about how good he looked. If no one else were there, she would have screwed him on the beach. She laughed to herself then looked around and spotted Kitana and Baron having small talk while looking over at Desmond. Taylor hoped they weren't talking about Kitana hooking up with Desmond. That was definitely a no-no.

Baron looked at Taylor with a sly grin while mouthing, "It's over, whore."

Thank God Taylor had her shades on, because her evil eyes would have killed him.

"Kitana! Kitana! Darling, we need you in a few shots," Hervé said.

Even without heels, Kitana worked her famous runway walk up to Desmond.

Taylor wanted to vomit as she watched her man and Kitana together. There was no breathing room in between them. In Taylor's eyes, it appeared that the two were really into each other.

"It's over between you and my son," Baron said to Taylor in a whisper.

Taylor looked over at him with snake eyes, ready to inject him with her venom.

"You're nothing but a washed up old gold digger, just trying to keep your name in the public. But do you see that sexy thing right there?" Baron continued.

Taylor looked back at the shoot to see Kitana rubbing her hands on Desmond's chest. She even started grinding her butt into his manhood.

"She's perfect for my son, and by the middle of next year, I'm going to make sure they're married and become South America and North America's hottest couple. So stay away, you money-hungry slut."

Taylor jumped when Baron lifted his hand and slapped her ass.

"Call me if you need some dick in that camel-toe vagina of yours." He laughed as he walked away.

Taylor's mouth was open. She was ready to fire back, but she didn't want everyone's attention to turn to her. She had a disgusted look on her face, and all she could think about was what would be different if her father weren't out of the game. She would have had him handle Baron for her. No matter what he'd said, she and Desmond would be together.

"A'ight! A'ight! Everyone, it's a wrap!" Hervé yelled, going over to Kitana, kissing her on both cheeks. He went over to kiss Desmond, who put up his hand to block Hervé.

Afterward, Desmond glanced at Taylor, who was pretending to look at some of the makeup and clothes. Without saying a word, she ran over to the limousine, knowing that Desmond was coming her way. She couldn't talk to him with Kitana or Baron there, so she jumped inside the limo, closing the door behind her.

Her driver looked at her, wondering what the rush was. Once she got herself together, all she told him was to quickly drive off. He did.

While riding down the streets of downtown Rio, Taylor felt broken. That was a feeling she hadn't felt in years. She didn't know why Desmond made her feel this way, so needy and insecure. It was supposed to be the other way around. She hated that it wasn't, but she also knew that love made a person feel this way sometimes.

As she was in deep thought, her cell phone rang. She looked at the screen to see that it was Duke. A smile was on her face. She thought it was good news. Now, she and Desmond could finally be together. Or, at least, that's what she thought.

Chapter 15

Taking My Place

"What!" Taylor shouted. "What do you mean you can't lock up Armand? What went wrong? Where is that undercover officer you had tracking my husband's every move? Come on, give me something."

"Well, we can't find the officer right now, and I'm not sending any of my men to any of Armand's locations, because I don't want a brutality case. The governor is already on my ass, and without the Americans confessing anything, we have no case."

Taylor sighed and looked at her freshly manicured nails. She rolled her eyes. "Well, what about the info me and the girls got for you? Will that bring Armand down? What about the meeting with Bruno Bello?"

"No. I'm sorry. The research I did on Bruno Bello proves that he is an extremely powerful man that can make any mountain of evidence disappear and show that he didn't have anything to do with your husband. So no way I have a case with your husband."

"Damnit! Damnit! Damnit!" Taylor was pissed off with a capital P.

Every time I try to get this bastard out of my life, he's always six steps ahead of me. Damn, am I slipping? I need to step up my game.

"Taylor, baby, you there?" Duke asked, interrupting her thoughts.

Tired of hearing his idiotic voice, she threw her phone to the side. Frustrated, she removed a photo of Desmond from her briefcase. He was looking so edible. Taylor licked her lips. "Don't worry, baby, we will be together soon." She kissed the photo.

"Where to, Ms. Monroe?" the driver asked.

Taylor put the photo back in the briefcase before crossing her legs. "Home, Samuel."

As soon as Taylor arrived home and got out of the limo, she noticed that a new gold Ferrari Spyder was parked in her driveway. She thought it was Sandino's. *Armand must pay him too much*, she thought. She then examined her five-million-dollar home with eight bedrooms, a four-car garage, and six bathrooms. As beautiful as her house was, she dreaded being there.

Opening the door, she glanced at the marble floors, crystal chandelier, and a grand stairway. She took off her sneakers and walked into the living room, which was all white with a white fur carpet and a crystal coffee table.

There was no sign of Armand or Sandino, but as she was just about to walk into the kitchen, she heard the smooth sounds of jazz coming from upstairs.

"What the hell?" Taylor whispered then pivoted to go upstairs to her and Armand's bedroom.

"To us," Taylor heard Armand say. The second she reached the doorway, she peeked through the crack in horror.

Armand and Ramon were in the bed, under the covers, drinking Perrier-Jouët and caressing each other. Taylor's blood was boiling, not because she loved Armand, but because this mess was going on in her house and in her bed.

At first, she wanted to rush in and break up Armand and Ramon's homoerotic love affair, until a lightbulb went off. *Why am I being the upset, jealous wife who thought she had the happy marriage? Hell, I'm the Head Bitch in Charge of Brazil, and it's time to get my Desmond plan into action now.* She went in her bag and pulled out her cell phone, pushing the video recording button. *This is so disgusting. My enemy at work and my weak-ass husband, actually fucking.*

"Armand, baby, I'm tired of sharing you with that has-been, ugly, fish-patty bitch! I don't know why you stay with her trifling ass, showing off her lovers. I think she and that model friend of hers, Milena, are having some kind of a lesbian fling. When are you planning on leaving that bitch to get with some real love?" Ramon was rubbing Armand's hairy chest.

"In due time. Divorcing Taylor isn't that easy. That woman has so many tricks and dicks up her sleeve, there's no telling what she'll do." Armand softly touched Ramon's face before kissing him. "Just remember that I love you and only you. Just give me a little time, okay?"

They kissed again.

Ramon smiled. "Okay, daddy."

"So, do you like your new car, baby?"

"Yeah, but I love this even more."

Ramon got on top of Armand and placed his rock hard seven-inch shaft between his ass cheeks, riding him like a cowboy going into the sunset.

Taylor's mouth was wide open. *Damn, Ramon can ride a dick better than I can. If this fool wasn't such an asshole, maybe we could've swapped sex tips.*

When it became unbearable for her to watch, she stopped recording, went downstair,s and made her way outside. Taylor looked at the car with disgust written across her face. She picked up a brick from the garden then got inside of the limousine.

"Where to, Ms. Monroe?" Samuel asked.

Taylor rolled down the window and threw the brick at the windshield of Ramon's new car. "Drive, Samuel, drive!"

Samuel sped off like a criminal who had just robbed a bank. Taylor looked back, smiling at her handiwork.

Riding through Rio with a heavy heart, Taylor looked at her beautiful city. There were plenty of couples walking, holding hands, and kissing. She broke down into tears, wishing that she was with Desmond. She was the type of woman who always got what she wanted, so she quickly wiped her tears, knowing that everything would soon be okay.

Feeling slightly better, she pulled out her cell and dialed. Within moments, someone answered.

"Hola," said a man with a thick Spanish accent.

"Are you ready to do business?"

The man laughed. "You don't mean . . . ?"

"Oh, yes, I do. Operation Destroy Armand and Make You the King of South America."

"Excellent!"

They both laughed.

Chapter 16

Hunger Games

"Man, this is some scary shit being in this elevator," said Travis.

"Yeah, tell me about," replied Stan, sitting on the floor, shaking his head. "God, I need some weed to help me forget this shit is real."

"Me and you both, playa," said Tyler, looking at his blurred reflection in the stainless steel wall.

Swag looked at them like they were all crazy. *I hate when dudes go through the motions.* "Would y'all chill out. We only been in here for a few hours. But since we are in here, man up! Be strong."

Stan sucked on his teeth, mumbling under his breath, "Stupid ass."

Swag looked down on him. "What was that, fat boy? What?"

Stan turned with a smirk on his face. "Dude, you heard my ass."

Swag wanted to kick that smirk off Stan's face, until Brad intervened. "Keep y'all heads to y'all selves while we in this small space. Once we get out this hellhole, then you both can kill each other. Can you both have a truce until then?"

"Whatever," said both Swag and Stan in unison.

Brad couldn't say he didn't try to be the peacemaker. He went into the duffle bag and opened it. It contained sandwiches and milk. "Who wants a sandwich?"

The fellas each took two or three sandwiches and a carton of milk.

Before the guys could take a bite, Brad yelled, "Hold up! Don't eat all the food up."

They all looked at Brad like he was nuts.

"Dude, we hungry and thirsty as hell. Plus, we ain't even gon' be in here that long. That detective is just fuckin' with our heads," said Swag as he took a bite of the peanut butter and jelly sandwich. The bread was stale. "Eh!" Swag spit it out, almost hitting Stan and wishing he had hit him.

"Damn, this bread is stale." He threw the sandwich to the side and put the other one back in the duffle bag. "Y'all can have that shit."

"No, we gotta make this last us," said Brad, concerned.

"Damn, B, how long you think we gon' be here?" asked Tyler, drinking the warm bottled water.

"Man, I don't even know, but we gotta keep up our strength if we wanna live to see another day." Brad opened the duffle bag again. "Come on. Put some of the sandwiches back, please."

They all did just that. The fellas didn't want to die from starvation, and they sure as hell didn't want to start eating each other, just in case they stayed in the elevator longer than the sandwiches lasted.

Brad ate the stale sandwich, trying to hold himself together. He was going to keep his strength up for this journey. He was determined not to crack and to keep the fellas in order no matter what.

Let the battles begin, Brad thought.

Chapter 17

Happy Thanksgiving

Brad was standing up, tapping his foot at the elevator door. Being in there was almost making him crazy. The fellas had eaten all of the food and drinks in the duffle bag, and were tossed some more food that didn't last long. Brad had a vision that he was as strong as Superman and opened up the elevators, and he and his friends ran for freedom, but he knew it was only a dream and it was impossible.

"Do y'all think Duke forgot about us?" Brad asked.

Swag shook his head. "No, B. Like I told you, that wannabe cop just fuckin' wit' our heads."

"I don't know, man," said Travis, leaning against the wall.

"I wonder how long it's been since we been in this elevator—or should I say our tomb," said Tyler.

"I think about for a week or so," said Swag, leaning against the other side of wall.

"A week!" shouted Brad. "Man, I don't wanna die in this elevator from lack of oxygen and starvation."

"Dudes, will y'all chill out wit' that dying shit? We gon' get through this. Be cool," said Swag. He was trying to stay brave but was scared shitless, not knowing what was going to happen to him or his friends.

"I hope you right, bruh," said Tyler. "Hope we get outta here soon, 'cause this place stinks." He held his nose.

Tyler was right about one thing: the elevator smelled like an outhouse. There was no way for them to take a piss or a dump unless they did it in one of the corners. The elevator stunk so badly. They never could have imagined being crammed in a space like this.

With beads of sweat dotted on his face, Stan licked his fingers, trying to fight the hunger and shaking hysterically. The others were very concerned for their friend. Almost every day Stan and Swag got into an argument, but today, Stan wasn't saying a word.

Brad looked at his friend, who was sitting on the floor in a daze. "Damn, bruh, you all right?" He touched Stan's shoulder, but Stan jerked away from him as if Brad's touch burned.

"Don't touch me!" Stan shouted, shaking and with tears streaming down his face.

Brad backed away from him, and the others just stared.

Stan's voice trembled as he spoke. "I should be at home with my family right now, eating all the good stuff for Thanksgiving, but here I am in a damn place like this."

The guys were so focused on getting fifty Gs that they forgot all about Thanksgiving with their families. The truth was, many never had a real storybook Thanksgiving dinner like Stan's family. Thanksgiving for Brad, Tyler, Swag, and Travis was eating hot wings, drinking Bud Light, and watching the football games.

"Why did I let y'all talk me into this?" He looked at each of them, one by one. "I hate you! I hate you all!" He balled himself in the corner, crying hysterically. "I wish I was dead!"

The fellas felt bad, and everyone left Stan at peace. They were just as scared, tired, hungry, and funky as he was. All they could do, though, was think about what their next move was.

"We can't stay in here like this forever. Banging on that door ain't getting us nowhere, and I'm not sure how much more of this I can take," Tyler said.

They all looked dumbfounded.

"If they hadn't taken our cell phones, I would have called my stupid-ass father to see if he would come here to help us," Brad said. "Then again, I ain't talked to that fool since he abandoned me. I don't have his current number or an address for his ass."

Travis pounded his fist on the wall. "Then what the hell we gon' do, y'all?"

All eyes shifted to Swag.

"Don't look at me. It's not like I have some kind of master plan or something."

"Come on, cuz. I know you got some connections somewhere," Brad said.

"Possibly, but how am I going to get in touch with somebody?"

"Shit, I don't know. If we had a phone, you could call Zaria and have her wire us some money."

Swag twisted his lips. "Bruh, please. I don't want that trick to know where my stash is. I would rather rot in hell than tell her where my money at and have that trick go spend it at the mall."

This was a dire situation, and no one appreciated Swag's reason. They all looked at him like he was crazy.

"You really gon' do us like that?" Tyler said. "For real?"

"Yeah, your own flesh and blood?" Brad said. "Come on, bro, forget what Zaria may or may not do. You got two sons, and you don't want to be stuck in a shitty overseas prison for the next several years, do you? I sure don't."

"I don't either, but no matter what, I don't have a way to call her. I'm not even sure if the money I have can help us out of this situation." Swag scratched his head, seeing a bunch of dry flakes drop on the floor. His lips were dry and sticking together. To some extent, he felt as if this was all his fault, but then he also felt as if the fellas had made their own decisions to come here—even Stan, who had his head down, shaking uncontrollably. Swag wanted to tell him that he was sorry for putting him in the middle of his bullshit, but saying that may have come too late.

Swag beat on the door, yelling for help for his friend. "Come on now! He needs some medical attention, fast! My boy is dying in here! We're all dying in here, so open the fucking door!"

Minutes later, the elevator doors opened. Stan's eyes grew wide. He charged the door and started running like a maniac, only to be grabbed by two officers.

"Let me go! Let me go, you bastards!" Stan fought, bit, and spit in the face of one of the officers, trying to get them away from him. No luck. The fellas stood in awe, watching Stan lose it. They had never seen him act like that before. He was like a wild animal until one of the officers used his Taser to calm him.

"Ahhhhhhh!" Stan yelped out in pain as the electricity shot through his body. He backed into the elevator and curled up into a ball, crying as the officer cuffed him. The officer forced him to stand up. Stan held his head down, wanting to die. So did his friends, but they had a little more fight left in them.

One officer had a gun on them. "Come on, you idiots. Let's go."

With weakened legs, they walked slowly out of the elevator.

One officer pinched his nose. "You Americans stink. Damn!"

They ignored him. What in the hell did he expect? They were told not to say a word and to follow the officer down the stairs. Two other officers dragged Stan along because he was too weak to move.

Outside, the guys squinted from the bright sun as they were brought to a white van.

"Remain silent. Do not look at us, and don't even think about running. Anyone who does will be shot in the back," the officer threatened.

The thought of running was on all of their minds, but no one wanted to be shot. They piled into the van in silence before it took off.

While in the van, the fellas didn't say a word to each other. They just shifted their eyes around, making contact with each other and shaking their heads. They had no idea what their next location would be or the next time they'd see the light of day again.

Within minutes, they arrived at Bangu, a middle class neighborhood in Rio de Janeiro, which was the location of their new home, the Bangu Penitentiary Complex. Ordered to get out of the van, Brad glanced at the beauty of the outside for what he thought might be the last time, before he was pushed into the building by one of the correctional officers of the prison. Once inside, the door was slammed shut.

Good-bye, world, Brad thought with tears in his eyes. *Sorry, Grandma. I let you down. I know you in Heaven saying I fucked up, but if you can, would you tell God to protect me and keep me from all evil?*

Inside, the fellas were being processed as inmates. First they were fingerprinted and then stripped down to take quick showers. They were not regular showers where there was a curtain with privacy, but a shower where they had to strip naked, stand against a wall, and be sprayed with water hoses. Their bodies quivered from the cold water being sprayed on them, and all they could do was cover their faces in hopes that they wouldn't drown.

"Damn!" Swag shouted while facing the wall. "That's enough!"

"I'll tell you when it's enough! And I'm the one who give the orders around here!" The prison guard continued to spray them all. After the water torture was done, they were ordered to stand in line for a cavity search.

Stan shook his head, refusing to let the officer go up his anus. "You can't use that same glove on all of us."

"I can do what the hell I want. Now turn your ass around!" yelled the officer.

Stan wasn't backing down. "You gon' have to fight me in order to do that."

The fellas looked at Stan, feeling as if he had lost his mind.

The officer had no problem fighting Stan, but at the snap of his fingers, he changed his mind. "You know what, American? You're right. The nurse will be here tomorrow to check you out."

Stan had a smile of relief on his face.

"But in the meantime, you can spend the night in the hole."

Two officers stepped forward to grab Stan. He resisted, so one officer punched him in the gut, causing him to double over in pain. They escorted him to the hole.

"Wait!" Stan shouted. "No! No! No!" He kicked and screamed as he was being dragged down the hall by the officers.

They were all wondering if they would ever see their friend again.

"Don't treat him like that,!" Travis shouted. "Damn, this is fucked up!"

"You're damn right it is," Tyler said. "Stay strong, man. Keep yo' head up!"

After Stan was taken away, the guys were given prison uniforms and white sneakers. Then, their mugshots were taken before they were escorted to their cell. The men in all of the cells were like animals who spoke in languages the fellas couldn't follow. The one thing they could understand were the mean mugs they got from the men that implied, *I'ma rape you real good.* That made them more nervous. They saw all kinds of races of men, from Japanese and Russian to Arabs. There were about thirty-five men in one cell.

On the outside, the fellas may have looked tough, but on the inside they were frightened for their lives. They stood huddled together when confronted by a muscular Ghanaian man, who was black as the ace of spades. He stood seven foot one and was 325 pounds of pure muscle. He was only wearing his prison pants and dirty white sneakers.

"You black bastards in my spot," he said.

Brad, Tyler, and Travis wanted to move, but there was no room to move without stepping on or bumping into someone. Swag, however, was the type of dude not to back down to anyone, no matter how big or small they were.

"Look, you Deebo-gorilla-on-*Planet-of-the-Apes*, banana-eating bastard, I got the right to stand anywhere I damn well please. Now, run up!"

The Ghanaian man balled up his fists, causing everyone to inch back. But to Swag, he was at a point where he felt he had nothing to lose. Nobody was going to disrespect him and get away with it.

"Midnight!" said a man with deep voice and thick Mexican accent. The whole cell went quiet. "Let the four Americans pass!"

Midnight gritted his teeth, but he let the guys pass through. He shot Swag an evil gaze; Swag flashed one right back at him. Other inmates cleared the path that led the fellas to a somewhat better part of the cell. It wasn't as crowded, but it was still stuffy nonetheless.

Sitting down in a chair was a very handsome Mexican man, who was lean but muscular. His olive skin was smooth, and he had a five o'clock shadow on his face. He also rocked a low-cut Caesar, and he didn't wear a prison uniform like everyone else. He was wearing a short-sleeve, button-down Hawaiian shirt that was unbuttoned to show off his six pack. Leather sandals covered his feet, and he had on jean shorts. He smiled at the fellas while inviting them to come closer.

"Welcome, gentlemen. Welcome to my pad. My name's Paco Hernandez," he said.

Swag tossed his head back. "What's up, bruh?"

Everyone else remained silent.

"So, you guys have names?" Paco asked.

"I'm Swag." Swag looked over at the crew. "This is my cousin, Brad, and the twins are Tyler and Travis."

The spoke in unison. "What's up?"

"From what I see, y'all some bold dudes to stand up to my man Midnight."

"Bruh, where we from, respect is earned, not given," Swag said.

"I feel you on that. So where you dudes from, and what brings you to Brazil?"

"We from St. Louis, Missouri, in America, and we got busted for trafficking," replied Travis.

"Dude." Swag frowned as he looked at Travis. "Shut the hell up, man. We don't know this cat like that."

Paco waved him off. "It's cool. But if you all was working for me back in Houston, Texas, you would've been in the clear and back home smoking a blunt or screwin' a chick or two." Paco and his crew started to laugh.

Swag responded. "Now that we told you about us, what's your story, playa?"

Paco laughed as he lit a Cuban cigar. "Well, I run the Hernandez Cartel in Houston and Mexico, along with my father, Paco Hernandez Senior."

The fellas had seen and heard everything about the Hernandez Cartel. They were ruthless, coldblooded bastards who ran the fastest growing illegal business, from supplying cocaine to illegal gambling and trafficking young girls and boys for pleasure. The Hernandez Cartel was worth over a billion dollars, and the numbers continued to grow every day. The Hernandez family ran Texas to south of the border. They didn't play when it came to money and would kill you right in front of your mother or child if you screwed them over in any kind of way.

"Let me introduce you to my crew." Paco looked over at his men. "This is Ike. That's Rock, Landon, Miguel, Nash, and of course you all met Midnight."

All the Hernandez soldiers nodded to the fellas, and they nodded back.

"Now that we all friends, sit and join us. We don't bite, unless you do. Let's play cards. Midnight, go in the cooler and get our new friends a beer."

The guys didn't know what they were getting into with Paco or the Hernandez Cartel, but if they could somehow protect them from the rest of the prisoners, it was okay with them. Plus, a beer didn't sound too bad. They needed a beer or two after all they had been through. Too bad Stan wasn't around to taste one.

As they started to play cards, Stan stayed on Brad's mind.

Chapter 18

Taste of Insanity

For the next few days, the fellas stayed close to Paco and the members of the Hernandez Cartel. Being that they moved around with them, none of the other prisoners bothered them. Brad, Swag, Tyler, and Travis explained to Paco and his crew their situation in Brazil, but Paco's story was way different.

Paco and his crew came to Brazil to have a vacation with no Hernandez Cartel business and no drama, period. Everything was going good, until Paco was at one of Brazil's hottest night spots, talking to a Brazilian firecracker. She was one of the many mistresses of a Vietnamese crime boss, and the night ended up in a blood bath, leaving eight murdered. After that incident, the Hernandez Cartel members were going through all kinds of hell, with the media saying that it was a war between them and the Vietnamese crime family.

Paco's father, Paco Hernandez Sr., and his lawyer were doing everything they could to get Paco and his team out and back on the streets of Texas. Paco even offered to help the fellas out if they agreed to accompany him and his people back to Houston to work with the Hernandez Cartel as their debt. To Swag, Tyler, and Travis, if they had a good chance to get out of that filthy hellhole, they were on board.

The main thing on Brad's mind was his freedom, but Brad for damn sure wanted to make sure Diamond had her freedom too. He couldn't understand why he was falling so hard for a woman he barely knew. Maybe he could save her too, and to keep his boys and Paco's gang off his back, he agreed to be a part of the Hernandez Cartel if they were released.

The cell door opened, and the guard put in one more inmate. Everyone turned to see the fresh meat, but Brad and the fellas knew it was Stan.

Stan looked a god awful mess. His face had many scabs on it. His eyes were puffy, and his teeth were yellow. His hair was matted and nappy. He wore a prison uniform that looked way too baggy on him, and with his head down, he kept fidgeting.

Paco looked at Stan, then at Brad and the fellas.

"Do you all know that crackhead?"

The fellas could look at Stan and tell his mind was gone. They couldn't afford to have him tag along if they were in Paco's gang, and they didn't want to lose that connection, because that gave them a good chance of getting out of Brazil.

"Hell, naw, we don't know that fool!" Swag spat.

Brad looked at his cousin, who had no emotion on his face. He knew Swag was a cutthroat kind of dude who would throw his own sons to the wolves in a minute to save himself. Stan meant nothing to him, nor did he mean much to the others, who were looking for a way out.

About twelve men went up to Stan, shoving him around like he was a common prison bitch.

"Ahhhh, leave me alone!" Stan cried out. "Just leave me alone and keep y'all hands off meeeee!"

Hearing Stan's screams and cries really disturbed the fellas, but there wasn't much they could say or do.

Interfering would mean serious trouble for them, so in the moment, silence was golden. Stan tried running, but he tripped over to the Hernandez Cartel side of the cell. He had on a tank top, and his face was bloody. His blood mixed with his tears as he glared at his so-called friends. He looked at Brad, who had so much sorrow for him in his eyes.

Stan extended his hand to Brad. "He . . . help me!"

Brad wanted to help him, but before he could, Paco pushed him aside and kicked Stan right in his face, breaking his nose that busted clean open and started gushing blood.

"Midnight and Rock, throw that piece of shit back out there."

Both Midnight and Rock stood on both sides of Stan, picking him up.

"Noooooo!" Stan screamed as they threw him back to his predators.

Paco and his crew laughed as they watched Stan get beaten and ganged raped. Brad and the fellas joined in the laugher. On the inside they wanted to cry, but their freedom was way too valuable.

Love you, bruh, thought Brad, closing his eyes as he continued hearing his best friend's screams.

Chapter 19

What About Your Friends?

On the prison courtyard, everyone had their own sections from the gang associations, nationalities, and so on. The fellas had never seen anything like this, except in prison documentaries they watched back home. Brad saw one of the Bosnian gang members do a drug deal with another inmate. Some of the gangs worked out on some of the equipment the prison supplied to them.

The fellas could see prison guards up and down, watching the place at all times. Security was real tight, so no one was going to escape anytime soon. If you tried, the guards would shoot you dead, no questions asked.

When the fellas were in the mess hall earlier, where the food looked like dog shit, one of the Asian inmates told them that a few days ago, his friend tried to escape. The guard let his friend climb the fences as high as he could, and when he was about to cut the barbed wires, one of the guards that was on the fifth floor of the building shot his friend in the face, letting him fall to his bloody death. To make the story even grosser, the Asian inmate told them that the guards just let the vultures eat his friend.

The fellas knew right then this prison was ruthless. Overseas prisons made American prisons look like the late Michael Jackson's Neverland. It was a good thing for Brad, Swag, Tyler, and Travis that they were under Paco's protection in there, especially since one of the gangs picked a fight with another gang.

The fellas sat on the bleachers as Paco and his crew played basketball with the Arabs. Paco offered the fellas to play, but they refused for now, so Paco gave them some courtesy marijuana to ease their minds. It was one of the many benefits of being under his protection.

The fellas sat there for a moment, not believing this shit was real. Everyone was hoping this shit was just a bad dream that would go away and they would be back in St. Louis, kickin' it.

Swag went over and over in his mind what had gone wrong with this. He knew Armand had something to do with the setup. Swag would never admit it, but deep down, he was sorry he had ever gotten his boys involved with this foolishness.

Brad looked over at the other side of the yard to see a room that men were coming in and out of. He knew they were up to no good. When a big German came out, Stan followed behind. Stan was butt-ass naked with his head down. *My God, Stan.*

Brad remembered back in the cell and in the mess hall, the Nigerians and the Russians were bidding on Stan. The Nigerians gave the Russians a piece they couldn't refuse, and from then on, Stan was the property of the gang called the Nigerian Warlords. As soon as they bought him, they made him in to a sex slave to pimp out to the men in prison and to themselves. The men were paying the Nigerian Warlords anything from money and drugs to renting some of their own slaves to get a piece of Stan's fresh meat.

The next guy that was going to run up into Stan was a Chilean man, who gave the Nigerian Warlords the latest issue of *Playboy* magazine and his watch. One of the Nigerian Warlords looked at the items and nodded. The Chilean man knew that was the signal to take Stan in the room. The Chilean man pushed Stan then followed

behind and closed the door. Brad noticed that when Stan
went with the man, he didn't fight or even speak.

Stan, who was in the dark and dirty room getting
banged out by the Chilean men, knew he had lost everything, from his job to his unfaithful-ass girlfriend. The
Nigerian Warlords had stripped him of his dignity, and
most importantly, he was betrayed by his friends who he
thought were so loyal. They used to talk about loyalty, but
he knew the fellas were full of shit.

Fuck 'em, Stan thought. For now, he was going to play
his role as the new prison bitch, until he got his bloody
revenge. The blood he wanted to taste was Brad's. As the
Chilean man was still hitting him, huffing and puffing
almost ready to cum, Stan thought about the day he
went into that cell and he reached for Brad to help him.
He knew the other fellas were for self. He just knew his
buddy Brad would help him, but in Stan's bloody red,
teary eyes, Brad had failed him. Stan was going to taste
the revenge on all the fellas that did him wrong.

Bitch ass, Stan thought, giving a twisted face, knowing
his anus was hurting bad. *Revenge will be mine.*

Brad sat there shaking his head. "What have I done?"

"What, bruh?" asked Tyler, taking his braids down.
"Damn, my shit is itchy."

"Dudes, do y'all see what I'm seeing?" said Brad, turning his head.

Swag turned around and looked at the room where
Stan was getting raped. "Man, chill out wit' that shit."

"Oh, so you just gon' pretend that's not our friend
getting pimped out by them damn Nigerian Warlords
like a ho and getting raped in that room," replied Brad,
pointing to the room.

The fellas were quiet for a moment until Swag spoke up. "First off, B, you my cousin and I love you, but you really need to chill out wit' that shit. Secondly, Stan blew his own fuse. If he had a strong enough mind, he wouldn't be a ho for 'em African dudes and getting his ass fucked right now."

"Yeah, man. You gotta remember he ain't really no friend of ours. We"—Travis circled his arm around Brad—"been friends. Nah, we been like brothers to each other for last ten years. Our bond is way stronger than what we had with that fool." Travis took a puff from his marijuana before passing it to Swag.

"Yeah, man, remember you introduced that dude to us. That dude was just someone you worked with," said Tyler coldheartedly.

"Yeah, he was never really one of us anyway, B. He didn't fit in to our crew anyway. Soft-ass dude," said Swag, taking two puffs from the marijuana, letting it take its effect. "See, B, me, the twins, and you, we fam. We been through too much with each other—good, bad, and as ugly as these prison walls. So do us all a favor and just cut Stan off altogether. It's for the better."

Brad just couldn't believe that his boys were saying this shit. Brad couldn't sell out his friend like that. He was going to make one more attempt to keep the group together.

We came to Brazil as a team to do this trafficking shit and get this money that completely blew up in our faces, thought Brad, lying back on the bleachers. *Now look at us, locked up in a shitty overseas prison that makes the ghetto of St. Louis look like a walk on the beach. And our boy is being beaten and raped constantly by inmates just to get their sick nut off.*

The one thing about Brad was that he was a loyal dude to the end. He was going to do his damnest to persuade his boys to help their friend and get whatever little sanity he had left. "Look, y'all, this ain't us. Look at how we doin' Stan, man."

They all looked at Brad like he had shit on his face.

Brad was determined to get through to his boys. "Swag, you know the street game better than any of us here, so I know you can handle a street dude like Paco. Can you at least talk to him?"

In Swag's mind, that was a definite no, but he decided to play his cousin along. He looked at Brad up and down. "Talk to that dude about what, cuz?"

Brad looked at his cousin, dumbfounded. "Swag, bro, you know how this underworld street game or whatever this shit you call it goes!" Brad took a deep breath, calming himself down. "Cuz, please. Can you at least talk to Paco man to man? Maybe he could buy Stan from them Nigerian Warlords, put Stan under his protection so that no one can touch him. We can work wit' him while we're here for now. So once when we get back to the States, Stan will be somewhat together in the head."

"Brad!" shouted Tyler, looking at him like he was crazy.

Travis gave him the "bruh, that shit ain't gon' happen" eyes.

"Man, we came into this bullshit together. We need to stick together. We got families back at home. Hell, Stan's got family the most. They like the damn Brady Bunch. They need to see their son sooner or later, and we need to return him somewhat straight in the head. Come on, y'all, for our friend. Let's help him." Brad looked back at Swag, begging him one last time. "Cuz, are you willing to talk to Paco into buying Stan so that we can help get his shit somewhat together?"

"Hell to the nah!" shouted Swag with no remorse.

Brad was disappointed but not surprised by his cousin's reaction. "Why?"

Tyler put his hand on Brad's knee. "B, look in front of you. This place ain't exactly Disneyland."

"Yeah, bruh, Paco didn't have to put us under his protection. What makes you think he'll ever buy Stan from them Nigerian Warlord motherfuckas?" replied Travis.

Tyler took down his last braid. "Yeah, that dude is just damaged goods now. B, just let him go, man. Stan is a lost cause."

"Yeah, man, just forget you ever met that dude," replied Travis as he was lying down on the bleachers, letting the marijuana take effect as he closed his eyes. "Damn, Paco got the good shit."

With no help from the twins, Brad looked over at Swag.

Swag gave him a crazy look. "B, cuz, don't be lookin' over here." He took another puff. "Look, my dude, that's your . . . friend, and if you wanna help him, then that's all . . . on you. Shit, cuz, if I have to live in this shithole, I may as well live like a king under Paco's protection. Now, if you decide you wanna stick up for Stan and become a new prison bitch yourself, go right ahead. Don't expect any help from me, Tyler, or Travis. You gon' be all . . . on your own with that one. So what's it gonna be, cuz?" Swag took another puff of weed and handed it to Brad. "Now, hit this shit and shut the hell up. That dude no longer exists to us. Period."

Brad took a deep breath. He took the marijuana from Swag and took a deep breath. He coughed a little since he hadn't done weed since high school, so he had to remember to puff-puff-give and fight the cough. He took another puff and let the marijuana fill his body, making it feel like Jell-o. The marijuana was just the thing he needed to take him out of this world for a moment and forget his problem. He realized his cousin and friends weren't as loyal as he thought they were. He was letting the weed soak in. He couldn't believe how his friends would sell a friend out for hood luxury in prison from a dude they hardly knew.

Brad laughed. *Hell, I would.*

Brad clearly knew his normal self was gone and the old weedhead asshole Brad was back. *Why am I laughing at this shit?*

In Brad's mind, he knew he was a loyal dude and a good-ass friend to the bitter end. He wanted all the fellas to stay together in one piece. But at the same time, Brad didn't wanna lose his protection from Paco, or the fellas having his back also. Brad, sooner or later, was going to get his boys to help Stan before he got in too deep and lost himself in this prison world. But until then, Brad was going to completely distance himself from Stan altogether. Brad took another puff of the good-ass joint before passing it to Tyler. He blew out the smoke, thinking he just blew all his troubles away.

Chapter 20

Plan B

Two weeks later, the fellas remained in the prison, but under Paco's protection, no one in the prison dared to touch them unless Paco said so. Stan was being beaten, raped, and passed around the other side of the cell constantly. After a while, he was getting better at his new prison bitch role and even getting some of the profit the Nigerean Warlords were making off of him. They would give him smokes, and cocaine to relieve the pain from the beating and in his anus. But the one thing he was grieving was the blood of the fellas, who had reduced him to this role. In his mind, they were going to pay. At night, he had visions of slicing their heads open and eating their brains. He knew that his vision was going to be a reality before long. He just stayed patient and waited for that day that kept somewhat of a sick smile on his face.

The guys, especially Brad, wanted to help their friend, but to stay under the protection of Paco they broke all ties and communication with their boy until their court date. They had no clue when that would be.

Being under Paco's protection had some greater benefits as well. Not only did other prisoners distance themselves, but they all got to shower in private, thanks to Paco's connections with the correctional officers. They also didn't have to eat the pig slop the prison served the inmates. With the hookups in the prison, Paco and his crew, plus Brad and the fellas, ate gourmet foods fit for kings in the dining area every night. For entertainment, they played cards. None of them were delighted about being in prison, but other than what had happened to Stan, it wasn't as horrific as they had imagined it to be, like on TV or the stories they had heard. They also knew, though, that with the snap of Paco's fingers, that could all change.

Aside from trying to make his own escape, Brad thought about Diamond as well. He promised himself that if he managed to get out of there, he would find her and take her back to America with him. For some reason, he felt as if she was still alive. Maybe suffering like he was, but definitely still alive. In private, Brad talked to his crew about his plans.

They also convinced Swag to utilize the clout he had to try to make a phone call to Zaria. They weren't sure if money could help them in this situation, but it was good to have something on hand, if needed.

Swag was escorted by one of the officers to go call Zaria and tell her where his stash was so she could send it to him. He figured she had been wondering where he was, but he didn't have time to get into details with her. All she needed to know was he would possibly need bail money for him and the fellas—nothing more and nothing less.

Swag strutted down the hall like he was the pimp of the place because of being under Paco's protection. As he was walking with the officer behind him, he turned around and looked in the conference room, where Paco and two other gentlemen were sitting down, discussing serious business. Swag shook his head. He couldn't trust anyone, and he damn sure didn't trust Paco.

Man, if I do get outta this shit, maybe I'll get a real job, go to Job Corps to get my GED, give my life to the Lord, and maybe marry Zaria.

***

Paco was in the prison conference room with his lawyer, Manny Louis, a slick-looking white man on the chubby side, who was dressed in a gray business suit. He was known as the white Johnnie Cochran of Houston, Texas, and was also known for getting gang leaders, drug lords, and even members of the Hernandez Cartel off by making all of the evidence disappear. It all came at the price of a pretty penny, but it left the judges no choice but to let some of Texas's most hardcore criminals go scot free.

Also in the room with Paco was the King of Houston, the most notorious man in the crime world. Deadlier than the Italian Mafia, they even feared him. Paco's father was named Paco Juan Hernandez, but everyone called him PJ, or the Cocaine and Sex King. He had some of the best cocaine in Texas, thanks to his connections in Colombia and from taking lessons from his late mentor, who was murdered. Her name was Griselda Blanco, also known as the Godmother of Cocaine. Her mentoring also helped him to venture into the sex trade. He kept that business strictly in his native land of Mexico. Kidnapping homeless kids in the Texas area and drugging them up, he'd put them in a whorehouse in Mexico. That new business was making him even richer, especially when the giants in the corporate world came all the way from New York, or even Africa, to get some young ass.

For a fifty-two-year-old man, PJ had total swagger. He was a very handsome man who resembled actor Ricardo Antonio Chavira. He was working with a very powerful physique that showed well in a Hickey Freeman navy classic-fit suit. He really could have easily graced the cover of *GQ* or *Men's Health* magazine. From the look on PJ's face, he wasn't pleased with the shit his son and his friends had done in Brazil, because the whole Hernandez Cartel was under investigation.

Manny explained to Paco that the incident had gone global, and the D.A. back in Houston was fighting hard to take the Hernandez Cartel down. He wouldn't rest until the Hernandez Cartel was brought down and PJ was behind bars for good.

"Papi, maybe we can pay that dickhead off to keep him quiet. Or you know, my favorite, we can always put him out of his misery to shut him up forever," Paco suggested.

PJ looked at his son like he was crazy. "Boy, are you stupid? You're the same fool your uncle was, telling me to give that jerkoff half of what the Hernandez Cartel worked so hard to build. I run Texas, not that asshole. Even if I did pay that ass off, he would blackmail us for the rest of our days, and no one would eat. Hell no. That shit is out."

Paco was getting so pissed off. "Papi, get me out this hellhole. Hell, get me out this damn country and back on U.S. soil. I got a family back in Houston. I got my woman and my little girl. Come on, Manny. You're a lawyer, so scheme."

Manny sighed. "Well, the good news is that I can get you out on bail, but you would have to lay low for a while so that me and your father can fix a lot of the bullshit you and your men caused."

Paco smiled. "Cool, whatever."

"But the bad news is you will have to leave your men behind." PJ spoke with an emotionless face.

Dead silence filled the room. Paco couldn't believe what he was hearing. The one thing Paco believed in was loyalty in the family business. Paco was a loyal dude until the end. No way was he leaving his boys, who had his back since he was in diapers, in that shithole. If they went down, he was going to go down with them like a true G would do.

"Manny and Papi, have you both lost your damn minds? What part of the game is that? Huh? I would never sell my boys out for not even one second of freedom. Both of you old bastards better figure out something so that my boys and a few of my new friends get out of here and back on U.S. soil."

"Come on, son. Take the offer, and I will figure out a way to get your boys and new boys released," PJ said.

Paco knew that his father was one of the biggest liars that God ever put on this earth. PJ lied about never breaking Paco's mother's heart. Paco's mother was a good woman with a heart of gold that would give you the shirt off her back. She was the most beautiful Mexican woman, with a tight body giving Salma Hayek a run for her money. She held her man down at any cost, even putting her own dreams of being a doctor on hold. In time, the perfect family she built started crashing down when she found out that PJ had another family in Dallas. Plus, he had women and children all over the state of Texas coming at him for child support. She even caught him in the act twice. With PJ not making an effort to make his marriage work, it caused Paco's mother to have a nervous breakdown. Soon after, Paco's mother was committed to a mental hospital on suicide watch.

Also, Paco knew that his father set his own brother up so that he could take over the Hernandez Cartel. Paco, himself, never understood why he had even gotten involved with the Hernandez Cartel, because there was no loyalty anywhere. Paco remembered when his grandfather was on his deathbed and he told Paco to get as far away from the family as quickly as he could, because he knew when he met his maker, the Hernandez Cartel was going straight to hell. When he closed his eyes, sure enough he did.

Paco's mind wandered until PJ slammed his hand on the wooden table, breaking his son out of his daydream. "Look, boy, you have to choose. Get out of this hellhole and go back to Houston to be with your family that loves and supports you. If you don't, you will be completely cut off from the Hernandez Cartel and the family forever. So, what's it going to be, son?" PJ smiled, knowing that his son was going to make the right choice.

That smile pissed off Paco. He stood up, looking as if he wanted to assassinate both his father and Manny. "Fuck you, Manny, and fuck you too, old man. I don't give a damn about the Hernandez Cartel. Our family died a long time ago when you screwed Mommy over with your whore and bastard children. I hope you burn in hell, old man. So, fuck you!"

After hearing those words, PJ and Manny both stood.

"Okay, Paco. Enjoy prison food, and don't drop the soap."

PJ and Manny walked out of the room.

"Fuck you both!" Paco gave them the finger.

Once PJ and Manny were out of the room, the correctional officer walked over to Paco, putting his hand on his shoulder. "You cool, boss?"

"Yeah, Mario."

"So, what now, boss?" Mario asked in a thick Spanish accent.

Paco smiled at Mario. "Time for plan B: To get the hell out of here!"

Chapter 21

Plan In Action

That evening, Paco and his crew, along with Brad, Swag, Tyler, and Travis were in the prison private dining area, enjoying the perks of being with Paco. They were having a good meal of fried chicken wings, collard greens, T-bone steak, fried rice, baked potatoes, cupcakes from Diamond's bakery, and all the beer they wanted.

As the fellas were eating like kings, they noticed Brad slowly licking a chocolate cupcake with pink frosting and sprinkles. Brad knew that those delicious cupcakes were from the bakery Diamond worked for—or, in Brad's mind, the bakery she was forced to work for. He imagined Diamond's beautifully manicured hands making cupcakes and mixing up the batter. In his mind, he was having a freaky vision of her in a Victoria's Secret bra and panty set. Her body was shaped like model Chanel Iman, with a Nicki Minaj booty. He could picture her working in a hot, steamy kitchen with sweat dripping down her sexy body as she was taking cupcakes out of the hot oven. He could imagine watching her frost every cupcake. Brad pretended that his fingers were hers as he licked them passionately.

The fellas were laughing at him, because they knew what was wrong with Brad. Being in the prison for weeks without any women around was hard on any man, and they all jacked off at night. But Brad had gone too far, and he was looking like a desperate fool. Tyler threw a chicken wing at Brad, knocking him out of his day dream. He looked over at his boys, who were laughing up a storm.

"Damn, playa," Swag said, laughing.

"He workin 'em fingers," said Paco. "Whose clit you imaginin' you eatin' out?"

They continued to laugh, and Brad gave them all the finger.

As they continued eating like kings, Paco cleared his throat. His crew knew when he did that, it was time to get down to business.

"Well, everyone, I have some bad news and some good news," Paco said.

Everyone was silent.

"The bad news is we ain't getting out of here, because my father wanted only me released, but I said hell naw. I'm loyal to the damn end. So I'm officially cut off from the Hernandez Cartel."

The fellas didn't say a word. They were stunned that their boy had risked his own freedom, wealth, and family to be in a shithole with them. To them, that was true friendship.

"The good news is I've been making contacts, and I'm now hooked up with a very powerful Costa Rican mob boss. We been talking business for years, and I'm thinking of joining that squad. The plan is to bring my father's piece of shit organization down and make the streets of Houston and Mexico mine, with you all as equal partners."

All the fellas clapped, including Swag, Tyler, and Travis, who really didn't give a shit about anything anymore except getting the hell out of Brazil by any means necessary. Brad felt the same way, but he had to find out what was up with Diamond.

"Shh!" Paco said. "Calm that shit down 'fore y'all wake up the whole damn prison."

The fellas silenced themselves again.

"But, Paco, if they gon' make us full partners, how we gon' do it from in here and they in Costa Rica?" Brad asked.

"Homies, if you just shut the hell up, I can tell you the rest of the story," Paco said sarcastically. "Yeah, I know this cat in Costa Rica, and the boss is going to take real good care of us. We all gon' make more money than we ever dreamed of. We can kick it in Costa Rica for a few years, until I can build my own dynasty and bring my father's down. Then, Houston can be ours for the taking."

Swag, Tyler, Travis, and Paco's boys were saying, "Hell yeah! Anything to get out of this hellhole."

Brad couldn't believe how his cousin and his boys were acting. He was highly disappointed. They kept making the same mistake over and over again, and even though Brad had agreed to go along with the plan, he didn't want to. There was nothing to be happy about. He just wanted out. He didn't give a damn about running the streets with men like Paco, and shame on the others for wanting to be down with him.

"Yo, B, you wit' us or what, bro?" Paco asked.

Brad pretended as if he hadn't heard him. "What you say, man?"

"You down wit' us or what?" Paco smiled.

"Yeah, I'm down for whatever."

"Cool. Gentlemen, in a few short days, we will be free and very rich men." Paco raised his cup. "To the future."

"To the future!" Everyone raised their cups.

Goodbye, fellas, Brad thought while taking a sip of his drink. *I'm so glad this is almost over.*

Chapter 22

It's Goin' Down

In the prison that night, Paco held a little party for all of the inmates in the cell, with jerk chicken, barbecue ribs, corn on the cob, white rice, and cake. No one, not even the faculty at the prison, questioned Paco about having the party. Since he was an ex-member of the Hernandez Cartel, he still had money everywhere, and with money, people still respected him. He had the power, no doubt. All of the prisoners ate like they never had food before. Hell, they hadn't had good food like that in a minute.

One prisoner said, "This feast is even better than sex and Christmas combined," and all of the inmates laughed.

Paco watched as everyone was enjoying the food. *Eat up, 'cause it will be your last meal.*

As everyone was enjoying their meal, the officer brought a big orange water dispenser, which contained red Kool-Aid. Each prisoner grabbed a cup, but Paco warned his crew, Brad, Swag, Tyler, and Travis not to drink it unless they wanted to meet their maker sooner than later. Paco proposed a toast to life and blessings, but in his mind, the real toast he wanted to say was, *Fuck you all, and good luck in hell.*

All the prisoners ate and drank, until it got quieter and quieter. The cell went to a deathful silence. Brad and the fellas were scared shitless. Brad looked over and saw his boy Stan, who was now dead to the world. His eyes were wide open and without a blink.

Good luck in the afterlife, my friend. He tried to hold in his tears. Brad knew that he did wrong by his friend, abandoning Stan when he needed Brad the most. He knew he had to reap punishment for it later, but for now, all he wanted to do was get the hell out of the prison, check up on Diamond, and get out of Brazil with her by his side.

There was a clicking sound, and the cell door opened.

"Come on," Paco said.

Everyone followed his lead out of the cell. Brad stopped one moment to look back at Stan. "Deuces, my friend," he said in a whisper.

When he was heading out to meet his boys, out of nowhere, someone jumped on Brad's back, pulling him down. The crew pivoted to see what was going on, and they saw that it was Stan, fighting with Brad, after everyone thought he was dead.

"You ain't going no damn where," Stan hissed like a demon. "You gon' stay in here with me and be the new bitch!"

"Get off me," Brad said, pushing him back and then putting him into a headlock.

Stan was no longer the nice, funny guy Brad used to work and hang out with. Stan had turned into a wild beast, thirsty for blood, but Brad couldn't blame him. Brad had sacrificed his friend to the wolves, seeing and hearing his friend being beaten, raped, and sold for cigarettes or soap. That would make anyone go crazy.

"All I can say is I'm sorry," Brad said in a low tone while trying to calm Stan.

"Fuck you and your *sorry*. I'ma—"

The sound of firecrackers went off. Brad was in a state of shock as he had blood splattered all over him from his friend's brains being blown out. Stan's lifeless body fell to the ground, and when Brad looked up, he saw the person who had shot Stan. It was one of the officers that worked for Paco.

"Move it, fat ass, and catch up with your friends if you want your freedom. I'll take care of this piece of shit. Go!"

Brad stepped over Stan's body and hurried to make his way to his crew so they could get the hell out of the prison.

Once the guys were outside, one of the other guards had a black van waiting for the fellas. Brad smelled the air. It still smelled so sweet. Now that he was smelling the sweet victory of freedom, he thought about how he was going to get away from everyone. He didn't know his way around, and even if he got to the airport again, how would he be able to board one of those planes and get the hell out of there? He was sure that Diamond could help him, and he could help her too. She appeared to be a trustworthy person, and there weren't too many other people that Brad trusted right now.

As the van drove off, they all lifted their hands, waving good-bye.

While the van drove down the streets of downtown Rio, the fellas, Paco, and his crew were shouting, laughing, and drinking beer while saying, "Thank God. Free at last. Costa Rica, here we come."

That was with the exception of Brad, who was looking out the window and smelling the fresh night air. He glanced at all of the buildings and at the ocean that had a reflection of the moon in the night waters. The scent reminded him of his arrival to Brazil, but then the flashbacks of his best friend being shot in the head came back to haunt him. It wasn't the first time Brad had seen someone being killed, but that was his boy. He soon snapped out of the flashback and gazed at his friends and cousin, not knowing who they were anymore. Paco had really filled their heads up with bullshit, and Brad refused to be one of Paco's puppets. He took a deep breath as he was preparing to make one of the biggest decisions of his life.

"Midnight, pull over," Brad said in a soft tone.

Everyone shifted their heads to look at him.

"Bruh, what did you just say?" Swag said, frowning. "We gotta get outta here asap."

Brad ignored Swag. To him, Swag was a perfect stranger, instead of the cousin who'd had his back growing up. All Brad had now was himself.

"Midnight, let me out now!" This time, he put a little more bass in his voice.

Paco sighed and shook his head. "You stupid fool. I figured you would change your mind, but go ahead and be an idiot. You won't get far. You will be killed by morning. I'm not going to stop you from getting out, and with one down, there will be more freaking money for us." Paco looked at Midnight. "Pull over and let this dumb-ass piece of shit out 'fore he get us all caught up."

Midnight waited until he found a dark alley; then he parked.

"Cuz, are you crazy? What are you doin'? You tryin' to get caught?" Swag asked.

"Nah, man, I just don't think this is the way forward. I'm gon' take my own route and see where it leads me."

"There is no other way," Travis said. "And I believe this is more about you trying to go back to that girl more than anything else."

"Right. It's a bad time for yo' big ass to be thinking about some punany," Tyler said. "There's goin' to be plenty of Costa Rican ass for you to bone."

"Man, to hell with all that!" Brad shouted. "I just need to get out of here!"

"All y'all, shut the hell up!" Paco yelled as he looked at Brad. "Go, you fool. I can't afford for you to slow us down. None of you will slow us down!"

Brad didn't wait another minute. He got out of the van, barely having time to look at his crew and give his final good-bye. They all shook their heads, thinking that Brad had made a horrible mistake by not staying with them. Midnight sped off, leaving Brad in the alley, wondering if he had made the right decision as well.

Before Brad started to walk, he removed his bloody shirt, throwing it in a dumpster. A tear fell down his face as he thought about the betrayal of his friendship with Stan. He hated that things had to end this way, but considering what was going on, he didn't have many options.

He proceeded on foot, but when he saw an apartment farther down the alley, with clothes hanging on a line to dry, he reached for a white hoodie to cover himself with. It was too tight for Brad, but for now, it would work. His plan was in motion, and he was on his way to see Diamond so they could figure out a way to help each other.

Chapter 23

The Quest

Diamond was outside, locking up her bakery that belonged to Armand. Once the doors were locked, she slowly walked to a black car, which picked her up every single night. The driver would often drive her from one hell to another, and even though he'd gotten out of the car to open the door for her, she knew what to expect.

Once she was inside, she quickly closed the door. The driver took off, moving at a slow pace that enabled her to look out the window and reminisce about the life she always wanted. More than anything, she wondered where her life was heading. She had dreamed of her freedom so many times, but at times she just gave up on life, love, and freedom.

The last time she was ever happy was at the age of nine, before her life went to hell. She hadn't smiled that often, up until a few days ago. That was when she and Brad had spoken. He made her smile, and she didn't know what it was about him that made her feel as if, one day, everything would be okay.

For years, she had been with Armand, a man who took her innocence, her hopes and dreams, and turned them all into nightmares. She trained her mind to hate all men and thought they were all the same, but Brad seemed a little different. That brief moment made her realize the good in some men. She wondered where Brad had gone, and as she imagined something bad happening to him, she closed her eyes to wash away the thoughts.

The driver reached her apartment building and opened the door for her to get out. She slowly walked to the building, figuring that Armand was probably inside waiting for her. So many times, she had tried to escape from Armand's prison, but every time she did, she would always end up getting caught. Armand had goons all over Rio to catch Diamond if she ever tried to escape. That was unfortunate, and she didn't know how long she would have to deal with this shitty lifestyle.

Once Diamond was inside her apartment, she was hungry, as usual. She hoped that something different was in the refrigerator, but as always, there were just vegetables and fruits. If the staff at the bakery weren't so tight around her, she could sneak a cupcake home, or eat some at the job. Unfortunately, the staff was so good at following Armand's orders because, to him, she was too valuable to get fat and ugly. So, like every night, to keep up her strength, she got two apples and a carrot.

She was glad to see that Armand wasn't there waiting for her, and when she was done eating, she took a long, hot shower, washing the funky smell of the bakery and Armand off her body. While in the shower, her mind wandered to her parents and the good life she had as a little girl. She thought about a life of happiness and even a little romance. She just couldn't let go of the thoughts of having a good life, and some way or somehow, she was determined to have it.

After she was done with her shower, she went into the living room, wearing a white robe. She sat on the sofa, turned on the TV, and started flipping channels. There was a note on the table, and when she picked it up, she saw it was written by Armand. He informed her that he wouldn't be there that night. He would be out of town for a few days, and she wasn't to eat anything that wasn't in the fridge. He warned her about causing trouble, and said that upon his return, she needed to be ready to please him.

Diamond ripped up the note and let the shredded pieces fall on the floor. She was thankful that he was away, but she knew that he would be back soon to get what he considered his property. That made Diamond sad. Nonetheless, she stretched out on the sofa to enjoy the next few days of freedom from Armand's sexual abuse. She still had to work at the bakery and have his stooges watch her every move, but as long as she didn't have to see Armand's face, Diamond was good.

A hard knock on the door interrupted Diamond's thoughts. She was just starting to feel good, but now she figured that Armand had changed his mind about going out of town. Then again, he had his own key to unlock the door. There was no need for him to knock, so she got off the couch and slowly made her way to the door.

Diamond's heart started to beat faster. She touched the knob and took a deep breath. When she opened the door, everything happened so fast. The next thing she knew, someone's hands were over her mouth, telling her to *shush*. After that, she heard the door slam.

She thought it was someone trying to rape her, but the vibes from the stranger seemed innocent as he led her over to the sofa. He removed his hands from her mouth, and as she attempted to see who he was behind the hoodie, she squinted.

"Who are you? What do you want?"

The stranger removed the hoodie from his head. "It's me, your knight in shining armor. I came to get you and me out of this hellhole, one way or another," Brad said.

Diamond was so shocked. She couldn't believe that Brad was that concerned about her and that he had come to get her out of there. She sat up and then reached out to touch his face. His face was smooth yet rough. Tears fell down her face.

"I . . . I can't believe you're here. I thought you were gone. Gone for good."

She threw her arms around Brad, holding him tight. He squeezed her tightly but made it clear that they needed to discuss a plan and get out of there—fast.

Chapter 24

King

Finally, after several hours of driving, Midnight arrived on the Port of Santos in the city of São Paulo. He nudged Paco, who was knocked out in the passenger's seat.

"Boss, boss, wake up. We here."

Paco slowly opened his eyes, still a little tipsy from the beer and blinded by the bright lights from the boats. Once he realized he was at the port, his eyes grew wide. *Yes, yes, yes*, he thought. *We made it with no distractions, except for that fat-ass fool Brad.*

Paco looked back at the backseat to see his boys, Swag, Tyler, and Travis were all out like lights from celebrating their escape from prison. Paco quickly got into boss mode.

"Wake up!" He clapped his hands. "Hurry up. We here now, and we need to go."

Swag woke up, wiping his nose and the corner of his mouth. He gazed out of the window, seeing all kinds of boats, from fishing boats and light boats to a huge, brightly lit cruise ship with weird foreign writing on it.

"Paco, what's going on? I thought we were getting out of Brazil," he said.

"What are you talking about, fool? We are getting out of Brazil." He was clearly irritated. All he wanted was some coffee and weed.

"But what's up with the boats?" Travis asked.

"Yeah, where's a getaway plane that'll get us outta here a little faster?" Tyler questioned.

"You fellas are some damn idiots. I can't afford for all of us to get on a plane. Y'all watch too many movies. The best way to get out this country is through a ship. It's the last thing the authorities will expect."

Paco removed a cigar from the glove compartment. He lit it and took a puff before whistling the thick smoke into the air. The fellas waved their hands in front of their faces to clear the air. With Paco's nasty tone, they were now starting to see the asshole he really was, not to mention how he had spoken to Brad. But the fellas had to remain cool. They owed him a lot for getting them out of prison.

"A ship is less conspicuous, and before long, the FBI and feds will be looking for us. We all can't look like targets. As I said earlier, my friend in Costa Rica got us, and once we get there, we'll be living like kings." *And I will bring my father's operation down and kill that bastard for what he did to my mother,* he thought.

"P, is that the boat that says *Malo La Perra El Rey*?" Midnight asked.

Paco looked at it. It was a big, beautiful cruise ship with numerous levels and a top deck that people could live on for the rest of their lives, sailing the ocean. Paco smiled. "Yes, that's the one. Park this van out of sight and let's go."

Once the coast was clear, they got out of the van and headed toward the ship. Paco reminded everyone to stay cool and not look suspicious. By making conversation with each other and laughing, they looked to be friends who were about to go on vacation.

Once they got closer to the ship, the guys were stopped by a husky man wearing a black suit. His face was full of pockmarks, and his devilish eyes made him look wicked.

Paco and the man spoke in Spanish for a moment, and then he spoke into his headset. Once the conversion ended, he looked at Paco and the guys with him. "Go up. The boss is waiting for you all."

Paco grinned as he and his men made their way up to the ship with smiles on their faces.

"Thank God," Swag said, taking a deep breath. "It's finally on and popping."

The others agreed, and they stood for a moment in disbelief. They were grateful for their newfound freedom, but they knew once they got on that ship, there was no turning back. They had to say good-bye to their families, St. Louis, their dreams, and goals. But as Paco said, they would live like kings, and to them, losing some to gain a lot seemed like the right plan.

Paco shouted as they stood in thought, "Y'all coming or what?"

Tyler and Travis rushed on the ship like there was no tomorrow. Swag slowly walked up the ship. He was thinking of the wise words of his cousin, Brad, who he was sure he would never see again.

"Man, you gon' get yo' ass caught up one of these days. You got your girl and your boys to think about."

While that may have been true for Swag, he also had to think about himself. Still, Brad's words wouldn't depart from his head. He thought about his sons and what life would have been like with Zaria if he had done right by her. He thought about his life, mainly being a high school dropout. Swag was thinking about how he should have been in college by now or in the NBA, because back in Swag's teen years, he was a great basketball player on the courts. One of his regrets was not telling Brad about his surprise. He wanted to let Brad know that after this drop, he was going to stop working for Armand and being a stickup guy altogether. He was going to return to St. Louis, study for his GED, and open up a business with the money he had been saving. Now, it was all too late to make things right. Now he was a fugitive, or whatever Paco and this new partner wanted him to be in Costa Rica.

Once on the ship, all the guys saw how amazing it was. The main attraction was the numerous sexy, topless women walking around and conversing with other men on board. Swag, Tyler, and Travis wanted to forget about their dealings with Paco. They stood with lust in their eyes, hoping that they would be given an opportunity to entertain with the women soon.

In the meantime, one of the security guards led the guys to the ship's dining room. It was so large that it could fit at least six thousand people. Gold and diamond chandeliers hung from the ceiling. All the tables were covered with white silk tablecloths, solid gold plates, solid gold silverware, and crystal champagne glasses. Swag couldn't believe his eyes. Money always excited him, and he loved this type of atmosphere.

The men sat down. Once everyone was seated, there was a loud horn, and the ship started to sail. Relief came over the fellas, and they were eager to make it to their final destination.

After the ship had sailed for about an hour, the guys were served a breakfast feast fit for kings, thanks to their new boss. They ate French toast, bacon, eggs, and biscuits with gravy. Also, there were Costa Rican dishes such as *gallo pinto* and fried plantains. Champagne was available as well. From Cristal to Dom Perignon, they were served it all. That included shoulder and dick rubs from the topless ladies. They felt as if they were in heaven, and compared to where they had come from, it was.

As they were eating, a bell rang. The guys looked up, and it was the large guy who had blocked them from entering the ship earlier.

"Gentlemen and ladies, may I have your attention please," he said. All eyes were on him. "It gives me great pleasure to introduce you to my boss and the king of all bosses. Give it up for King!"

The man stepped aside, and everyone's eyes shifted to the grand staircase.

Swag, Tyler, and Travis were expecting a Marlon Brando–type *Godfather* mob boss to come down, but all the guys were amazed by a five-foot-seven Costa Rican chick, who looked to be no more than twenty-one years old. She appeared to be mixed with Italian ancestry, and she cascaded down the stairs with the vision of billions of dollars blowing around her. She had long, curly, honey-blond hair that went pass her shoulders. Her makeup was flawless, but her natural beauty didn't require her to need much at all. She had a body that would put many video girls out of work. It showed well in a black lace teddy that left nothing to the imagination. Her black heels were at least seven inches, and her arms and legs were toned. On her left arm she had a tattoo of a leopard, and on the right of her 32DDDs was a tattoo that read: *Femme Fatale,* with a crown on top.

After her foot touched the dining room floor, she sauntered over to the table where Paco, Midnight, Swag, Tyler, and Travis were sitting. Going over to Paco first, she passionately kissed him while rubbing his face. "Hello, Paco." She sat on his lap then snapped her fingers. One of the topless girls gave her a glass with champagne.

Paco smiled.

"Fellas, this is our new business partner, who is going to make us all very rich. Meet King Kia Costello."

She smiled. King had the most beautiful, pearly white teeth, and her green eyes sparkled with excitement.

Swag was in total shock and disbelief. He sensed something very wrong, and he didn't like doing business with women. *Oh, shit! Now me and my boys are doing business with an even deadlier mofo.*

Swag remembered seeing something about her. It was on *Gangland*, on the History Channel. The episode was titled "The Green-Eyed Beauty King—Not Beauty Queen: The Rise of a Costa Rican Gangstress."

King Kia Costello, aka King K, aka K.K., aka K.C., was an international female don of the Leopard Clit. The Leopard Clit was a crime organization that specialized in smuggling diamonds, gold, and military machine guns all cross the globe. She was also a madam running a very powerful prostitution ring that ran from Costa Rica, Japan, and Puerto Rico. Also, she was a very deadly female assassin, who would kill you without even blinking twice. She was even offered two million dollars from the Ku Klux Klan to assassinate President Barack Obama when he first got into the presidential office, but two million was chump change to a femme fatale that was worth $150 billion.

King was born to an Afro-Costa Rican prostitute, Ivy. Her father was believed to be notorious Italian mobster Bruno Bello, head of the Bello Family, an American Mafia crime organization. In interviews, Bruno denied King being his child and said that Ivy was a liar, but Ivy knew the truth. That family didn't want any Negro or Hispanic biracial bastard child's blood messing up their perfect Italian, pasta-eating bloodline. To them, all women of color like her were good for was a good time.

Ivy told King that when she first met Bruno, he was charming and made all kinds of promises to get her out of the whorehouse she was in, promising to take her back to America, marry her, and make her a proper lady; but like all men she'd slept with, he left, and she was stuck with his seed. When King was born, her mother wanted to name her something special, so King fit perfectly. It was a way of letting her know that she came from royalty as the child of Bruno, who her mother once believed was her king.

King and her mother were kicked out of the whorehouse to fend for themselves. King grew up on the hardcore streets of La Carpio, one of Costa Rica's dangerous ghettos, where there was crime, drugs, and prostitution everywhere. Ivy got a small apartment in the area. To support herself and King, she became the one thing she knew how to be: a whore, once again. Ivy soon became addicted to cocaine.

King hated the way her father played her mother like a doll and threw her away. She made a promise to herself to not end up like her mother and to get revenge on the Bello Family, who she knew would never claim her.

Through her youthful years, without any proper education, she taught herself to read, learn about art, different cultures, and fashion. She began her life of crime by seducing men, just as her mother had done. She learned the art of killing from one of her mother's clients, and she looked to seduce some of the wealthiest men in Costa Rica by robbing them blind and sending them to meet their maker. The art of smuggling came from a drug powerhouse in her neighborhood. First, at the young age of fourteen, she smuggled drugs from Costa Rica to Miami with success, but the drug thing wasn't for her. She wanted to smuggle things with extreme value, and that's when she learned the art of stealing jewelry. At the age of sixteen, King was the diva of the crime, commanding over a hundred soldiers who would lie, kill, and steal for her.

King was tried seven times in places as varied as Costa Rica, Miami, Germany, and Korea for stealing, smuggling, and possibly assassinating many political leaders. Seven juries saw her beautiful face, but with her sweet, well-cultured voice and her enchanting smile, no one believed she could've done it. The evidence always seemed to just disappear.

Now, at twenty-one, she was loved and feared by many in Costa Rica as a boss. She owned one the most beautiful properties that she shared with her now sober mother. All she wanted was to get revenge against her father, who had left her and her mother in poverty while he lived a life of luxury in America. The only way to do that was to team up with Paco and get a taste of the drug world. Once she got rid of her father and the Bello Family, she would be the number one kingpin.

Swag knew she was a dangerous chick, and he could see how someone so beautiful could be so deadly. He remembered from the documentary that she was well known for her many sexual vices. King was openly bisexual and said that "The one type of person I love to have sex with is transgender, because you get the best of both worlds." Swag knew he had to stay in her good graces. She was not the one to be messed with.

"King? What kind of name is that for a chick?" Travis shouted. He was slightly tipsy from the wine.

Everyone, including his boys, glared at him like he had just lost his mind.

"You a chick. You supposed to be a queen." Travis laughed.

Man, would this dude just please shut the hell up? thought Swag, who was no longer calling the shots. *This dude doesn't know who he fucking wit'. This chick is a monster.*

King looked at him like a lioness hunting for her prey. She got off of Paco's lap and went over to Travis. She leaned forward to kiss his bottom lip. He could feel his dick rising and seriously thought she was interested in him. She licked his cheek, and then her lips traveled to his left earlobe. She sucked on it for a second, but then she chomped down hard on it with her teeth.

Travis screamed like a bitch. "Ahhhhhh! Shit, shit, shit!"

King bit off a small piece of his earlobe, spitting it out on the floor. As blood rushed from Travis' earlobe, he held it with his hand in tears.

"Only a king can do that," she said, reaching for a napkin to wipe her bloody mouth. As she walked away, she put her long, manicured black fingernail in her mouth, licking more blood before returning to Paco's lap. The smile returned on her face as everyone stared in silence.

The other thing that Swag remembered from the documentary was that, for some sick reason, she loved to lick the blood of her many victims and enemies.

Travis looked at her, still holding his wounded ear. She kept smiling at him, admiring her handiwork. Paco and his men began to laugh at Travis.

"You punk little pussy," Paco said. "How can you let a female punk you like that?"

Travis was embarrassed, and he wanted to get her back, but he ventured in the wrong direction. "You bitch!"

He got up, but almost immediately, he noticed that something didn't feel right with his right hand. He looked, seeing that his right pinky finger was gone and his hand was bleeding profusely. He glared at King, but now she had his pinky finger in one hand and a pair of pliers in the other.

"Looking for this?" she said, taking his pinky finger and stirring it in her glass of wine. She removed the finger then licked the tip.

"Damn, Paco," Midnight said. "This woman is a straight up beast—and a G for real."

Paco laughed. "I know. That's why I wanted to do business with her. You always want someone this coldhearted and ruthless on your team."

"Fuck that, Paco! That bitch got my pinky finger!" Travis tried to charge at her, only to be stopped and have guns pointed at him by her team of security, which was made up of numerous topless women, who pointed everything at him from a nine millimeter magnum to a machine gun.

Oh, shit. I'm fucked, thought Travis, who could have been meeting his maker sooner than later.

Swag and Tyler rushed up to pull him back to chair.

"Be cool, man," Swag said.

Guns were still pointed at Travis, and he figured they would blast him in a second.

Swag went over to King, got on his knees, and held her hand. "King, please don't kill my friend. He's drunk and stupid. He don't know any better. If you spare his life, I'll do anything you ask me to."

King smiled at Swag. She admired his courage. She would usually cut out an eyeball and eat it, but something about him just mesmerized her. "All right." She raised her hand, and everyone lowered their guns. Swag took a deep breath.

"Thank you, King. I promise he will be no trouble."

Swag got up, heading to his seat. He watched as Tyler wrapped his brother's hand with a napkin.

King stood with her wineglass, throwing the pinky finger aside. "Let that be a lesson to you all. I am a king, not a queen, and if any of you fuck me over, you will be sleeping with the fishes or worse."

They all nodded at their new leader as she proposed a toast. "To a new future of making money, being rich, and bringing down the Bello Family and Hernandez Cartel so that we can be on top of the food chain. To a new future!"

"To a new future!" all the guys said—even Travis, who didn't want to lose any more fingers.

Swag looked around for a moment. He still couldn't believe how elegant the ship was, but deep down, he felt as if it were leading him straight to hell. He had finally gotten his wakeup call, and he wished he could turn back the hands of time. He wished he had never gotten involved with Armand. Now he could only dream of being back in St. Louis, smoking a blunt or two with his boys. He stared at the food on his plate in a daze, and for the first time in a long time, he prayed.

Lord, protect me and my boys, including my cousin Brad. I hope he's okay. And Lord, I ask for one more request. If you can, one day, I would love to see my sons again. I love them, and I need you to protect me on this unfortunate journey, just so I can get back to them. Amen.

Swag looked up and saw King undressing him with her lustful eyes. She was known for getting wherever she wanted, even if it was him. Swag put on a fake smile, trying to stay in her good favor.

And, Lord, please give me strength.

Chapter 25

The Awakening of a Boss Bitch

The next evening, Milena decided to invite Taylor over for a girls' night in. They were having dinner at her luxury penthouse apartment, a seventeenth birthday gift from her father. The penthouse had an amazing view of downtown Rio. The décor was modern, with all-white furniture. It was nothing but the best for this Brazilian model, part-time actress, semi-escort, socialite, and heiress to the Diaz boxing empire.

More than anything, Milena wanted to be a supermodel like Taylor was back in the '80s, '90s, and early 2000s. Taylor, her mentor, told her that the fashion industry had changed and the word *supermodel* was dead. According to her, now it was a package deal. Taylor told her you had to be a model, video girl, actress, dancer, singer, and even a reality TV star.

Milena worked as a highly paid showgirl in the Brazilian show *Queen*. Her modeling career wasn't going anywhere, and she was pissed off that she wasn't landing campaigns for Marc Jacobs or Calvin Klein. She was always being beaten out by many American actresses or French models. Her biggest heartbreaker was when she was the runner up to be the face of Versace. After many call backs, test shots, and semi-runway shows, she was beaten by Kitana. Milena always felt as if Kitana had the entertainment game on lock, from the fashion world to

TV and the movie screen. Milena's main focus was to be in the movies, and with the help of the money she was getting from the show, her admirers, and her father, she would take high-end acting lessons with the world's best acting coaches, until she got her big break.

Milena decided to put life aside and have Taylor over for dinner after the big release party for the *Brazilian Kouture* December release for its first male issue. Milena knew that something was not right with Taylor lately. She wasn't the usual bad bitch she had first kicked it with. She decided to fix her dinner, with all of Taylor's favorites: risotto barolo with roasted vegetables, spiced lamb shanks with blood orange relish and lobster salad in potato leek nests.

Taylor was in the living room, sitting on the sofa, looking semi-fab in a white tank top, black dress pants, black flats, and very little make up that showed signs of her real age mixed with stress. She was gazing at the fireplace, drowning her sorrows in Moët. Her mind was not focused on the magazine. After the *Brazilian Kouture* release party, she had just let the whole magazine get out of control. She was canceling meetings with big advertisers, failing to make guest appearances at other fashion vendors, and leaving work early to go to a hotel suite to drink her sorrows away with her new friends, vodka and Jack Daniel's.

Ramon was so tired of carrying the load of the magazine on his own shoulders that he had decided, of his own free will, to take a vacation to New York. Taylor knew that he was going there to meet her man-whore of a husband, who claimed he was going on a business trip that she referred to as "booty-hole business." Taylor just let the magazine go to hell. Hell, it wasn't even her magazine; it was Armand's, and she didn't care if it went bankrupt.

Taylor spent her days thinking of Desmond and the way he totally disrespected her at the magazine's male issue release party. She was also hating on the photo of Desmond and Kitana that Ramon had picked for the cover. Taylor didn't want that media whore in her magazine. The entire time at the release party, all media from MTV to CNN kept asking if they were dating or engaged. Desmond was even getting new endorsements and more movie deals. He didn't acknowledge Taylor at all. He told her that she had less than ten days to make a decision, and the clock was ticking.

Milena went over to Taylor. She was tired of seeing her best friend/mentor drink her life away for a man. She was sick of her not being with a man that she truly loved with all of her heart. Milena took the glass and wine bottle out of her hand.

"Hey, Milena, what are you doing with my medication?" Taylor slurred her words.

Milena looked at the half glass of wine and the bottle, throwing them both across the hallway.

"Hey!" Taylor yelled. "What are you doing, doll? I . . . " Taylor stood up but stumbled backward and fell on the couch.

"Taylor, I've been quiet for weeks, and I can't keep quiet anymore. What you are doing is so wrong. I should have stopped you the night of the release party, when you saw my brother hugged up with that hooker in front of the media."

Taylor remembered that night completely. Desmond was hugged up with that trick Kitana, and she loved every bit of it. After seeing how happy they seemed, Taylor went up to her office, allowing that jerk Ramon to take over for the evening while she drank two bottles of whiskey and one bottle of scotch. That was something she hadn't done since her days on the runway. That's where Milena found her passed out. Milena should have said something then, but tonight was as good a time as any.

"Chica, look at yourself. You're turning yourself into a lush, and for what? A man? What happened to you? I used to look up to you. Hell, I wanted to be like you, a true bad bitch with smarts, the clothes, the money, and the men. You let my brother's demands affect your better judgment. If you want to leave Armand to be with my brother, then so be it. You have more power than he ever will. You are the princess of a very powerful crime family, remember. Bring back the hustler/vengeful chick I liked from day one."

Taylor was so shocked that Milena said that. After Armand's glory coming to an end went bust, then Desmond's ultimatum, Kitana, and the release party, Taylor had really lost her bad bitch side. She turned around for a moment, only to see a reflection of herself. What she saw was not the supermodel who had a killer's instinct, dressed to kill with a deceitful heart, but an old woman who was washed up, drinking her life away and dressed for her own funeral.

"Oh my God." She sat back on the couch and busted out crying. "Milena, oh my God, doll, have I really gotten that bad?" She covered her face. Milena sat beside her and rubbed her back.

"I'm so ugly," Taylor cried while leaning on Milena's shoulder.

"Shh, no, that isn't true. You're beautiful. You just need to get your shit together and don't ever let a man bring you down. Not even my brother. You hear me? You're too bad of a bitch to be going through this shit."

Taylor looked into Milena's eyes and hugged her. Milena hugged her back.

"You are truly a loyal friend, Milena. I mean it, and it's not the Moët talking either. Other chicks would've just let me drink myself into an insane asylum, but not you.

You are one of the most loyal chicas ever, and I'm glad you're my best friend." Taylor kissed Milena on the cheek. "Thank you. And I won't let any man ever, ever bring me this down again."

"That's my girl," Milena said.

They smiled. "Just one thing, doll."

"Yes, sis," Milena said.

"What is my next move into reclaiming my bad bitch status?"

Both ladies laughed.

"First off, get out of your grandma's clothes. Secondly, put on some makeup, and lastly, claim your man, girl."

Taylor nodded. "You're right. What in the hell was I thinking, wearing this? And lastly, my Desmond. There is no way in hell I'm losing my man to that media whore, Kitana. She may look pretty, but there is no way in hell I'm going to let another woman dig her claws into him. As for Armand, I have some connections I need to get in contact with about his reckless behavior. But first, let's eat."

When evening set in, the ladies ate like pigs. Milena did Taylor's makeup, and she converted to the boss she really was. For the rest of the evening, the ladies looked at TV and ate candy bars.

As they were watching TV, the news popped on with a breaking story about a massacre at the Bangu Penitentiary Complex that left many prisoners dead and a few missing. They flashed the missing prisoners' faces on the screen. This caught Milena's eyes.

"Chica, those are the Americans who were working with Armand and made the bust a flop."

"So?" Taylor said, rolling her eyes.

A mug shot of Brad Carter flashed on the screen.

"Taylor, that was the American who had a thing for Diamond and ignored the other girls. I can only wonder if she is into something with him."

"Doll, please. You watch too many romance movies. I don't think that American is stupid enough to chase one of Armand's li'l whores. He'd better be trying to figure out how to get the hell out of Rio before he's killed."

"I agree, but that girl isn't as bad as you think. She looked so lost and scared, as if she was with Armand against her will. When I saw her and that American together, she looked happy. I just have a feeling about them."

While listening to Milena, Taylor smiled and came up with her next scam. "You know what, Milena? I think we should pay this little girl a visit tomorrow, but first we are going to the mall to get me a brand new wardrobe."

Both of the ladies laughed, but all Taylor could think was, *Good-bye, Armand, the magazine, and Brazil. Hello, Desmond and my new life in America. The boss bitch is back.*

Chapter 26

The Proposal

During most of the day, Brad stayed in the penthouse, watching his back while Diamond worked at the bakery. If Diamond hadn't shown up for work, people would have been suspicious and called Armand to return. They didn't want that to happen before they came up with the perfect plan to get out of there.

Before Diamond left, she had given Brad some of Armand's clothes. Brad took a bath to clean the filth and blood from his body that still lingered from being in prison. He came out of the shower, smelling like raspberry crème, wearing a white Polo shirt, which was a little tight on him, and khaki shorts that fit him okay. He spent most of the day sitting on the sofa with his clean bare feet up on the coffee table, eating veggies and fruit. Being his size, what he really wanted was a triple bacon cheeseburger with a large order of fries and a jumbo chocolate shake from Steak 'n Shake back home. He even looked at TV, CNN in particular, where he noticed that what happened at the prison had made international news.

News anchor Don Lemon stated: "In Rio de Janeiro, drug lord Paco Hernandez and members of the Hernandez Cartel, along with fellow American traffickers—twin brothers Tyler and Travis Evans, and cousins Solomon and Brad Carter—managed to escape one of Rio's deadliest prisons, The Bangu Penitentiary Complex, leaving behind thirty-four inmates, murdered from drinking what they thought was Kool-Aid. One inmate was shot in the head. The prison will be under investigation by the city of Rio de Janeiro to find out why this happened. They are also conducting a massive manhunt to find the escapees."

Flashes of the mug shots of Brad, his friends, Paco, and members of the Hernandez Cartel came across the screen.

"If you know the whereabouts of these men, please call the police in your area. They may be armed and are very dangerous. We will resume this story soon."

Brad turned off the television. He couldn't believe any of this. How could he be in St. Louis one day, and many weeks later, he was a trafficker, a prison inmate, and now a fugitive? He had to get out of there fast. Going back to the U.S. would be difficult, and without identification, it was damn near impossible.

That evening, after Diamond got off work, she and Brad sat at the table, where Brad had sliced some tomatoes, cucumbers, and green grapes with ranch dressing on top. Even though Diamond was tired of veggies and fruits, Brad's dish tasted so good that it was making her want to have seconds. Brad smiled at her as she ate. To him, she looked so miserable, and she deserved better. He had never met a woman like her, and he suspected that the feeling was mutual.

As he lifted a tomato to his mouth, there was a knock on the door. In panic mode, Diamond looked at Brad, but he placed his finger over his lips.

"Shhh," he whispered. "Go open the door and I'll go hide. Just stay calm." Brad gave her a kiss on her cheek. He went in the coat closet and closed the door.

Diamond was a nervous wreck. She knew that it couldn't be Armand. *Who could it be this time? Maybe it's the police looking for Brad. If Armand finds out Brad was here, he'll kill me.*

Diamond took a deep breath, went to the door, and slowly opened it. She couldn't believe her eyes. It was none other than fashion icon and wife of her biggest nightmare, the one and only Taylor Monroe, at the door. Diamond was stunned and amazed at the same time. One thing she couldn't deny was that Taylor was an extremely beautiful woman. Her makeup was flawless, and her long hair was in thick curls that flowed down her back. She wore Linda Farrow sunglasses, a red strapless dress, red satin Manolo pumps, and diamond studs in both ears. Diamond also noticed that Taylor wasn't alone. She was accompanied by Milena, who looked even more gorgeous than the last time Diamond had seen her. Milena's hair hung down in waves. Her makeup was done to perfection. She wore a sleeveless waterfall dress with matching heels.

"Hi, ladies," Diamond said nervously.

"Mmmm." Taylor didn't think twice about walking into the apartment.

Milena walked in, smiling. "Hello, Diamond."

Diamond nodded as she closed the door, wondering what they wanted. Both Taylor and Milena sat on the sofa. Diamond sat in a chair next to them, continuing to smile.

"Can I get you ladies something to drink? Tea or water?"

"No!" both ladies shouted.

"Darling, just relax. Shut up and listen," Taylor demanded while looking at Diamond with coldness in her eyes.

Milena glanced at Taylor, knowing that she was being too hard on Diamond. "Taylor, stop it. This girl hasn't done anything to you." She looked over at Diamond, who had a blank look on her face. "Diamond, sweetheart, excuse my BFF. We just want to talk to you for a few minutes."

Diamond faced the two women. "How did you find me? How did you get by Armand's undercover stooges, who guard this place around the clock?"

Taylor flipped her hair back. "Honey, don't worry about Armand's goons for security. I paid the underground stooges way more than Armand pays them to take the night off. Plus, I added a bonus with my girls to keep them too busy to think about you. One thing about men, they always think with their dicks."

Milena laughed.

True, thought Diamond, nodding her head. She felt a breath of fresh air thinking all the security watching her was gone for the night. She thought it was a great time to get out. Forgetting Brad was even in the closet, Diamond wanted to burst right out from her seat and run out of the apartment building.

Taylor could see the pleasure on Diamond's face, but Taylor wanted Diamond to see she was still the captain of this ship. "Uh, little girl, don't get any ideas." Taylor patted her new Michael Kors purse where her "baby" was.

Diamond's thoughts of freedom were short lived, seeing that Taylor would kill her in a heartbeat.

"Well, what do you want with me?" asked Diamond in a worried tone. Maybe Taylor was one of those crazy wives who wanted to beat up her husband's mistress. She didn't know, but she did know that she wasn't his mistress. She was more like his sex slave.

Taylor looked over at Milena for a moment before going into her bag. She removed a cigarette and lit it, blowing smoke in Diamond's face. "For the sake of my best friend and sister, I'm going to give you the benefit of the doubt. What are you to my husband, besides a trophy whore?"

"What?" asked Diamond in confusion.

"Little girl, I am a woman who doesn't like to repeat herself. When I ask a question, I demand an answer. So if you don't want to be dead when my husband comes back, I suggest you give me the answer I want," said Taylor in a rude tone. "Now, for the last time, how are you and Armand connected?"

"First off, I'm not a whore." Diamond was still in fear of what Taylor was going to do, but she still stood her ground. She was tired of being called Armand's whore. No one knew the whole story of her struggle. "I am just property, payback for a debt. When I was a little girl, I was taken from everything I ever knew or loved." Diamond breathed heavily, trying to hold back tears. "For the past ten years of my life, I've been physically abused and sexually abused by Armand. I was forced to work like a slave at the bakery and eat nothing but veggies and fruit." Tears came down her face. "He took me away from my family and my home. I hate him with every fiber of my soul. Every day I just wished that bastard would burn in hell for his deeds of evil." She cried unstoppably.

Taylor's icy heart, hatred, and ugly thoughts toward Diamond melted away. She no longer saw Diamond as the whore she had painted in her mind for years. Taylor now just saw a scared, lost little girl.

"So if you come here to kill me, then do it. Shit, I have nothing or no one to live for," Diamond said. But then Diamond regretted saying it.

Brad. She looked back at the closet for a moment and then went back to eye contact with Taylor, though still teary eyed.

Milena went in her bag, getting out a tissue and handing it to Diamond.

"Thank you," said Diamond, wiping her face.

"Armand has been touching and keeping you prisoner here since you were a child?" asked a still disbelieving Taylor.

Diamond nodded. "Yes."

"That man is sick, Taylor," said Milena with a twisted look on her face.

"I knew Armand was a freak that'll fuck anything that had a hole, but a child? A baby? That bastard. That . . . child molester!" shouted Taylor. Just thinking of Armand and the ordeal of him touching Diamond as a child made Taylor heated. Taylor had to get another cigarette to calm her nerves.

"Diamond, I don't say this to many people: I'm truly sorry." Just saying the word "sorry" was hard for Taylor, but this situation was too much. Taylor's heart softened for Diamond at that moment. "I'm so sorry for calling you a whore all these years without knowing your truth. No child should ever go through what you went through, especially with a nasty pig like Armand."

"I'm sorry for you too," said a misty-eyed Milena.

For Taylor, it was getting too emotional. She needed to get focused, immediately going back to bad boss-bitch mode. She took a puff of her cigarette and blew smoke in Diamond's face.

Diamond coughed.

Taylor took another puff. "Darling, you can't change the past. The best thing to do is to move forward. And that's why I'm here to give you a gift."

Diamond was stunned. "And what is that?"

"My dear, I am going to help you get your freedom," Taylor said, putting out her cigarette.

Diamond's eyes grew wide. Those were the most beautiful words she'd heard in a long time. "Excuse me, ma'am?"

"Babe, you heard her. We are going to help you get your freedom," said Milena.

While in the closet, Brad could hear the ladies' conversation. It was his chance to get the hell out of Brazil and start a new life. Then he sneezed.

Diamond looked at the closet, and her heart dropped to her stomach. She wondered why Brad had to sneeze at that moment.

"We're sorry for intruding," Taylor said, touching her chest, smiling. "Well, Ms. Diamond, I see there's another rooster in the hen house. If so, come out, come out, whoever you are in the closet."

Brad stood still, wondering what would happen if he did come out of the closet. Maybe this was a trick. Maybe Armand's ass was out there ready to kill him for not completing the job. He wasn't going to budge.

"For the last time, come out of the closet!" Taylor reached in her purse, pulling out a 9 mm. She pointed it at the closet.

"Noooo!" Diamond screamed and ran over to the closet.

"Don't move!" Taylor stood and pointed the gun at Diamond.

Diamond stood there, frozen.

"Come out now or Diamond gets it!" Taylor pointed the gun at the lamp, shooting it.

The loud bang caused Diamond to scream. Brad burst out of the closet with a coat hanger as his only weapon.

"Diamond!" He looked at her to see if she was okay. She confirmed that she was when she wrapped her arms around his waist.

A quick soft spot came over Taylor. She could tell this couple had an interesting connection, but she quickly went back into bitch mode with a wicked grin. "I knew that would get you out."

Brad was heated. "Lady, are you crazy? Someone in this building could've heard that!"

Taylor just laughed. "Little boy, or should I say big boy, this little penthouse is completely soundproof, just the way Armand wanted it. If I wanted to kill her, no one would've heard it."

Brad looked at Taylor. He knew exactly who she was. He remembered his dad having magazines with her pictures on them in the bathroom that he would jerked off to. Now that he was face to face with the supermodel, all he thought was how crazy she looked with the gun in her hand. He looked at the broken lamp.

"You could've hurt someone up in here," he said.

Taylor put the gun back in her purse then walked back over to the couch to sit. "Now, both of you come here. Sit down." She patted the spot next to her.

Diamond sat back down, but Brad looked to his right. "Milena?"

Milena cocked her head back. "Brad?"

Taylor looked at them both. "You know him?"

"Yes. He was the one who was helping Armand with the drug thing here."

Milena was amazed that he was still in Brazil, but deep down she'd had a feeling that he would be right here with Diamond. Her intuition was correct.

"I thought you were with your cousin and friends. It's not safe for you here."

"I had to come for Diamond so we could figure out a way to get out of here together." He looked back at Diamond and then looked at both Taylor and Milena. "Now, tell us more about how we can get our freedom and get the hell out of Brazil for good." Brad sat next to Diamond and put his arm around her shoulders.

Taylor looked at the two lovebirds, whose love seemed so pure, innocent, and risky. She didn't want to separate them, so she came up with a new plan.

"Diamond, tomorrow there will be a big surprise at your bakery. I mean, at my husband Armand's bakery."

Armand's wife? Oh my God, thought Brad. *Should we even trust her ass?*

Taylor continued. "When you get your surprise, go out of the back door and the rest will be taken care of."

"What about me? I want me and Diamond to get out of Brazil together." Brad was frustrated, and he damn sure didn't want to be left out.

"Hold on, okay? I have plans for you too." Taylor removed a key from her purse then tossed it to Brad.

He looked at the key then back at Taylor. "What is this?"

"A key, silly," Taylor answered.

"I know that, but to what? How is this gon' help me?"

"Well, smart guy, you know that basement you and your little friends were in?"

Brad had to think back, but he did remember going to the basement of the apartment building, with all the drugs and money inside. "Oh, yeah, I remember. What about it?"

This man must have a few brain cells missing, Taylor thought, shaking her head.

"Genius, that is the key to your chance at a fortune. Later this evening, go downstairs to the basement and get all the money you want."

Brad looked at the key, but reality quickly set in. Greed was what got him there, and he didn't want to travel down that road again. All he wanted was for him and Diamond to get out of there without dealing with anymore bullshit. Besides, bad thoughts came to mind about the dangers that came with getting the money. He had to reject Taylor's offer.

"Mrs. . . ."

"No need for the Mrs.," Taylor said, cutting him off.

"Taylor will do."

"Well, Taylor, what about those guards Armand have guarding that shit? How am I supposed to get past them without getting killed? I'm not interested in going that route. Thanks, but no thanks."

Taylor laughed sinisterly. "First of all, darling, you need not worry about them. Don't let this opportunity pass you by. And think hard before you speak. When you come to the right conclusion, I'm sure you'll be in the basement by midnight. You'll be granted only a few minutes to get enough money to last you and Diamond for the rest of your lives."

Brad hated to admit it, but that did sound pretty good. He wasn't sure why Taylor had made this offer, but he asked her something else. "May I ask you for another favor?"

Taylor shrugged her shoulders. "Depends."

"Is there any way you can get a private plane to fly me and Diamond out of Brazil to somewhere safe where no one will recognize us, especially me? Can you arrange that for us?"

Taylor smiled, loving Brad's determination. "I may be able to help you with that one, my dear, but in the meantime, get that money!"

Brad didn't reply, and he wouldn't until he talked this over with Diamond. He just wanted to make sure this was the right move to make.

"I just have one more question for you, Taylor. Who are you? Really?" asked Brad.

Taylor laughed, knowing he would never get that answer. "Besides being a powerful woman, I am many things, including deadly."

Taylor's cell phone alarm went off. She didn't answer, but she stood to leave. "Please forgive me, but Milena and I have another engagement."

Milena stood and headed to the door behind Taylor.

Before Taylor left, she looked at Brad and Diamond again. "Diamond, don't forget about the surprise, and Brad, don't forget your money. After Diamond leaves for work in the morning, I'll have a car pick you up, and my friends will take care of the rest."

Taylor and Milena left the apartment.

Brad and Diamond stood in awe. They couldn't believe what had just happened. After a long, thoughtful discussion, they came to a conclusion that would make them rich and get them out of Brazil.

Outside, Taylor and Milena kissed each other on the cheek. Milena got into a cab and left. Taylor walked over to a black limousine, got in, and it pulled off. Things stayed quiet in the limousine, until a deep male voice with a thick Spanish accent spoke.

"Is it done?" he asked.

Taylor smiled. "Yes. Once I destroy my husband's reputation, businesses, and fortune, the Colombian Mob will reign over South America once again."

The man rubbed his hands together. "Excellent. South America will be mine. Desmond will be officially yours once I see your husband's blood flow."

Taylor smiled and leaned over to kiss the man. "Uncle Sandino, we are the baddest sons of bitches on this earth. It's no wonder why my daddy left you his operation."

Sandino smiled at his niece. "Yeah, baby girl, he is a very smart man."

Taylor smiled because she knew that it was about to go down in Brazil.

Desmond, baby, I'm almost there.

***

It was two minutes until midnight, and Brad had the big duffle bag ready to go. Before he left, he and Diamond shared a passionate kiss like it was their last.

"I need to say this before you go," she said tearfully. "Thank you for everything, Brad. Thank you so much, and please be careful. Come back to me, okay?"

"I promise," he said, giving her another kiss on her sweet lips. "I will be back."

With the hoodie thrown over his head, Brad went downstairs to the lobby. To his surprise, there were only a few people browsing around, many who were conversing with each other and paying him no mind. The two guards who usually guarded the basement door were outside being distracted by two beautiful women. One was Latina, and the other one was Japanese. They looked familiar to Brad. Then he realized the Latina chick was Sasha, and the Japanese chick was Aoki. He remembered hanging out with them and his boys during their good times in Brazil. Stan had been talking to Sasha, and one of the twins had been talking to Aoki, who also had a twin. Brad hated to think of Stan at a time like this. He knew he was wrong for fucking over his friend, but that was a cross he had to bear.

Aoki nudged her head, signaling for Brad to go down to the basement.

Damn, they work for Taylor too? Everyone is settin' everyone up, thought Brad, shaking his head.

Brad pulled out the key, opened the door, and rushed down the stairs. Once he was down in the basement, he turned on the light and saw all of the kilos of cocaine and money. He went over to the money, nervously stashing as much as he could into the duffle bag. When the bag was full, he stuffed money into his front and back pockets. There was some in his socks, the front and back of his underwear, and also in his shoes. He had about ninety-five percent of the cash, damn near cleaning house before heading upstairs. On his way there, he spotted a 9 mm. He snatched that up then sneaked back upstairs to return to Diamond as promised.

Chapter 27

Dawn of a new Era

The next morning, Diamond got ready for work as usual. She looked over at Brad, who was sitting on the bed, nervously counting and stuffing the money back in the duffle bag. He'd completely lost count, but he knew that there was enough money to last him and Diamond for a good while.

As Diamond was putting her hair into a ponytail, she sat down next to Brad. "Brad?"

He looked over at her. "What's up, ma?"

"Brad . . ." She paused. "Brad, I'm scared today. So many things are running through my mind that can go wrong. What if I get killed? What if you get killed? If something ever happened to you, I—" Diamond started to cry.

Brad put his arm around her, pulling her close to his chest. "Baby, listen. Nothing is going to happen to you, or to me, for that matter. We gon' be all right. Trust me."

He wasn't so sure if that was true, but his words put a tiny smile on her face. "You promise," she said.

Brad wiped her tears away with his thumb and smiled. "I promise. Now, go do your thang, and we'll meet up soon." Brad rubbed her cheek and then her neck softly.

Diamond placed her hand on his. She loved his touch, which was a feeling she had never experienced.

They were so lost in each other that they almost didn't hear the loud banging at the front door.

"Damn, who is that?" Brad said, trying not to show how nervous he was.

"One of Armand's goons. He's here to pick me up. If I'm not down in a certain amount of minutes, he'll bang on the door like a damn cop. Gotta go. See you soon." Diamond kissed Brad's cheek. She got up from the bed, but before leaving her bedroom, which she hoped to see for the last time, she looked at Brad again. "I can't thank you enough for coming into my life at the right time. I don't know where we go from here, but I hope it'll be somewhere where there is nothing but peace."

He smiled, hoping the same thing.

Diamond walked out of her apartment, thinking, *Good-bye, Hell.*

An hour after Diamond left, Brad poked around the apartment, looking at how Diamond had been living. All Armand had provided for her was a roof over her head, clothes, fruits, vegetables, underwear, and a pot to piss in. Brad was sick and tired of eating fruits and vegetables. He did, however, eat a few grapes before stepping into the shower. He came out smelling like butterscotch and then put on Armand's tan khaki shorts, a wife beater, and sneakers. As he was about to turn on the TV, a knock came at the door. Brad's heart started to beat faster.

"Brad, open up!" a male's voice said on the other side of the door. "Hurry up, man, we gotta move."

Brad assumed it was Taylor's people, preparing to get him and Diamond out of Brazil. He hurried to Diamond's room to get the duffle bag with their future inside. When he went back and opened the door, his steps halted. His stomached tightened, and he finally felt as if it was all over with when he saw Sandino standing there.

"San—" Brad was scared out of his mind. He figured that Armand had found out about him and Diamond's planned escape, or the fact that Brad had a huge chunk of Armand's fortune in the duffle bag. He wanted to reach inside of the duffle bag for the gun, until Taylor stepped in front of Sandino, telling Brad to relax.

She removed her Fendi sunglasses. "Brad, meet my uncle Sandino. Uncle Sandino, meet Brad Carter. Oh, I forgot you two know each other already." She laughed.

"Uncle? You mean sugar daddy?" Brad said in a sarcastic tone.

Sandino laughed a little, but Taylor rolled her eyes. "No, don't get things twisted. My uncle, as in my godfather. Watch the sarcasm, because I could make a quick, anonymous call to the authorities and have them come get your big ass. You'll then be in a shithole worse than you were before. I'll have Armand doing anything that he wants to your li'l girlfriend, so remember not to burn your bridges, especially not with the one who's giving you and Diamond your freedom."

Brad nodded and corrected himself. "Sorry. Please forgive me."

Taylor smiled. *Now he knows who's in charge of this operation.*

"Fine," she said. "Come on. We have to pick up Diamond."

Diamond was in the breakroom in back of the bakery, taking her fifteen-minute break. So many thoughts were running through her mind. Today could finally be the day she got her freedom. She didn't know what to do with it or how to act. She didn't want to go back to Belize until she was mentally ready. She also wondered what life with Brad would be like. Would the two of them stay together or decide to go their separate ways? She just didn't know, but she was sure of one thing: The clock was ticking.

Diamond took a sip of water, thinking of the good and the bad that would come as a result of getting her freedom. She also thought about what Armand would do once he discovered she was gone. Would he come after her? She was very fearful of that. She didn't believe there was a place on earth where he couldn't find her. Armand had taken so much from her. If anything happened to Brad, she would be devastated. He was her last chance of being completely happy, something she totally deserved. She had been through pure hell in the past ten years with Armand, and getting away from him would be her revenge.

As she was about to take another sip of her bottled water, all she could hear were screams and gunfire from the work and lobby area. Diamond locked the door to the breakroom, making sure that no one was trying to kill her. She was petrified, hearing the loud gunshots and customers and workers screaming for their lives. Tears came from Diamond's eyes.

"Help me, pleeeeease!" one woman shouted. "Please don't shoo—"

More gunfire rang out, and the woman's cries went silent. More screams and cries continued, and it broke Diamond's heart when she heard a little girl calling for her mother.

"Mommy, nooooo! Please don't hurt my mommy anymore."

The little girl's voice was silenced too. Diamond shielded her ears with her hand, and started praying. *God, please don't let them find me. Lord, I prayed to you all of my life for my prince to save me from Armand. I just want to get out of here safe and alive. Don't allow my life to end like this. Please, Lord, please.*

Tears continued to stream down Diamond's face, and after several more minutes, the gunshots and screams died down. Diamond took several deep breaths to get herself together. She wiped the sheen of sweat from her forehead, and then she slowly opened the door. Stepping out, she saw nothing but broken glass, mashed pastries, blood everywhere and dead bodies of even some of Armand's goons, who were there to make sure Diamond never tried to escape.

She carefully stepped over one dead body after another. Her legs shook, but before she could step any farther, a big hand was clamped over her mouth and she was dragged out the back door of the bakery. She tried to scream for her life and break away, but whoever was holding onto her was as strong as an ox. Then, in the alley of the bakery, was a black limousine. The limousine's back door was opened. The stranger carried Diamond to the limousine, and someone pulled her inside as the stranger closed the door. The limousine took off.

Inside of the limousine, Diamond looked up, and it was like the archangel Michael was in her presence. "Brad." She hugged him tightly.

He held her close, not wanting to let her go. Brad looked over at Taylor and Sandino on the other side of the limo.

"So what happens next?" he asked.

Diamond was still afraid. She was scared of Sandino. She thought he would tell Armand.

Taylor helped to calm the wary look in Diamond's eyes. "Relax, Rhinestone. Sandino is on my side. He's my uncle."

Diamond still didn't trust them, but she nodded anyway. "So, where are we going?"

"First, I'm taking you to a remote location to stay for a day or two, until I get you to a safe place where no one will recognize you both."

Brad didn't like the idea of that. He wanted to leave now. "Why can't you get us a private plane today? Why do we have to stay here another day or two? I can't take this anymore, and I want to leave now. Please help us leave now."

Sandino spoke before Taylor did. "Relax. I have to make a few calls to some friends to get a private jet for you. Just give me time. Me and Taylor are going to put you both in a safe area where no one will find you. It'll have everything you both will need for a day or two. I promise you and Diamond will be off Brazilian soil forever. Okay?"

Brad and Diamond looked at each other and then back at Taylor and Sandino. They had no choice but to agree. "Okay." They held each other all through the ride.

Within a few hours, they arrived in Santa Catarina, the southern part of Brazil, where it was mostly countryside, mountains, and the beach. The limo had pulled up to a small cottage that sat on twenty acres of land. The outside of the cottage was a mess, but the inside made up for it. The style was very modern, mixed in with traditional.

"Okay, Big Boy and Rhinestone." Taylor laughed at her little nicknames for Brad and Diamond. "This is where you will stay. No one will find you here. There's fresh food in the pantry and the fridge. Brad, you will find some clothes and new underwear in there, so you can burn my husband's shit up when you take them off. Diamond, you're going to love the dresses. Have a good time. Don't worry about anything, and enjoy yourselves. We'll be back." Taylor looked over at Sandino. "Come on, Uncle. Let's leave the lovebirds."

Once Taylor and Sandino were gone, Brad and Diamond looked around the place. Everything looked legit to them, but they realized they didn't have a TV, which was fine. All Brad cared about was that Diamond was now finally safe and free. They were together at last, and for the first time, they felt hopeful that this would soon be over. They'd be even happier once that private plane took them off Brazilian soil for good, but for now, they stood in the middle of the living room, hugging each other with tears in their eyes.

As the limousine was driving back to Rio, Taylor and Sandino laughed.

"The destruction of Armand Castro begins tomorrow," Taylor said.

"Yes, and the family will rise again, and you will have Desmond."

"Yes." Taylor smiled, thinking about Desmond. She looked over at her driver. "Can you drive a little faster? I don't want to miss the fireworks."

"Yes, Ms. Monroe," said the driver.

Taylor crossed her legs, thinking about all that tomorrow would bring.

Chapter 28

A Taste of Freedom

The next day was beautiful and sunny outside in Rio. Diamond was feeling better than she had in a long time, now that she had left Armand's prison. She was in a comfortable cottage, looking over at the man who had saved her from her miserable life with Armand. He was so beautiful as he slept, although his snoring could wake the cows up. She got out of bed, went in the backyard, and noticed that it had a small garden of flowers. She picked a few before heading back to the cottage.

She went into the kitchen to get a few grapes out of the refrigerator. She looked at the grapes then put them back when she saw a big chocolate cake. She cut herself a huge slice and grabbed two slices of turkey meat. She went in the freezer and got three scoops of vanilla ice cream.

She then reached for a can of Coca-Cola. She took the plate of food and the flowers to the bathroom. It was very average looking, had marble floors, and was painted a peach color with a marble sink, toilet, and huge tub. She put her food and flowers down on the toilet seat. Turning on the water in the tub, she poured some bubble bath in.

Once the tub was full, she put the flower petals in, took off her nightgown, and stepped into the tub. Letting the warm water relax her body, she ate some of her cake, ice cream, and a slice of turkey meat. She was so happy to be eating something that wasn't nutritious. She laughed as cake crumbs fell into the tub. She lay back and closed her eyes, thinking about her future.

Minutes later, the bathroom door opened, and Brad walked in wearing only sweatpants, with sleep in his eyes. He squinted to see Diamond's naked body in the tub.

"Oh." He turned his head. "I'm sorry. I'm so sorry. I'll come back." He slowly backed out of the bathroom.

"Stop," Diamond said with a laugh. "Come sit, but watch the plate."

Brad smiled as he put the half-eaten plate of food on the floor and took a slice of turkey. He was glad that she was eating more, and he predicted that she would be pretty thick in no time. He sat on the toilet seat, grabbed the washcloth, then dipped it into the sudsy water. Diamond leaned forward so Brad could wash her back.

"Damn," said Brad, licking his lips. He couldn't believe he was washing his dream girl's back.

"What?" Diamond slightly turned her head.

"Nothing. Just lean forward again."

She did. Brad was on cloud nine. He kept eyeing Diamond's 38B breasts. They were perfect, and her nipples were rock hard. They looked like oversized Hershey's Kisses waiting to be licked. Brad tried to control himself as he took the washcloth and slowly wiped Diamond's beautiful, broad shoulders up to her neck.

Diamond closed her eyes, thinking about how much she loved his touch. Being around Brad made her feel like a virgin all over again. She took his hand, kissed it, and guided it to her right breast.

At first he was hesitant, but he massaged and caressed her breast tenderly.

"Ahh," Diamond groaned, also feeling another kind of wetness between her legs. "Oh my God."

Feeling the heat from her body, Brad could tell that Diamond was aroused, and it was starting to wake up the woody in his sweats.

"Brad, can you get me a towel please."

"Sure."

He went over to the closet to get her a towel. When he turned around, he saw Diamond standing up in the tub. She looked even more beautiful, standing there naked and wet. She reminded Brad of that famous Botticelli painting, *The Birth of Venus*. He was completely lost in thought as he drooled over Diamond's near-perfect sculpted body.

"Are you going to stare at me all day, or are you going to give me that towel?"

"I'm going to stand here and look at you."

Diamond laughed, and so did he.

"Just kidding. Here you go." He passed her the towel.

"Thank you," Diamond said, wrapping the towel around herself. Brad took her hand, helping her out of the tub.

She glanced out the bathroom window, seeing nothing but acres of land. For a second, she thought about running away in the middle of the night. She didn't know if she could trust Sandino and Taylor, but Brad seemed as if he surely did. She walked over to the sink, picking up the bottle of Oil of Olay lotion and leaving the bathroom to go in the backyard.

Brad looked at her, wondering what the hell she was doing. He still had a woody in his sweats. The next thing Diamond did completely shocked Brad. She removed the towel, revealing her naked body to God and the trees. Brad followed her outside to watch.

"Diamond, are you crazy? What if someone sees you? You never know. Someone could be watching us."

"Maybe so, but I don't care." Diamond gave Brad the lotion before laying the towel neatly on the ground. She then lay flat on her stomach.

Brad examined her nice, firm booty. Right then and there he wanted to have sex with her. Diamond wasn't a common whore, so he wanted to make love to her. He got on his knees, put a nice amount of lotion in his hands, and rubbed them on her shoulders.

"That feels good." Diamond turned her head to the side, looking at Brad with a smile.

His hands traveled down her back and finally to his favorite part, her ass. Brad took his big hands and caressed her cheeks, using the tip of his middle finger for Diamond's crack.

"Mmmmmm," Diamond moaned as she could feel more wetness between her legs.

Brad noticed her cumming on the towel. He also noticed some spots on his pants from his pre-cum. Diamond slowly lifted up, and Brad moved back. She gazed into his eyes. Brad didn't know what to think as Diamond softly touched his face. He kissed her hand. She pulled him closer to her, and they shared a romantic kiss. Brad wrapped his arms around her as he slowly leaned back, with her now on top of him.

Diamond could feel his hardness. She stopped kissing him.

"Brad, make love to me."

He stared at her with so much concern in his eyes. He could tell that she had been through a lot with Armand. He didn't want to push or pressure her in any kind of way.

"You sure? We don't have any protection."

She kissed his chin. "I trust you." She kissed him again. "Make love to me." Diamond slightly lifted up so Brad could slide his sweats down to his knees. She looked at his eight-inch penis, appreciating the length and thickness "Be gentle with me."

"I will." He positioned her.

Diamond felt him slide inside of her. "Ahh." Her mouth opened wide.

Brad slowly grinded, holding on to her hips. "Ohhh, baby, yes . . ."

Diamond leaned forward, and they shared a passionate kiss as Brad rubbed her back.

"Ahhhhh." Diamond released her fluids on Brad's manhood. She'd never felt so good in her life.

Brad sped up the pace, and many of their moans escaped into the air. "Ahh . . . yeah . . . oh . . . God, this feels so good."

Brad sat up, grinding faster as he and Diamond remained in a lip lock.

He kept looking at the pure pleasure in her eyes as she rode him and they released more of their sexual energy together.

"I . . . I'm cumming. Are you ready?" she said.

Brad nodded and came with her. He could feel all of his juices flowing inside of her. They searched into each other's eyes, wondering how all of this was made possible. Love was written all over them, and there was no moving forward without each other.

Chapter 29

Campfire Stories

Throughout the day and evening, Brad and Diamond grew closer. They were getting to know each other and made love all over the house. It was the best day Diamond had had in years. She felt so comfortable around Brad. She wanted him to love and know every part of her before she would give her heart to him completely and possibly spend the rest of her life with him. Brad had to know the girl outside of Diamond.

That night, the happy couple spent the evening outside, around a small campfire making s'mores. After Brad was done with a few of them, Diamond was still eating them like there was no tomorrow.

Brad smiled at her. "I'm glad to see you eating something different for a change."

"Carter Marie," Diamond said with a mouthful of s'mores.

"Excuse me?"

Diamond swallowed and cleared her throat. "My name is not Diamond. It's Carter Marie Lily Levy."

Brad nodded. "That's cute. I like that."

"I haven't said my real name in years." Diamond got a warm feeling of relief as she laughed and cried.

Brad hugged her tightly, taking in all of her pain. He knew that it was time to get to know the real her, instead of the girl he fell so hard for at first sight. He used his thumb to wipe her tears away. "Shhh, it's okay." He kissed her nose.

Diamond touched Brad's face so softly while looking into his eyes. She couldn't help but feel so much trust and love from him. She sat on his lap, and he wrapped his big arms around her, not wanting to let her go. They looked at the fire.

"Before I give you all of my love and heart, you must know where I been," Diamond said as she looked at the flames rise.

Chapter 30

The Memoirs of Carter Marie

Born and raised in Belize City, Belize, Carter Mario Levy was the son of Carter Levy Sr., aka Big Carter, a fisherman, and Marisol, a maid. Both of his parents worked hard every day, but they still lived in a one-bedroom apartment in one of Belize City's toughest neighborhoods. They wanted so much better for their son and wanted him to leave Belize, going to a good college in America like Harvard or Yale University. They thought he'd have the opportunity to become a doctor or maybe a judge. He would not have to work paycheck to paycheck like they had all their lives.

At the age of fifteen, he was getting into all of kinds of trouble and hanging out with the wrong crowd. He was friendly with the leaders of two of Belize's biggest gangs, The Whitesides and The Belize Lords. Then, during a big drug riot, he witnessed the Whiteside gang leader being killed. The authorities were sure that he knew what had happened or was somehow involved in the riot. Because he would not tell the Belizean authorities anything, they harassed him every time he stepped out the front door of his apartment. Everywhere he went, from the market to school, the authorities were on him hard, doing everything in their power to make him talk. The biggest scare was when the Belize Lords gang leader left a tongue on his family's doorstep with a note saying: Keep yo' damn mouth closed or the real cat will catch that tongue.

Big Carter and Marisol knew that Belize was no longer safe for their son with the Belize Lords and the police threatening Carter's life every day. So, Marisol called her big brother, Joseph Ferguson, who lived in the United States in Miami, and she begged him to take her son in until things cooled down in Belize. Finally, her brother agreed.

Carter was so disappointed that he had to leave Belize, and he even went into his tough guy role, telling his mother and father that he wasn't afraid of the Belize Lords or the authorities. Big Carter wasn't having it any other way, so the next day, he and Marisol took all of their life savings and got Carter on the next flight to Miami to live with his uncle Joseph.

When Carter went to his uncle's home, he was completely blown away. He had heard from his parents and old friends back in Belize that Joseph was a very rich man. Joseph's home had thirteen bedrooms, a basketball court, a tennis court, and indoor and outdoor pools. It was known as one of the hottest homes in Miami. Carter thought he had died and gone to heaven. Hell, to him, living in a mansion beat living in a hot-ass one-bedroom apartment with barely any running water.

Joseph enrolled Carter in one of Miami's exclusive private schools, where he excelled and even met his new best friend, Ian Castro, a light-skinned pretty boy with good hair. He was half black and half Brazilian, with a well-to-do family who welcomed Carter into their family like he was their own son.

Even though Carter was enjoying the playboy life in Miami, one thing always stayed on his mind: How did Joseph get so rich? He hardly ever left the house for work. Joseph was either at home chilling out, in his home gym, or wining and dining a beautiful woman in Miami. His uncle was not a mean man at all. He was more of a father figure or a mentor to him. They talked about life, women, money, and sex. On Carter's seventeenth birthday, Joseph gave him a Haitian woman, and that was a happy day for Carter.

Then, on another occasion, Carter was coming home in his red Corvette, and he saw the police, the newscasters, the mayor of Miami, as well as IRS and FBI agents all over the property. Soon, the cops brought Joseph out of his mansion in handcuffs.

"What the hell?" Carter jumped out of the car and made his way over to his uncle. A police officer blocked him. "Let me go! This is my uncle's house! Let me go! What is this? What the hell is going on?"

Joseph held his head down in shame. Carter tried to break away from the police officer's embrace, but to no avail. "Let me go! This is my uncle's house!"

"Look at what I got here!" said an FBI agent, coming out of Joseph's home with bags and bags of money.

"Well, son," the officer said, holding Carter, "that may be your uncle, but he's one of Florida's most notorious bank robbers, and we finally got his ass. Now, why don't you go home to your mama."

Carter just couldn't believe it. He watched as Joseph was put in the cop car and all of his servants and girlfriends were questioned. Carter looked at Joseph, who tried to keep his pride and hide his shame. The direction of his eyes traveled to his rose garden, and he hoped that Carter would get the signal before the police pulled off.

Carter cried, predicting that he would probably never see his uncle again.

That evening, when the FBI and police officers were gone, Carter went back to the mansion and dug up the rose garden. He found a suitcase, pulling it out of the dirt. He left the property right away and checked into a cheap hotel. After that, he took a long, hot shower,

reflecting on the day's events. He came out of the bath-
room with only a towel wrapped around his body. He
wiped some of the dirt off the suitcase before opening
it. To his amazement, he was shocked to see all of the
money inside. When he was done, he had counted about
$250,000.

"Well, at least 5-0 didn't get this as their bonus."

He turned on the television, seeing Joseph's face on
every news channel. The newscaster said, "Today, the
Miami Police Department and FBI have finally captured
Florida's notorious mega bank robber, a Belizean man
by the name of Joseph Ferguson. Ferguson was caught
when undercover cop Miriam Baker posed as one of the
criminal's many girlfriends."

"Damn, Unc," Carter said, shaking his head. He knew
that his uncle's weakness was beautiful women.

The next day, Carter called the bondsman to see how
much his uncle's bail would be. He found out it was a
million dollars. He knew that $250,000 wasn't enough.
Carter stayed in the hotel for two days, not knowing
what to do. He didn't want to go back to school with
the shame of his uncle being a bank robber. He damn
sure didn't want to go back to his poor life in Belize,
ending up a fisherman like his father, or working in the
fields. He finally found the nerve to call his boy Ian for
help. He ended up staying with Ian's family, who didn't
give a damn about Joseph being a bank robber. Carter
graduated from high school and went to the University
of Miami to major in business, but all of that came with
a price.

Because the Castro family had saved Carter by taking
him in, Ian's father, Master Ian, thought that Carter
and Ian should now know the truth about the Castro

Family business. Carter had always believed that Ian's family was a well-to-do family because they owned many night spots in Miami, Palm Beach, Atlanta, and Brazil. He learned that they were all operations to cover up for their illegal prostitution and gambling ring.

Carter and Ian met Master Ian's brother, Armand Castro, who they learned was an untouchable drug lord in South America. He was well known for drug trafficking. Master Ian wanted to expand the family brand more in the United States, so he and Armand trained the boys to be traffickers who would be transporting drugs from Brazil back to American soil.

The first time the boys did it, they were scared shitless, but when they saw the money coming in, they learned to love it, using the university as a cover. They were both big men on campus with their top of the line clothes, new whips, and the mansion they shared. They were also known for having every kind of chick from black to white to Puerto Rican on their jocks.

Carter was getting accustomed to the rich playa lifestyle, boning the campus freaks every day and night. He still focused on making money, getting his degree, and figuring out how to get away from the Castro Family. The one girl that stole his heart on campus was a Somalian beauty, Lily Ail. She was the most stunning woman he had ever seen. Her skin was the color of bronze, her hair was a deep brown color, which she kept in thick curls, and her body was sick. She resembled the model Iman. He knew that she was going to be his wife.

When they first met, Lily tried not to notice him, but she was getting so turned on by the campus hottie, Carter Mario Levy. The other chicks on the campus only wanted him for his dick and his money. None of that mattered to Lily. She just wanted to know the real Carter.

When they finally went out on their first date, which consisted of a movie and a sexy candlelit dinner on Miami Beach, Carter learned so much about Lily. She was born and raised in Mogadishu, Somalia, to a father and mother who were both Harvard University graduates and doctors. She was also the granddaughter of a well-known DJ in Somalia, who was living the good life.

When civil war broke out in her country, her family lost everything, from her parents' wedding photos to her collection of custom made dolls. Her family found shelter in the university, which was the only place with running water. Missionaries gave them food, and her father sold some of the food to other refugees so that the family could save up money. Her family went from one refugee camp to another, until they moved to America and ended up in Portland, Maine.

Carter also found out her majors were human rights and psychology. She was hoping to one day return home and help her country, especially the little girls in Somalia that didn't have a voice.

Carter knew that she had a beautiful and pure heart. She was also the only woman he wanted to spend the rest of his life with, but he was worried about keeping her safe from all his bullshit with the Castro Family.

So, in his last semester at school and still trafficking for Castro, Carter found and bought a beautiful home where he knew Lily would be safe and, hopefully, one day they would live in peace and harmony.

On graduation day, Carter proposed to Lily, but Lily told him, "If I say yes to be your wife . . ." She paused and put Carter's hand on her stomach. "You have to soon get away from the Castros and make us your main priority."

Carter nodded with tears falling down from his eyes. He was surprised that he was going to be a daddy. "I will."

"Then, yes, I will marry you."

After the graduation ceremony, they went straight to the courthouse and wed quickly. The next day, they moved to Ambergris Caye, Belize, into their new beach-front home, having the happiest nine months of their lives. This made Carter and Lily even closer and their love even stronger.

The biggest light of their life was when their beautiful baby girl, Carter Marie Lily Levy, came into the world. To Carter, his daughter was the most beautiful thing he'd ever seen. He knew he had to get away from the Castro Family. He wanted to do and give his baby girl things he never had. He wanted her to be well rounded, go to school in Paris, learn six languages, and be a queen of a country. But for now, Carter Marie was going to be his little princess.

When Carter came back to Miami, he confronted the Castro Family. He said he wanted to get out of the drug trade once and for all, for the sake of his wife and newborn child.

Master Ian and Armand weren't going to let him go that easyly. He was their best guy. Both of the Castro brothers made a deal with Carter. If they appointed him lieutenant of the Castro Family, and within the next nine years he made them rich, powerful, and unstoppable, they promised to cut all ties with Carter so that he could live his life for him and his family. Like the G Carter was, he accepted the offer, knowing that Lily wasn't going to be happy with his decision.

Returning to Belize, he told Lily about his deal to work with the Castro brothers for the next nine years, until he built their family business, making them number one.

Of course, Lily was against the whole thing. "Are you stupid? Why would you agree to do some dumb shit like that? You have a family now that loves and needs you. Why don't you, me, and Carter Marie run away to Paris and never look back? We have enough money to do that shit."

Carter wrapped his arms around Lily and kissed her cheek. "Come on, Lily. It's just nine years. Please. I promise you once that time is up, we will go to Paris. Please, I promise. Nine years will go quickly. Trust me."

Lily took a deep breath, and more tears fell down her face. "Okay. Nine years. That's it, and no more. No excuses once the nine years are up."

For the next nine years, Carter commanded traffickers along with Ian, who made sure that everything went to the supplier and the right destination. They were making money and never slipping. He'd made the Castro Family the top of the food chain like he had promised.

When it was time, he had to face Master Ian and Armand, hoping they would release him from the family business and keep their end of the deal. He was face to face with both Castro brothers, hoping they'd just shake his hand and say, "Have a good life," and walk out. Carter had it all wrong. The men laughed in his face.

"What's so funny?" Carter questioned.

The Castro brothers continued to laugh.

"You are," Armand said.

That really pissed Carter off. He was confused.

"Did you think it was going to be that easy to just leave the family business? Once you get into the family business, you're a part of this organization forever," Armand said with an evil grin on his face.

Carter's blood started to boil. "But you and Master Ian both said if I helped build your business and make it number one in the food chain, I could be free to do whatever. I made you all more money than God, and I made no mistakes. We had a deal, and I think we should honor that deal."

"And the Castro Family is very grateful for all your work," Master Ian said, pulling out a Cuban cigar. "Carter, I love you like a son, but frankly, there was never really a deal, and now this meeting is over."

No, no, no no! No deal. I promised Lily. I can't do this shit anymore. No this isn't right, thought Carter.

Armand laughed sinisterly.

Out of nowhere, Carter got up from his chair and punched Armand in his nose. Before he could finish him off, Master Ian grabbed Carter, though he was barely able to hold onto him. Carter had turned into a wild man.

"You lying snake bastards! Fuck you! Fuck all y'all!"

Master Ian pulled him out of the room and took him outside to the limousine.

Carter pushed Master Ian off him. "Fuck you!" He got in the limo and closed the door.

Master Ian went to the limo driver and said, "Take Mr. Levy to the airport, please." He stepped back and looked at Carter as the limo took off. He stood there, waving him good-bye, pissing Carter off even more.

There was silence the entire ride. Carter was so pissed with the Castro brothers. He was the loyal one. He made their product the top of the food chain. He brought in new business, and all they did was laugh in his face and tell him he was never going to get out of the family. Like many hustlers in the drug trade, there was no damn loyalty in this business. There was nothing but snakes and deceit.

All through the ride, he thought about how he was going to explain things to Lily. He made up his mind that he was going to get richer, break down the Castro Family, and get his family out of the country for good.

For the next couple of months, Carter stole money, little bit by little bit, from the Castro Family in ways that they wouldn't find out. He started making anonymous calls to the FBI to get the traffickers busted. He just didn't give a damn anymore.

Many months later, the Levy family was packing up their lives in Belize to move to Paris in a nice château Carter had bought. Their plans were cut short when armed members of the Castro Family surrounded the home, and there was nowhere to run. The Levy family felt so hopeless, holding onto each other closely.

Armand, Master Ian, and Ian pulled Carter away from his family, beating the shit out of him. Master Ian pointed his 9 mm in Carter's face as he kicked him in his face.

Nine-year-old Carter Marie and Lily were screaming and yelling, "Stop it!"

One of the soldiers slapped the shit out of both Lily and Carter Marie. "Shut up! Shut your mouths or else!"

Master Ian looked down at Carter as blood and some of his teeth dangled from his mouth. Master Ian tried not to cry, because he loved Carter like son, but stealing from the family was a big no to him.

"Carter, how could you do this to me? I loved you like a son. I welcomed you into my family, and this is how you pay me back? Stealing from me, your father?" He wanted to shoot Carter right then and there, but he couldn't.

Carter looked up at Master Ian. "What are you talking about? I would never steal from you."

"Oh, really?" Master said, snapping his finger.

Ian came over, revealing black and white photographs of Carter stealing money from the family vault and photos of him at different phone booths in Miami and Tampa, making his famous calls to the FBI.

"Any more questions?" Ian spat in his face. "Stupid ass. You was my brother. Why?"

Carter was so ashamed. He looked over at his family and back at Master Ian and Ian. "Please just kill me, but let my wife and daughter go. They had nothing to do with this. Please let them go."

Armand looked over at Lily and Carter Marie. He had another bright idea. "Wait, brother, don't kill him."

Master Ian looked at Armand as he walked over to Carter Marie, who was in so much confusion. She moved her head around so Armand wouldn't touch her. Armand roughly grabbed her face. Carter Marie was so scared as she looked into Armand's eyes, knowing that he was evil.

"Brother, what are you doing to that child?"

Armand smiled at Master Ian. "Big brother, don't you see that the girl should be the price that Carter owes the family?"

Lily held onto Carter Marie tightly.

"What do you mean, Armand?" Master Ian asked, looking at his brother and knowing he was a sick bastard because he was attracted to young flesh.

"The child is worth more than money. She is our repayment. Look at her. She will be a true beauty one day."

"Nooo! Not my baby! Not my child!" Lily yelled, hugging Carter Marie tightly and not wanting anyone to take her child. She looked over at Armand. "Take me instead."

Armand went over to Lily, pulling her away from her child. He was gripping her arm tightly, and then he slapped the taste out her mouth. "Bitch, no one wants your old ass. Boys, get the child!"

"Carter Marie, run!" Lily yelled.

Carter Marie did as she was told, but with no hope, she was caught by Armand's thugs and tied up. She was screaming for her mom and dad to help her.

Armand smiled at Lily then looked at Carter Marie. "Say good-bye to Mommy, little one."

Lily's eyes widened as she saw Armand pull out his gun and point it in her face. He fired, causing Carter Marie to scream for dear life. "Mommy!" Tears came from her eyes as she looked at her mother's lifeless body.

"Noooo!" Carter yelled. "Not my Lily."

Ian kicked him in the face. "Shut the hell up!"

One of the soldiers used his hands to cover Carter Marie's mouth. Armand looked back at Carter Marie and the soldier with his hand over her mouth. "Take the girl to the car. All of you leave, except Sandino, Master Ian, Ian, and myself."

All the soldiers exited, leaving the heads of the Castro Family looking at a half dead Carter, who was now in a daze from seeing his true love murdered in front of his eyes.

Master Ian said, "Any last words, my son?"

Carter looked up at Master Ian. "I'm not your son!" Carter yelled, trying to get up.

Armand shot him in his head, smiling at his lifeless body.

A stunned Master Ian asked, "Are you stupid? I didn't want to kill the boy. He was family. Why, Armand?"

Armand laughed. "You asshole. I don't know why our father put you in charge of this operation."

"What are you talking about?"

"You are the reason this family is so weak, and every-one else thinks so as well. Maybe it's time for a new leader and a new era. But"—Armand turned to look at Ian— "before I can claim my throne, I must take care of the future heir of the throne first."

"What?" Master Ian yelled.

Armand nodded his head at Sandino.Another gunshot went off, and a lifeless Ian fell to the ground after being shot in the head by Armand's main man.

"Why? What did you just do?" Master Ian ran to his son, kneeling down to hold his bloody body. "My son, my only son." Master Ian cried.

The plan was to finish what he'd started, and Armand had done just that.

Smoke came from his gun as he looked at his now lifeless brother. "All hail the new head of the Castro Family, new and improved."

Both he and Sandino walked out of the house and got into the limousine. As the limo took off, Carter Marie was kicking, screaming, and crying her eyes out.

"Mommy! Daddy! Help me! Help!" Her screams continued until one of the soldiers pulled out a needle, injecting a tranquilizer in her arm. It calmed her down, forcing her into a deep, dark sleep.

In Rio de Janeiro, Brazil, twelve hours later, Carter Marie woke up thinking that what had happened to her parents was all a bad dream. She got up from the bed, only to be caught by a fat, olive-skinned Brazilian woman in a maid's uniform, spotless white nurse's shoes, and her black hair in a bun.

"Let me go! Let me go!" Carter Marie tried to get away from the maid, but she was too strong for her. "I want my mommy and daddy!"

"Shut up, you little whiny bitch!" The maid shook her. "You don't have a mother and father anymore! This is your home now. Now, come on!"

Too afraid to fight her, Carter Marie went along with the woman, who was ordered to give her a bath and a good scrub down.

"That hurts. The water is too hot, and you're scrubbing too hard," Carter Marie complained.

"Sorry, dear. Orders from Armand. He wants me to scrub every last bit of Belizean dirt from your body. You are worth a lot to him now, so fight through the pain of the hot water and my scrubbing. Oh, and forget you came from Belize, and never think of your family again."

Carter Marie cried and cried.

"Let it all out, sweetheart. Let it out. I cried just like you when I was your age. My family sold me to the Castro Family years ago, and I cried just like you. It's just best to forget everything." The woman bathed her, easing up on the scrubbing.

Carter Marie looked at the woman. "What's your name?"

"Olga."

Carter Marie started to shake and continued to cry.

For weeks, Carter Marie worked in Armand's house, cleaning the mansion from top to bottom. She was never allowed to go outside, and as soon as her chores were done, she slept in the attic, where the windows were completely cemented. Carter Marie was determined to break away from Armand's jail, one way or another. What kept her sane was Olga, who talked to her, gave her advice, and filled her up with courage that her Prince Charming would one day save her.

Carter Marie tried to escape so many times, but she was always caught and punished badly. One time, Armand locked her in the attic for a month with no food or water.

By the time Carter Marie was fifteen, she blossomed into a true beauty, and soon Armand took notice. On her fifteenth birthday, Armand bought her a Versace dress and Dior pumps. He had Olga bathe her with the best oils, put makeup on her face and perfume on her body. He took her to a suite in São Paulo, and that was the night when he took her virginity. She tried to fight him off, but he was too strong.

The whole night, while he was raping her, she prayed and asked God to get her out of that hellhole and away from Armand, who was Satan himself. That was also the night that Armand gave Carter Marie her new name, Diamond, because he hated the name Carter. It brought back old memories of the man who betrayed the family. It also reflected that she was worth a lot to him.

After that day, the more she was around Armand, the more she hated him. She had even gotten pregnant by him twice. He made her get an abortion both times, which suited her just fine. He had a doctor give her birth control shots so she wouldn't get pregnant for the next three years.

When Diamond tried to escape one more time from the house and failed, Armand made it official to move her out of the mansion, believing that she was more trouble than she was worth. He put her in an apartment in downtown Rio, where she was heavily guarded. If she left, they would kill her.

Since she liked to be outside and Armand wanted her to pay her debt for her father's crimes, he formed Diamond's Bakery Boutique, where she worked 365 days of the year with no pay. She wanted to escape so *many times, since the bakery was always so packed, but Armand had eyes everywhere. Diamond feared for her life every day in the bakery. She waited for the day when someone wasn't watching her every move.*

Throughout the years, Diamond continued to pray and remembered what Olga had said: "Your Prince Charming will come to save you soon."

In her eyes, he was finally here.

Chapter 31

Rebirth

Brad was so amazed by Diamond's story. It was power-ful and sad. The main thing was that it was going to have a happy ending—well, that was if they survived it. The thing was she was safe now. So many women were not blessed to have a man like Brad who would save them.

Brad held her tightly. "It's okay. I'm here now. Honestly, after that story, I will always be here, and no one will ever hurt you again. I promise."

Diamond looked up to give him a kiss. "Thank you."

He smiled.

"Brad?"

"Yes, bae?"

"Go in the house and get those clippers please?"

"Sure." Brad got up and ran into the house.

Diamond looked at the fire, feeling so free because she had told her story to someone who cared for her. She was going to make one of the biggest changes in her life.

"Here." Brad gave her the clippers and sat beside her.

"Brad?"

"Yes."

She gave him the clippers back. "Cut all of this hair off. Please."

Brad cocked his head back, looking at her like she was crazy. She had the most beautiful long black hair he'd ever seen. "You sure, ma?"

"I'm sure. This is my rebirth. I'm saying good-bye to Diamond and resurrecting Carter Marie Lily Levy."

Brad smiled, knowing that the haircut was a way for her to release all of the pain and sexual abuse of the past. "Okay, I'll do it under one condition."

"What's that?"

He got down on bended knee. "Look, I know we haven't known each other that long, but I feel something in my heart that I ain't never felt before. I can't give back your innocence, but I know I can give all of the love you missed out on and fill that hole in your heart. If we make it out of this alive, will you, Carter Marie Lily Levy, be my wife?"

Tears filled Diamond's eyes. "Yes!" She nodded. "Yes!" She hugged him. "I would love to be your wife."

Brad had tears in his eyes too. He couldn't help but to think about his boys, wondering how they would feel if they knew he had asked a woman to marry him. He thought about their journey, hoping that they had found some success like him. For now, though, it was all about him and Diamond.

"Stop thinking so much and cut my hair," she said.

Brad laughed. "Okay." He got up, turned on the clippers, and cut his fiancée's long hair off.

Diamond felt reborn as she watched her hair fall down. *Good-bye, Diamond. Carter Marie, I got you now, and I'm not ever letting you go again.*

Chapter 32

New York

Even though it wasn't officially Christmas yet, it was truly a Merry Christmas for Ramon Lopez. In New York, even before Christmas, he was going up and down Fifth Avenue, Times Square, and Fashion Avenue between West 26th Street and 42nd Street, buying in every last store in Manhattan from Versace to Gucci and Fendi. He went to the theater to see *The Lion King* three times in a row, and then to different modeling agencies, from Ford Models to Wilhelmina Models to IMG Models, in hopes of a new shot at modeling again. He damn sure didn't want to work for Taylor for the rest of his days. He'd rather go back to porn than work for her.

He thought no one would remember the reputation that got him blackballed from the fashion world, but all he heard every modeling recruiter say once they gave him back his portfolio was, "Don't call us; we'll call you," or "You're not for us right now," and "I don't think we can sell your look to the public. Sorry." This surely devastated Ramon, and if he could turn back the hands of time, he would. Hell, he thought he should have been on the same level as Tyson Beckford or Antonio Sabato, not some ex-porn actor and editor-in-chief at some low-rate, trashy fashion magazine with a has-been, super-gold-digging, pushing-forty model whom he despised seeing on an everyday basis. He was only working there because

she was married to the one man he ever loved, his
Armand Castro, who was making his trip to New York an
excellent one.

Armand was so open with him in the streets of
Manhattan, from kissing him in public, holding his hand,
and having romantic evenings in fancy restaurants and
in between the sheets. Ramon wished it could last like
that forever, wishing Armand would just divorce Taylor
for good. They could move to New York and live happily
ever after. Still, he knew in his mind that was all a fantasy,
but he hoped for the new year that Armand would have
a change of heart, come out of the closet, and be his one
and only.

That evening, the two men spent the night in their
penthouse suite at the Plaza Hotel, where Armand, but
mainly Ramon, enjoyed opening up their gifts the day
before Christmas. They'd had a lovely stroll down Central
Park, looking at the beautiful snow covering the city of
New York. Now they were having a romantic dinner in
their suite. The real dessert was in their huge bedroom
fit for a king and a queen. Ramon rocked Armand's
world. He thought a man like Armand was feared in the
streets of Brazil and South America, but he was the total
package when it came to being a bottom bitch. Ramon's
motto was: *Don't judge a book by its cover. Check that
bank account first.*

After their third round of sweaty, hot, and steamy sex,
Ramon rolled off of Armand, who was in complete sexual
ecstasy after he was done jacking himself off. He was
breathing heavy from getting pleasure from his lover and
himself. Ramon went over to his side of the bed, got a
cigarette, and lit it. He took a puff and gave it to Armand.
Ramon got another one for himself.

Ramon looked over at Armand, who was taking puffs
of the cigarette, trying to get his breathing under control.
"How you feel, baby?"

Armand looked over at Ramon, smiling, "Good. How are you enjoying New York so far?"

"I finally got you all to myself." He laughed as he took two more drags from the cigarette that was clenched between his fingers.

"You know, nothing means more to me than being here with you. I wish it could be like this all year long, or forever. I want you to myself. I'm tired of sharing you with that witch and everyone else in Brazil. I want to make us official at the beginning of the new year."

Armand felt Ramon's words, and he could see the hurt and determination in his face, but he really didn't give a shit about anyone but himself. Hell, in his mind, he was still a young man who could screw and bust a nut into anything he pleased, whether it was a woman, a man, or a sheep, if he was into sleeping with animals. All he cared about was himself, the drugs, the business, and making even more money. He didn't want Ramon catching feelings for him, but he thought since he was so fine, naïve, and had a good dick game, he'd string him along for the ride. Before long, he'd have to get rid of him before his ass got too obsessed and possessive. Sooner or later he was going to put a bullet right through Ramon's temple. The last thing Armand wanted was a gay version of *Fatal Attraction*, because that would be bad for business. But, until that time, he just played his little mind games with Ramon to keep him in line.

"You want to be with me forever, darling?"

Ramon deeply kissed Armand. "You know I do, baby."

Armand smiled. *I got him. Sucker.*

"Listen, when the new year comes in, I promise no more drugs, no more killing, no more sexing strangers, no more being in the family business, and definitely no more Taylor. From now on, it'll be just you and me. No in between, okay?" he said to Ramon.

***

Ramon was hyped while looking into Armand's eyes, believing that every word he was saying was genuine and true this time around.

"You promise?"

How stupid can this guy be? thought Armand.

"I promise this time around it'll be me and you only. Our happily ever after is coming true, darling."

Ramon smiled even harder, but it went away. "But what about Taylor? With the divorce, she is destined to get everything. That includes the magazine, the house, and of course, half of your money. You better get a very good attorney for that shit."

"Well, my love, I already have that planned out. I promised you no more killings, but in this case, I have to kill Taylor. Once she is out of the picture, I will officially make you Publisher & CEO of *Brazilian Kouture*. What do you say to that?"

Ramon was ecstatic. He hated Taylor anyway. "Baby, if it makes you feel good to kill her, do it as long as we are together forever."

In his mind, all Armand could say was, *Idiot, idiot, and idiot.*

He laughed. "Anything for my baby."

"Yay!" Ramon clapped his hands and got out of bed. He was overjoyed and excited that Armand Castro was going to finally be his and only his. "Baby, we gotta celebrate." He thought for a second, with a big grin on his face. "Champagne. Let's celebrate this moment with a toast. I'll get the champagne." He ran out of the room like a little butt-naked fairy.

Armand wiped his smile off real quick as he sat up in the bed. *Now, this is going to be one bullet I'm going to be glad to put in someone's head. Damn. But I did promise him one thing, though. I'm going to kill Taylor's ass soon enough. This marriage shit ain't for me. Why did I marry that bitch anyway? Oh, yeah. My weakness for beautiful women. All I need is my sex drive, my money, and business to keep me going. And also Diamond's little quickies here and there.*

He laughed and looked at the cigarette. *Now, he knows I only smoke Cubans after sex. Stupid fool.*

Armand got out of bed and went to his bag to get a Cuban cigar. His cell started to ring. He looked at it, seeing that it was a 911 call from Sandino, who had been warned not to call him. Since it was a 911 call, Armand knew it was urgent. Maybe something had gone wrong with one of his suppliers. He wasn't sure, so he pushed the talk button and put the phone up to his ear.

"Yeah, what? You know I'm on vacation!"

"Boss, this is important. Turn on the TV to CNN now!"

"What, Sandino? What the hell is going on?"

"Just do it!"

Armand grabbed the remote, turning the 60-inch flat plasma TV on. When he turned the channel to CNN, it showed multiple buildings up in flames. Then he saw a news anchor, who came on the air and said, "This evening, a tragedy struck Rio De Janeiro, Brazil. Yesterday, a bloody massacre took the lives of thirty-four people in a Rio bakery called Diamond's Bakery Boutique, before it was blown away this evening, along with the Castro apartment building in downtown Rio. The blast killed all of the tenants and guests. Also, there was an explosion that destroyed a beloved South American fashion magazine house called Brazilian Kouture, killing all of its employees, except its CEO and publisher, the former supermodel Taylor Monroe. Its editor-in-chief, Ramon Lopez, is away on vacation. Monroe's attorney will have a statement ready in a few hours."

Film footage showed all the explosions from different angles. Armand dropped his phone. "What the fuck!"

He immediately picked up his phone, pissed off at what had just happened. What he had built was all gone. His most prized possessions were now dust. He'd lost Diamond and his money—all his money. He didn't believe in banks, so he would put all of his money in each building so it wouldn't get taxed by the government. He stood there for a moment, attempting to process that he was now broke and was going to be in some deep shit with the law and with his suppliers.

Armand had to come up with a plan fast. He put his cell phone up to his ear. "Sandino, what are we going to do?" All he heard was dead air. "Sandino! Sandino! Hello? Shit!" He tried to call Sandino, but all he got was a recording, telling him that the number he was trying to reach had been disconnected.

He redialed Sandino's number, but he still got the same message. "Shit! Shit! Shit!"

Armand was going crazy, and he was in disbelief that all his money and drugs were gone. He turned his attention back to the TV.

The CNN news anchor went on. "Authorities have recovered new evidence that suggests all of the buildings were stash houses for money and drugs. One of the forensics team's analysts found many ounces of cocaine in the apartment of Armand Castro, the owner and operator of the businesses."

Suddenly, his picture flashed across this screen.

"He has not been found yet, but is wanted for questioning. No one knows if the bombing and massacres were due to terrorist attacks, or perhaps a drug war. Keep watching, and we'll bring you more on this story in a moment."

Pissed off, Armand turned off the TV. "Shiiiiit!" he shouted.

His phone rang again, and he answered without looking at the screen. He just hoped the caller was Sandino. "What the hell happened to you?" he yelled into the phone.

"So, how is your little sex session with Ramon going, you piece of shit?" a seductive female voice said.

Armand's eyes widened because he knew that it was Taylor. "Bitch, what the fuck do you want?"

"Oh, nothing. Just enjoying the fireworks of the city. Merry Christmas!" She sounded jolly. "My early Christmas gift to you. Do you love it?"

Armand was in so much disbelief. *My wife,* he thought. *When did she become Ma Barker mixed with Griselda Blanco? Who the hell did I marry?*

"Bitch, what in the fuck were you thinking? Do you know what you have done? You know what kind of shit you're going to cause?"

"Just enough to get rid of your fudge-packer ass and be with a real man, not some wannabe *Godfather*."

Those words angered Armand even more. "Bitc—"

"Oh, and don't have none of your henchmen come after me. I already took care of that."

"What?"

There was silence, and he soon heard the dial tone.

"Hello? Hello? Hello? That bitch!" Before he threw his phone on the bed, it chimed, alerting him that messages were arriving. He picked it up and went through all of his messages. There were pictures of all of his workers and henchmen, killed or being tortured to death. They were coming from an anonymous source.

"Daaaamn." He shook his head. Then the clicking sound came back. This time, he saw pictures of him and Ramon in New York, kissing, shopping, and in their bedroom, making love, with a message that read: SAY GOODBYE.

Right then, Armand knew that the source was Taylor. Then more messages came to his phone. This time, it was messages from his suppliers and the distributors, stating that they could no longer do business with him. They couldn't handle doing business with a gay man. Armand's wonderful vacation was now shot to hell, so he threw his cell phone across the room.

"Fuck!" He threw a chair at the wall and tore the room apart. He was going crazy like a wild beast, knowing that world he had worked so hard to build was now crumbling.

A butt naked Ramon came running in with a bottle of Moët in his hand. When he saw that Armand had totally lost his damn mind, he eased the bottle down on a table then went over to Armand and tried to calm him.

"Stop it, baby! Stop it!" While wrapping his arms around Armand, Ramon sat him on the bed. "Calm down, okay? Tell me what's the matter. Whatever it is, the two of us can work it out."

Armand slowly started to calm down, but all he did was stare at Ramon.

"Armand, baby, please tell me what's wrong."

Armand laughed. "Nothing. I'm just having a moment." He smiled at Ramon. "Ramon, do you really want to be with me?"

"Of course. Nothing more will make me happy."

"Good. We'll be together sooner than what you think. Listen, why don't you get the Jacuzzi going, and I'll join you in a few, okay?"

"Cool." Ramon kissed Armand on his cheek then went into the luxurious bathroom. When he heard water flowing into the tub, Armand used the suite's telephone to call his pilot to get back home to Rio.

When his pilot finally answered, he was tired as hell.

Armand yelled in his ear, "Get your ass to my jet in White Plains in an hour. I need to be back in Rio as soon as possible."

The pilot tried to speak, but Armand cut him off, warning, "Don't ask any questions. Just be there." He finished by saying, "I'll be in a special suit," knowing that the pilot would understand what that meant.

After hanging up, Armand lay down on the bed. *Taylor, you better have your running shoes on, because I'm going to cut, slice, dice, and mutilate that entire pretty face and body of yours.*

The whole thought of how he was going to kill Taylor was making him so hot that his dick got hard, but passion could wait. He had to get the hell out of New York and back on Brazilian soil. He got up, going over to his suitcase to get out his special accessories.

"I'm ready for my close up." He smiled, wanting to taste the blood of Taylor.

Taylor and Sandino enjoyed a candlelit dinner on the balcony at the penthouse at the Belmond Copacabana Palace overlooking the beach and enjoying the fireworks in downtown Rio. While laughing their heads off, they toasted to their new futures.

"I can't believe this shit worked out," Sandino said.

"I know. Me either, but you and my parents mapped it out. Before long, this will be all Luis's area, with you as head commander."

"Selena, you are one bad-ass chick," Sandino said, using Taylor's real name.

"And don't you forget. Before long, I will be in America with my true love, Desmond. I will be known as Taylor Monroe-Diaz." She laughed, thinking about her genius plan that would have Desmond holding her in his arms again and forever.

As they toasted, her cell phone rang. She picked it up.

"Hello."

"Taylor, hi. This is Elroy. I just wanted to let you know that we have your arrangements set up for tomorrow. Everything is prepared and ready to go. Instructions are in the living room, so give us a call if you need anything."

"Thank you, Elroy. The check will be in soon."

"Anytime, Taylor," said Elroy.

Taylor hung up the phone.

"Who was that?" Sandino asked.

"You'll see very soon. Let's finish dinner. Then you'll see why I love movies about ancient Rome."

"My little niece," said Sandino, taking a sip of his drink. "I wonder how Armand will get out of New York and back to Rio."

Taylor laughed. "Uncle, if it's one thing I know, it's that Armand is the master—or should I say the queen—of deceit and masquerade."

In New York, Armand was leaving the hotel in his best disguise. He had on a realistic face mask, making him look like a 70-year-old man. He wore a tan khaki suit with matching shoes.

When he got down to the lobby, he put his acting skills to use and even walked like an old man. He noticed three big, muscular dudes in black suits walking his way.

Oh, shit. I hope this ain't FBI, thought Armand, hoping the men didn't realize it was him.

The men ended up passing him, heading up to the elevator. Armand took a deep breath and rushed outside. He waved for a taxi, and luckily, one stopped. Armand got in, quickly ordering the driver to go. It was a good thing he did, because within seconds, police surrounded the hotel.

"Suckers," Armand said softly.

"Where to, boss?" asked the taxi driver in a thick Jamaican accent.

Armand cleared his throat, ready for another great performance. "To White Plains, and step on it!" he said in his old man voice.

The driver nodded as he turned on his radio.

The radio news announcer was talking about the whereabouts of Armand and about the Rio massacres.

"Boss, this is a crazy world we live in," said the taxi driver.

"Yeah," said Armand dryly.

If only he knew he was talking to the king of Brazil.

Chapter 33

Blood, Love, and Fashion

It had been a long day of explosions, blood, massacres, and the fall of Armand Castro. The next was an even busier day for Taylor. She had Brad and Diamond out in hiding, but she had to get them out of Brazil that day for sure, and she needed to prepare for the destruction of Armand.

For now, Taylor was feeling horny.

Pulling up to Desmond's place, she stepped out of her limosine, feeling like the glam goddess she was. She stood there for a moment in her long fur coat that covered her sexy lingerie. Her face was beat to the gods. She smelled the fresh morning air. To her, the sun looked so beautiful and bright. Sex was heavily on her mind as she strutted up to the front door, getting the spare key from under the mat. She unlocked the door, entering the house like she was the queen of the castle. After closing the door, she looked around for a few moments, thinking, *I'm home.*

Desmond's home felt so welcoming and peaceful, more than Taylor had ever felt at her former home or at her husband's magazine house. "Dez! Dez! Your Pinky is home."

No answer.

She smiled, thinking he was upstairs in bed, sleeping. Taylor wanted to feel her man inside of her. Her pussy was going to put him to sleep, where he was going to be calling her DayQuil. She took off her heels, leaving them in the middle of the entryway. She tiptoed upstairs, slowly taking off her fur coat, revealing her two-piece Victoria's Secret lingerie.

Upstairs, she slowly walked up to Desmond's room. As she got closer to his bedroom, Taylor heard weird noises coming from behind the closed door.

She put her ear up close. The noise she heard was two people having hot sex. Then she heard Desmond groaning like some random chick was really turning his ass out. More moaning and groaning came from behind the closed door, like they were really getting it in.

Taylor stepped away from the door with tears falling down her face. She couldn't believe it. Thoughts of Kitana were fresh in her mind—Kitana's good punany going up and down on Desmond's dick.

That bitch!

Thoughts of Desmond's father came into play. That old bastard wanted them to be together, and he probably was the one who'd set the whole thing up. The tears kept flowing as she stepped back, thinking of all the hard work she had just done so they could be together.

I sacrificed my business, I'm about to save two love-sick lovers, and I'm finally going to destroy Armand. She felt all her hard work was done for nothing. *How could I have been so stupid?*

She started to walk downstairs, but then she stopped.

Hold up! I ain't a weak bitch. I'm way past that. I'm an ultimate bad bitch. No. I'm an ultimate bad-ass boss bitch in charge. Desmond was the only man I gave all my heart and soul to, and he does me like this? I don't think so, honey. To the world I'm Taylor Monroe, but I'm also the blood lust princess, Selena Luis, the heiress to the Colombian Mob.

Taylor wiped her tears as she headed downstairs to look at herself in the mirror. She was perfect, as always. She wouldn't allow this to set her back, so she went into Desmond's study to take a deep breath. She turned around and saw Desmond's collection of ninja swords. An evil thought came to Taylor's mind. She walked up to the swords, removing one from the wall and carefully taking it out of the holder. The sword was real. It was beautifully made out of silver, but soon it was going to be covered with Desmond and Kitana's blood. Cutting, slicing, and chopping up their bodies played in her mind.

She left the study, quietly going back up the stairs with so much rage and anger inside of her. When she got up to the bedroom door, she could still hear Desmond groaning. Also, to her, it sounded like him crying, as if Kitana's pussy was that good. That angered her more, because she felt as if she were the only woman with good pussy that could make a grown man cry. She held up the sword, ready to make her presence known. After taking another deep breath, Taylor whispered, "Good-bye, Dez."

The groaning and moaning got louder, as if they were about to climax. She finally kicked open the door, holding the sword high and ready to charge.

Desmond looked up at her. He stopped jacking off and quickly jumped off the bed before Taylor almost sliced off his foot. Desmond looked at her with both shock and fear, but he managed to stand up and play the macho, tough guy.

"Taylor!" He breathed heavily. "Damn, woman, what the hell is wrong with you?"

Taylor still had a little rage in her eyes while looking at his sexy naked body. She turned around to see a Brazilian woman on his 46-inch plasma TV, getting fucked by a well-endowed white guy in a porno.

Taylor dropped the sword on the ground, feeling relieved and downright embarrassed. She should've known that Desmond, her Dez, would never, ever cheat on her—and not with some B-list model like Kitana, at that. He was a good man. She felt so ashamed for her actions.

"Taylor, bae, what the hell is the meaning of this? You damn near cut off my foot. What's gotten into you?"

Taylor was at a loss for words, which was a first for her. "I . . . I—"

Desmond laughed at her. "I guess it's some of that Luis blood in you, huh?"

This really caught Taylor off guard. *What? How did he know about my family?* "What did you say?" She trembled.

"You heard me, Taylor—or should I say Ms. Selena Luis, princess of the Colombian Mob?" He smiled at Taylor, loving the amazement on her face after she'd tried to kill him.

"How do you know about me and my family?" Taylor asked, panicking. "Please, don't tell the media. I couldn't bear for the public, who worshipped me as a supermodel, to think of me as heiress to the Colombian Mob. I worked hard to create a name and identity for myself. Please don't take that from me. I'll pay anything, if you just keep this quiet. Please." Taylor was so nervous. She began to feel lightheaded and fainted, landing on the bed.

"Baby, baby," Desmond said, grabbing a pillow to prop up her head. He then put on his boxer briefs. He went into the bathroom and wet a washcloth. He went back to Taylor, patting her face lightly with the cloth. "There, there, Pinky. Come on, baby. Come on, Pinky."

Taylor started to wake up, still a little lightheaded. "Desmond, darling. I'm sorry about what happened. That wasn't me at all. I just had visions of you and Kitana. The

way she was all over you at the photo shoot and release
party, I just—"

"Really, Pinky?" Desmond cut her off. "You really think
I would go with a self-absorbed, stuck-up chick like that?
My dad tried to hook us up, but all she talks about is how
she looks, what magazines she's on the cover of, if she
needs any plastic surgery done, or what celebrities she
knows. Plus, that chick is a straight-up cokehead. I don't
have time for that." He kissed Taylor's forehead. "Pinky, I
only have eyes for you, no matter what our age difference
is. I haven't touched another woman since I asked you to
choose between me and Armand. That's why I'm watching a porno, jacking off and thinking of you."

Taylor blushed and lifted herself up. "I should've
known better, Dez. I'm so sorry. I hope you know how
much I love you."

She leaned in to kiss him. They shared a romantic
kiss as she rested her hand on his sculpted chest. "But
one more thing I wanna know. How did you know who I
really am and about my family?"

"Do you really have to ask? My father has been snoop-
ing around. He has been close friends with your father
for years. I would sometimes come along to Miami to
visit your family, and when I was a little boy, I would look
at photo albums of you when you were young, up until
your modeling covers. I recently asked for your father's
blessing to marry you. He said yes, but only if I got rid of
Armand."

Taylor was happy, knowing now they could officially be
together forever. "Dez, baby, I have some good news. We
can be together."

Desmond was delighted to hear the news, but it was no
surprise. "Pinky, I already know that. But what are you
going to do as far as Armand is concerned?"

Taylor was so amazed that Desmond knew who she really was. Now they had no secrets between them anymore. "Let's take care of Armand together as an official couple." She smiled.

He laughed, thinking back on all the news about the explosions and massacres of Armand's business. "Damn, Pinky, I should've known that you were behind the shit that happened in Downtown Rio." Desmond shook his head. "You a cold chick."

"And don't you forget it," said Taylor, laughing. "So, are you in with helping me with Armand?"

"Pinky, just to have you in my life forever without that bastard in the picture, I'm in all the way," Desmond said as he kissed her. "So, what's the plan?"

"Oh, Dez, I have that all worked out, and our costumes are ready to go."

Desmond was curious. "Costumes?"

"Don't worry. I'll call you with the detail in a few hours," Taylor said, holding his hand.

They kissed.

"But in the meantime, be ready for what's about to go down," Taylor said, getting up and walking to the door.

"Where you going? You got me hard and shit," Desmond said, pointing at his jock.

Taylor looked back at him. "Dez, baby, passion can wait. I have another little job to clean up, and then feeding time at the zoo." She laughed.

Desmond looked at her like she was crazy, but it was turning him on so much his nipples were hard.

Before she walked out of the room, she smiled at her man. "That'll teach you not to give me an ultimatum." She walked out, going downstairs.

"What am I supposed to do about this woody?" Desmond yelled from upstairs.

"You got lotion and pornos. Like Tim Gunn say, 'Make it work!'" Taylor yelled, laughing as she exited the house.

She went to her limo and got inside.

"Where to, Ms. Monroe?" Samuel asked.

"I wanted to pay our two lovebirds a visit," said Taylor.

"As you wish."

Taylor smiled. *Some shit is going down.*

Chapter 34

Bonjour

Sleeping in the Victorian bed in peace and harmony, Brad was holding Carter Marie's naked body close to his after making passionate love all over the house. They'd been going at it all day and into the night, making this their only break all evening. It was the first time they both had slept that well in a long time. They were dreaming of a new life of happiness, loving, and maybe having a family of their own.

Brad still had dreams, even though they were on the run from the law and possibly from Armand. He was going to do any and everything to keep his freedom. He was even more determined to keep Diamond, or should he say his future wife, Carter Marie, safe from all harm. Even though he couldn't change the evil that was done to her in the past, he was going to make damn sure that he would give her a secure, loving, and happy future.

As the two lovers slept, they didn't know that in the middle of the room, Taylor was looking at them with a lustful grin on her face. Seeing the two lovers was really making Taylor's panties wet, but to her, there was something beautiful about the two sleeping in bed together. They looked so innocent, like two souls that had been searching for each other for years and were finally one with each other. She also noticed that Diamond had cut all of her long, beautiful hair and was rocking a buzz cut like the model Amber Rose. Taylor loved the fact that Diamond was a natural beauty and she could really be model material. Even though Brad was a big guy to Taylor, he and Diamond would have made a beautiful spread in a fashion magazine.

Soon, Taylor thought that was enough of the peaceful sleep, so she shouted, "Okay, my sleepyheads! Wake up! We gotta move out!"

Both Brad and Carter Marie slowly opened their eyes, seeing that it was Taylor standing there looking at all of their nakedness. They immediately jumped out of the bed. Brad put his hands down, covering his penis. Carter Marie took the sheet off the bed, wrapping up her body.

"Taylor, are you crazy? What are you doing, especially looking at me and my girl in the bed naked? You could've knocked!" yelled Brad in shock.

Taylor laughed. She sat on the edge of the bed, crossing her legs, and took off her Gucci sunglasses. "Relax. You both ain't got nothing I ain't seen." She looked at Brad's hands covering his penis. "And for a big guy, not bad. Not bad at all." She smiled then looked at Carter Marie. "And no wonder Armand kept you locked up. If I was still into women, well, ain't no telling what I would have done to that body. Damn!" She licked her lips.

"What do you want, Taylor? 'Cause I'm freezing. I hope you have good news for us." Brad was grumpy.

Taylor's smile quickly vanished when she turned to look at Brad. "Look, Big Boy, this is my house, and I come up in this bitch whenever I damn well please. Don't ever raise your voice to the queen who is going to get you both out of Brazil right now."

Brad's and Carter Marie's eyes were filled with amazement and shock.

"Damn, Taylor, you quick. And thank you. Sorry for my tone, again," Brad said.

Taylor's smile quickly came back.

Carter Marie cleared her throat. "So, Ms. Monroe . . ."

"No need for the Ms." Taylor cut her off.

"I mean Taylor. Where are we going?"

Taylor lay down on the bed. "I'm glad you asked." She took off one of her heels. "Well, you and Brad are going to France, in the countryside of Normandy. I have an eighteenth-century cottage home that one of my many admirers built for me many years ago. Everything you will need is there, and there's a little town called Blangy-Sur-Bresle, where you can get food and so on. Also, I will have a French tutor come by to help you learn the French language so you both can blend in."

Carter Marie's mind was in a daze when Taylor said they were going to France. She thought about her mother and father, who'd had dreams of living in France.

"Yeah, you both can stay there as long as you'd like, and maybe when I get some time off, we can get together." She used her perfect size-seven manicured foot to go up Brad's bare leg to where his hands were covering his tool.

He backed up. "Would you stop that and just get me and my fiancée out of Brazil?" Brad tried to keep a mad look on his face, but he had to admit to himself that her touch felt good. It gave him a woody.

Taylor laughed and got off the bed, knowing she still had her seductive powers. She put her heel back on. "Passion and our little threesome can wait. Right now, get dressed and meet me outside in my car in thirty minutes, no less." Before Taylor walked out of the room, she looked down at Brad, whose erection was peeping out. "Oh, and Big Boy, two words: cold shower." She walked out of the room, giggling as she closed the door behind her.

Both Brad and Carter Marie took deep breaths. They walked up to each other and hugged.

"You will finally be free, Carter Marie Lily Levy—or should I say Mrs. Brad Carter." Brad touched her face so softly.

Carter Marie smiled with tears in her eyes. "Yes. Free at last."

Through most of the ride Taylor, Brad, and Carter Marie sat in silence. Brad held Carter Marie close to him.

Finally, Taylor cleared her throat, demanding attention. "Here are your passports and more info so you both won't stick out like sore thumbs." She passed them an envelope.

Brad took it and looked inside, noticing that it had social security cards, passports, birth certificates, and a driver's license. It had them as a married couple, Maury Ventura and Liza Ventura.

"Guard that with your life, and be careful to the both of you, especially you, Brad. You're a man that is wanted worldwide. In the basement of the cottage, there's a home gym in there. I suggest you use it."

Brad and Carter Marie didn't say a word.

Soon, they reached a big country field with acres and acres of land. In the middle was a huge luxury helicopter. Brad and Carter Marie knew that Taylor's crazy ass wasn't playing. That helicopter was their passport to their new life and freedom.

The driver parked the car, and Taylor, Brad, and Carter Marie got out. Brad went to the trunk of the car to get the bags that had his and Carter Marie's future in it. They rushed up to the helicopter just as the pilot came out.

"Brad and Diamond, this is your pilot, Pierre. Pierre, this is Brad and Diamond. Pierre will be taking you to France."

"Bonjour, Monsieur Brad. Bonjour, Madame Diamond." Pierre took her hand and kissed it. "Come on, get in. Get in."

Carter Marie got in first, and Brad followed. He put the bags to the side. Pierre closed the door and went around to the other side.

Taylor stepped back as the helicopter started and began to take off, leaving Brazilian soil. Taylor waved. "Enjoy France."

Now that I have done my good deed before the year is out, I have to get ready for my performance. And once it's over, I can be with my Dez.

Taylor rushed back to the limousine, hoping for a happy ending as well. She pulled out her cell phone to three-way Desmond and Sandino. When they finally answered, Taylor said, "It's going down tonight."

Chapter 35

Ancient Rome

Within hours, Armand was back on Brazilian soil, and he had no problem getting a limo to pick him up, taking him back to his home. Armand still had on his old man costume, just in case anyone recognized him. So far, the driver hadn't, which was a good sign. During the ride home, Armand tasted nothing but blood and revenge for his wife. That was all he'd thought about on the plane ride home.

The limousine pulled up to Armand's mansion. He had his gun in his hand, knowing that he had nothing to lose. All he wanted was his beautiful wife to tell him where his money was and to have Sandino get him her pretty little head on a silver platter.

Armand had been trying to call Sandino all day. He was hoping that he would pick him up at the jet location, but every time he tried to call him, all he got was that his phone was disconnected. Before he got out of the limo, he made one more attempt to call him, and he still got the message that his phone was disconnected.

The limo driver got out of the limo and opened Armand's door. Armand got out of the limo, pissed off. He ended up throwing his phone across the estate, feeling frustrated and tired of all the shit that had happened to him. All of his businesses were burned to the ground, his money was gone, all his contacts dissed him after they saw homoerotic pictures of him and Ramon, and his main prize, Diamond, was gone. She must've wanted him to believe that she was killed in the massacre at the bakery. Everything he had worked so hard for was now gone. The only thing he had left was Ramon, but he had no plans of being with a man anytime soon. The only thing that was somewhat keeping a smile on his face was killing Taylor slowly and seeing her blood flow all over the mansion.

As he was walking toward the door, the limo driver tapped Armand on the shoulder. Armand quickly turned around. "What?" he yelled.

"Uh, can I get paid, please?" The driver smiled and held his hand out.

Armand looked him up and down. "Get lost."

As he was about to open his door, the limo driver tapped Armand on the shoulder again. Armand quickly turned around, but this time, he pointed a Glock 9 in the limo driver's face, blowing his head off.

The limo driver's lifeless body fell to the ground with his brains oozing all over the mansion's driveway. Armand smiled then tucked the gun in his pants.

"There's your fucking payment: a one-way trip to hell. Enjoy," Armand said, ripping the mask off and throwing it to the side.

He opened his front door. His blood was boiling, and he had one bullet left in his gun. It was for Taylor. While walking through the house, he looked both ways and yelled out "Taylor! Tay-lor! You bitch! Where the fuck are you? Tay! Tay!"

Before Armand knew it, he was knocked clean on the ground after being hit with an expensive marble statue. All he could see were pieces of the broken statue and his blood on the marble floor. His head was aching, and the only thing he could hear were voices saying, "Hurry up! They're getting hungry." After that, Armand blacked out.

***

What seemed like hours later, Armand woke up with his head still aching. He slowly got up, touching the back of his head, which was bleeding. He felt a breeze and realized that he was naked and in his backyard.

"What the hell?" He tried to get in the house through the back door, but it was sealed shut. "Damn!" He then tried to climb the fence, but he got an electrical shock that made him quickly back away. "Ahhhh!" he shouted then fell to the ground. "Shit! When did we get an electric fence?"

This was so confusing to Armand. His back door was sealed shut, and his fences were electric. The thing that made him scared shitless and made him shit on himself literally was in the backyard. There were three caged lions, looking at him like he was their dinner and dessert. He thought he was dreaming.

"This can't be happening."

"Oh, yes, it is, my no good darling."

Armand slowly turned around and looked at the balcony of his home. There stood Taylor, looking even more ravishing than the last time he'd seen her. She was dressed like the Greek goddess Athena, in an all-white garment. Her face was beat to the gods, and she was wearing a real solid gold Roman helmet.

"Taylor, what the hell is going on?"

Taylor looked at her manicured nails. "You're about to die, husband, so I can be cleansed of you."

"You cold-blooded bitch! After all I've done for you? This house, that wardrobe, jewels, and let's just top it off with that magazine. You do this to the hand that feeds you?"

"That material shit don't mean a damn thing to me, because I'm in love with a real man, while you're bare-backing that wannabe fashion model/ex-porn star, Ramon."

Armand was in total disbelief, but he was going to try to pull his famous reverse psychology on her. "Okay, Taylor, you had your fun. Now let me out of here. We have both wronged each other, but I do still love you, my dear. Always and forever."

"Desmond!" yelled Taylor.

Desmond walked up dressed like a Roman emperor, with a gold civic crown on his head.

"This little shit is who you picked over me? Bitch, you really downgraded badly. All you want is that young dick!" yelled Armand.

"Fuck you, ol'man," said Desmond as he wrapped his arm around Taylor.

They shared a romantic kiss.

Armand was ready to vomit, but he wasn't giving up yet. "Son, you're young. Don't let this old bitch trick you. She uses men like dolls. She'll rip you apart and get a new one."

"Man, don't play that bullshit with me!" yelled Desmond as he spit down at Armand.

Armand wiped it off his face. Not knowing what else to do, he only could think of one thing. "Sandino! Sandino!"

Taylor looked down at him, smiling and clapping her hands. Sandino appeared, dressed like a Roman captain of the guards.

Armand's heart sank to his stomach. He felt as if he had just died and gone straight to hell. "Sandino, what are you doing? Help me!"

Sandino laughed. "I quit being your bodyguard, because you're broke as shit. Help yourself. I only work for the Colombian Mob, who are in the works of taking back Brazil as theirs."

"You all are some bitches!" Armand was on the brink of insanity. The backyard was spinning.

"Oh, and Armand!" Taylor yelled.

Armand was now on the ground, crying like the scared little boy he really was.

Taylor laughed, loving to see her husband at his weak point. "Armand!"

He curled up in a ball. She looked at Sandino and nodded. He picked up a big ice bucket filled with blood and other morsels of meat, dumping it on Armand. Forcing Armand to get up, Sandino was making him even crazier. He was covered in blood, cut up toes, and a penis.

"Oh my God! Oh my God! What the fuck is this?" He looked up and Taylor and Sandino. "Whose blood is this?" He demanded to know.

Taylor looked at Desmond and Sandino, then back at Armand, who was losing his mind. Sandino threw down another package for Armand. Armand looked at it, realizing that it was the head of Ramon. He screamed like a little girl.

"Noooooo! Whyyyyy?"

"A little something called assassins and overnight delivery, with a little extra kicked in," Taylor said, laughing at her husband, who now knew that he had nothing left.

Armand had a little flashback to the three muscular men in New York who came to the hotel as he was leaving. "Oh my God. No! Not Ramon! Damn!"

She watched as he curled back into a little ball again. "Any last words, Armand?"

Armand was shaking and sweating nonstop.

Taylor knew that his mind was gone. "Oh, and Armand, one more thing, my dear. Diamond is alive and safe."

That really got his attention. "She is?"

"Now!" Taylor yelled.

Sandino pushed a button on a remote control, and the cage doors opened. The lions displayed their sharp teeth, and as they growled, they started to charge at Armand. He tried to run, but it was too late. The lions were eating at his flesh like they hadn't eaten in years.

It was grossing both Taylor and Desmond out. They went inside the house to enjoy Armand's screams of agony. They shared a lustful kiss, using Armand's dying screams as a romantic song.

Sandino followed them inside. "Taylor, are you okay?"

They stopped kissing.

Taylor took off the helmet. She walked over to Sandino and kissed him. "Thank you. I know you're going to make a great commander for my parents' business."

She walked back over to Desmond, putting her arms back around him and kissing him.

Sandino smiled. He loved seeing his niece happy now, and he knew she was going to be in safe arms now. Sandino cleared his thoat. "Well, I see you two want to be alone. I'll be downstairs."

Taylor waved him off as she continued to kiss Desmond.

Sandino left the room, and Taylor and Desmond continued their little love fest as they sat down on the bed.

"Pinky, baby, I can't believe we did that shit." Desmond was hyped up with excitement now that he had his lady.

Taylor laughed. "I can't either. But did you enjoy the show?"

Desmond laughed also. "Pinky, baby, you are wild as hell, but I'm glad you got rid of his ass."

"Anything for you, Dez. My Dez. Now make love to me, 'cause my body needs it."

She tried to kiss him again, but Desmond blocked her.

"What is it, Dez?"

"Baby, I have something I want to tell you," said Desmond.

"What?" Taylor was so horny.

"Look, Pinky, I don't care who your family is. I loved you the first time I saw you in person. You're the only woman for me. I love you."

They shared a passionate kiss and a lovable embrace.

"I love you too, Dez."

"Do you love me enough to be my wife?"

Taylor was stunned, even though she always knew that they would one day be married.

"Well, Pinky, will you?"

Tears flooded from her eyes. She nodded. "Yes, yes, yes, yes."

He kissed her. "Tonight!"

"What?" Her eyes grew wide. "Tonight?"

"Marry me now. Tonight. Let's go to Las Vegas in the North America."

Everything was moving so fast for Taylor. "Las Vegas? Tonight? That's a very long flight to get there. I have on this, and—"

"Let's go like this."

"What? Me and you in theses ancient Rome outfits?" Taylor laughed.

Desmond laughed at himself, realizing he sounded foolish to say they should go to America with nothing but crazy-ass costumes.

Taylor had a better idea. "Well, first, let's make love and take a hot bubble bath. Then I'll buy a new dress, and we'll take my private plane to the Americas."

That was the plan. Taylor grinned before laying Desmond down on the bed. She got on top of him, rubbing his chest and teasing his nipples with her long fingernails, removing the top of his outfit. She leaned down to kiss him seductively. She could feel the hardness underneath his garment, and she sure wasn't going to let a good hard-on go to waste. She helped him get out of his emperor outfit fast, admiring his naked physique.

"Before I become your wife, you have to give me my medicine for these pink lips. They have been suffering from withdrawals without your Johnson inside me," she said.

Desmond looked at her, confused.

"I said give my pussy its medicine. That dick of yours makes mama want to cum right here, right now." She pinched his nipple.

Her actions really turned Desmond on.

"Now, screw me like a little slut!" Taylor said, pinching his nipple even harder while she was grinding her ass on his penis. It was definitely making Taylor wet, and pre-cum was seeping out the top of Desmond's penis.

"A slut, huh?" he said.

"Yeah, daddy, turn this slut into a housewife." Taylor removed her outfit, throwing it to the side. The only thing she had on was her panties.

Desmond looked at her breasts, licking his lips. He was so ready to suck the life out of them, but he was ready for the main course. He put his hands on her hips, flipping her over. Now he was in control.

Taylor laughed, loving the fact that Desmond was a man that took charge. They kissed roughly. Then Desmond navigated his way down, taking one of her breasts in his hand, caressing it. He started to suck and lick on the other one like a newborn baby.

"Ohhhh," Taylor moaned, feeling the wetness between her legs. "Yes!"

That aroused Desmond more as he licked her flat, toned stomach. He then used his strong hands to rip off her panties like a kid on Christmas day opening a present. He definitely liked his toy. He smiled while gazing at her wet, pink lips.

"Damn, Pinky, you're so wet. You really missed daddy, didn't you?"

"Oh, yes. This is yours and nobody else's. Now eat, Dez, eat."

Taylor didn't have to tell him twice. He dove right into the center of her pink walls. He did every possible trick with his mouth and tongue. He spelled out her name, his, and the whole alphabet—making her cum three times and causing her whole body to shake like she was having a seizure.

Taylor was breathing heavily. "Damn, Dez." She massaged the back of his head, not wanting him to stop. "I missed this tongue. Give me more! I want more."

Desmond was tired of tasting her. He wanted to feel his future wife. He lifted her and gave her a juicy kiss before sliding his manhood inside of her.

"Ohhhh," Taylor moaned as she was unable to catch her breath. This was total satisfaction to her. She had missed her man's cinnamon stick inside of her.

He worked his woman like there was no tomorrow. He loved to hear her moan and groan. That let him know he was doing his job.

"You're going to be my wife, ain't you?" Desmond said, digging deep for a yes.

Taylor massaged her breasts and licked across her lips. "Oh, yes, I will . . . be . . . your . . . oh, yes . . . wife!"

"Uhhhh!" Desmond grunted with a smile while thrusting fast inside of her like he was trying to make a baby.

Taylor was in total ecstasy, feeling like the queen of the universe.

What a damn day. I saved two young lovers, I watched my husband—or should I say ex-husband—become dinner and dessert for the real Lion Kings.

While thinking about all of that, she rubbed her titties, still on a natural high with Desmond rocking her world. She warned him that she was cumming, and seconds later, they screamed in pleasure together.

Desmond fell on top of her, trying to catch his breath. Even though he was heavy and sweaty, Taylor didn't mind. To her, it was just a great feeling having her man's body next to hers. She rubbed his sweaty back then kissed his earlobe and neck. She whispered in Desmond's ear.

"Get your ass up so we can get married in Las Vegas."

He laughed as he raised his head to look at her. To him, Taylor was even more beautiful than the first time he'd seen her. Even though she was fourteen years older than him, he thought she looked like a young, attractive lady. He kissed her.

"Yeah, let's go, especially before you change your mind," he said.

"Not a chance in hell."

After their lovemaking session and bubble bath, Taylor and Desmond came downstairs, fully dressed and ready to go to Las Vegas. Sandino was in the living room, looking at the happy couple.

Taylor smiled at him and looked back at Desmond. "Dez, darling, can you wait in the limo while I talk to my uncle for a second?"

"Okay, Pinky," said Desmond, smiling. They kissed.

Desmond looked over at Sandino and nodded. Sandino nodded back, and Desmond exited the home.

Taylor went over to Sandino and sat next to him.

Sandino smiled. "Don't worry. Someone will be around to get the lions and clean up this mess."

"Thank you, Sandino. But just one more thing," said Taylor.

"What's that?"

"Get the lions out and burn this shit of a house to the ground." Taylor had a serious look on her face.

"As you wish."

Taylor smiled and kissed him again. "Thanks again. Now, I'm off to Vegas. Take care, Sandino."

She got up, heading to the door. As she was about to walk out the door, Sandino yelled out.

"Taylor!" She turned to look at him. Sandino walked over to her and took her hand. "I just wanted to let you know that if Desmond doesn't treat you like the princess you are, you know you can come back to me. I'll take care of you. I love you. I'll cherish and protect you with my life."

His words brought tears to Taylor's eyes. "Oh, why, Sandino?" She knew that he had a genuine soul like Desmond. "I will, but if I don't,"—she softly tongue-kissed him down—"use that to remember me by. And call Milena. She's totally digging you." She patted him on the shoulder. "Good-bye, Uncle Sandino." She walked out of the house toward the limousine, smiling about her life with the one man she loved.

Good-bye, Brazil. Hello, America.

Chapter 36

Beating the Odds

While in the helicopter, Brad sat by the window, look-ing at the night sky and enjoying a full bottle of Dom Perignon. The helicopter could fit at least fifteen people, and it had a mini bar, a refrigerator with many snacks, and white interior leather seats. Brad took time out of his "I'm a king" moment and started to think about the last twenty years of his life: the good, the bad, and the ugly. He thought about his grandmother, who by now was rolling over in her grave, seeing that her only grand-son had become a fugitive; his father, who had made it clear that he wasn't thinking about him; his former boss at the restaurant; and his ex-girlfriend, who had dissed him. He didn't have good thoughts about her, but he now knew why things had turned out as they had. He thought about his boys, not knowing if they were dead or alive. He especially thought of the main thing that would bring him nightmares, his boy Stan. Brad knew he would one day have to pay for that betrayal, but he asked God to go easy on him.

Thinking back to what seemed like yesterday, when they were all together and hanging out, he shed a few tears. He looked at one of the stars, feeling so sad that he was leaving everything behind just to have a better life. He looked down at Carter Marie, who was sound asleep with her head on his lap. He smiled, because if he was going to be on the run, there was no one that he would rather be with. He saw it all as God's plan. They had beaten the odds, but Brad was sure that there was so much more to come.

Epilogue

Taylor and Desmond Diaz

Months Later

With Armand out of the picture and her family reclaiming Brazil, Taylor was living life to the fullest. Only this time, she was now sharing her happiness with her new husband, Desmond Diaz. When they eloped in Las Vegas, it had shocked the media and pissed off Desmond's father.

Later, they did have a big Hollywood wedding at the Hotel Bel-Air in Los Angeles, with a celebrity guest list of thousands, including Beyonce, LeBron James, and all the Kardashians. Surprisingly, Desmond's father showed up, but with his new girlfriend, Kitana. All Taylor thought was that Baron Diaz was a dirty old man, trying to get some of that young punany. At her wedding, all she could do was smile at him and think, *Good luck with your lifelong prescription for Viagra.*

Taylor and Desmond shared a beautiful life in Los Angeles, where they were living the good life. Also Desmond signed a seven-figure deal with Jay Z's company, Roc Nation Sports, making him the highest paid mixed martial artist in the world and the first mixed martial artist in the company's mixed martial arts division.

Also, he had inked a deal with one of Hollywood's hottest directors to star in his new epic film.

Taylor, now known as Taylor Monroe-Diaz, was enjoying the limelight that her hubby was getting. With the extra publicity she received for being his wife, she was getting guest spots on TV shows, from *Project Runway* to the *Steve Harvey Show* to *Ellen*. She was even a frequent guest co-host on *The View*, talking about love, marriage, fashion, dating, modeling, and getting the man of your dreams. She was also a free-lance writer/guest editor, writing about fashion, modeling, and being an athlete's wife in publications such as *Vogue, ESPN*, and Vibe. Taylor even appeared on *The Real Housewives of Atlanta* as a guest speaker/modeling coach for one of the RHOA businesses. After her appearance on the show, Bravo offered Taylor and Desmond their own reality show. The network was willing to pay them whatever they wished. They both turned down the offer very quickly, not wanting the whole world in their business, but Taylor got the media's attention even more when she invested three million dollars into a fashion blog called Gal Fab. The blog was started by four young ladies who had been best friends since college. The blog was about makeup, the latest trends, food in the St. Louis, Los Angeles, and Las Vegas area. Also, Taylor was planning to open up her modeling agency.

Her first client was going to be her sister-in-law, Milena, but Taylor learned that Milena put modeling on hold to be a good wife to her husband, Sandino, who was now the kingpin of Brazil. Milena was pregnant with their first child. Even though Milena gave up the dream of being a supermodel, she remembered the hustling tips Taylor gave her, and never depended on a man.

Taylor put the idea of a modeling agency on hold, and instead, she inked a six-figure, three-book deal with

Random House. Her first book was going to be *Fashion & Blood*, which was somewhat inspired by her own life and the shit that had happened in Brazil last year.

Taylor sometimes just smiled as she looked at the sunset outside one of her and Desmond's million-dollar homes in Hollywood Hills. She couldn't help but think that life was so sweet. The next thing that would make her life complete would be a baby. She was ready for one, and as often as she and Desmond made love, she was sure that a baby was coming soon.

The Fellas

Swag, Travis, and Tyler were living it up in Costa Rica, sharing a mansion on the beach with Paco's men. Paco lived with King in her downtown loft in San Jose, where they were both loved, respected, and feared.

Tyler and Travis were being trained to be smugglers for King and to smuggle diamonds to a big spender in Russia. Travis learned to live without the pinky finger, but he was still on King's shit list until he could prove himself in Russia. Tyler, on the other hand, who remembered some of his hairstyling skills, was hooking King up. She almost hated making him one of her smugglers.

Swag was in training to be one of King's many assassins. She was his teacher of seduction, and she taught him how to get his prey and also the art of killing. He had been a stick-up guy back in St. Louis, but he never killed anyone. Killing someone frightened him, but the way King seduced him turned him on and made him feel like he was on fire.

Paco, however, wasn't too happy about that, and he wasn't going to let Swag ruin his good thing with King. He was going to be the number one man in King's bed. Once Swag's training was over, he was ordered to assassinate all the members of the Hernandez Cartel and the Bello family, but Paco knew he had to take care of Swag before King ordered him dead and made Swag her main man.

But that, however, was another story. . . .

Brad & Carter Marie Carter

After a few months of being in the countryside of France, the two lovers had made new friends. People didn't know who they were, because many of them didn't own a television. They mastered the language to a T. Brad even lost fifty pounds by using the basement gym, making him look very different than most of the most wanted pictures they used to show on CNN. The news about him and his boys had started to die down, but Brad knew not to sneak back into America. He wanted to wait a good five to ten years, but they did plan on going to Paris in a few months. Hopefully, they'd feel more comfortable.

The main thing that made Brad happy was seeing his wife, Carter Marie, happy. She was living life to the fullest, running, planting flowers, dancing, smiling, and laughing more and more every day. Even though he could never give her back her childhood and erase her past, he was going to make her happy and make her want to live life again.

The beautiful thing was that she was a few months pregnant with their first child. Brad knew they really had to be careful and keep their secret, in order to keep the child safe from the evil of the world. They had beaten all of the odds to be together, but they suspected that in the near future, trouble was going to strike. Until that time, they were going to live in love's bliss, knowing that they couldn't change their pasts, but they could damn sure build a better future.